SARAH COURT

CRAIG DAVIDSON

ChiZine Publications

FIRST EDITION

Sarah Court © 2010 by Craig Davidson
Jacket design © 2010 by Erik Mohr
Author photograph by Lisa Myers
All Rights Reserved.

LIBRARY AND ARCHIVES CANADA CATALOGUING IN PUBLICATION

Davidson, Craig, 1976-
  Sarah Court / Craig Davidson.

ISBN 978-1-926851-00-6

  I. Title.

PS8607.A79S37 2010   C813'.6   C2010-903133-4=20

CHIZINE PUBLICATIONS
Toronto, Canada
www.chizinepub.com
info@chizinepub.com

Edited by Brett Alexander Savory
Copyedited and proofread by Halli Villegas

Printed in Canada

SARAH COURT

TABLE OF CONTENTS

PROLOGUE   9

BLACK WATER—Riverman and Son   17

BLACK POWDER—Stardust   49

BLACK BOX—The Organist   88

BLACK CARD—Noseratu, My Son   165

BLACK SPOT—Pipes   257

EPILOGUE   302

PROLOGUE

Squirrels cause suburbanites more grief than any creatures under your sun.

Squirrels tore up my garden! Squirrels ate the seeds left out for the robins! Goddamn those marauding buggers!

I'd laugh, were I capable.

The Eastern Gray Squirrel, *sciurus carolinensis*, is, on average, fifteen inches from nose to tail tip. Weighs, on average, one pound. Pick up a pair of wire cutters. Snip your pinkie finger off below the nail. The size of a squirrel brain. A homo sapiens' synaptic clusters produce enough bioelectricity to jumpstart a Chevrolet. A squirrel's fail to produce enough to jumpstart a wristwatch.

Yet despite their many handicaps, they consistently outwit humankind. I've seen a grown woman crouched in her nightgown on a freezing winter morn lubing her bird feeder pole with bacon grease. Saw one man shoot a squirrel with a twelve-gauge Remington. Obliterate it. To quote an old aphorism: *There's a difference between scratching your ass and tearing big lumps out.*

Sarah Court had squirrel problems for years. Until its residents domesticated them. "Ushering hobos from gutter to penthouse," according to one disgruntled homeowner.

Sarah Court: a ring of homes erected by the Mountainview Holdings Corporation. Cookie-cutter houses put up quick. Residents digging gardens will encounter broken bricks and wiring bales haphazardly strewn and covered with sod. In a town twenty minutes north of Niagara Falls. Grape and wine country. Crops harvested by itinerant Caribbean fieldhands who ride bicycles bundled in toques and fingerless gloves even in summertime. A town unfurling along Lake Ontario. Once so polluted, salmon developed pearlescent lesions on their skin. Ducks, pustules on their webbed feet. They seizured from contagions in their blood. Children were limited to swimming in ten-minute increments.

You really are such magnificently grim bastards. Trashing utopias is how you party.

A town where, as they say, everybody is in everybody's pocket. Where any resident can ask another resident if they have seen any other resident and the answer will be: "I've seen him around." Everybody is always seeing everyone else, around. A town where those who suffer a flat tire are apt to drive on the emergency spare for six months. Whose more corpulent residents have been spotted wearing T-shirts reading I SURVIVED THE 24-HOUR FAMINE with no discernible hint of irony. Whose denizens have been collectively referred to by graceless out-of-towners as resembling "your standard roller derby audience." A town you cannot truly label multicultural, though its undertaker does craft specialty coffins for Muslims to be interred on their sides facing Mecca. He also receives a fee from town coffers for indigents who are interred in industrial rollpaper tubes: basically, toilet paper rolls roomy enough to fit one deceased hobo.

A town where young men barrel out of downtown boozers to find their gaze fastened upon the star-studded sky, gibbous moon tilting over the low architecture and streetlights of St. Paul street, knowing this is it—their place in the world. A town where if you get away, you get away young. Otherwise inertia locks you into acceptance. A town where men return to their old high schools after the bars shut down. Always a case of warm beer in somebody's trunk. The "Mobile Party Kit." They huddle on bleachers talking about that football game they lost but how afterwards they scrapped the winners and sent them home bust up. A town adept at reconfiguring losses as wins. One friend inevitably challenges another to a hundred-yard dash— "Track's right there, fucko. You chickenshit?"—so they run drunkenly yet somehow desperate, warm beers in hand, on legs already turning soft round their bones.

A town where most work at fabrication plants, dry docks, Redpath Sugar. Half a lifetime at one mind-crumbling task: pressing sheet metal into fenders or arc-welding ships' hulls or filling bags with ice tea mix. Drive past the GM factory at six a.m.: greenhorns coming off skeleton shifts pin-eyed and pasty as arctic zombies while older men with tin lunchboxes festooned with Chiquita banana stickers punch in. Men forever smelling of acetylene sparks, industrial glue, unrefined sugar. Who smell of such on their marriage altars and will smell of such in their coffins. Or should their lives spin terribly awry: rollpaper tubes.

A town like so many others, with a "right" and "wrong" side, delineated by the CN Pacific tracks cleaved through its heart. How is it so many of your kind's habitations are thus separated? As if when railcars offloaded the town founders, all the promising citizens disembarked out one side while the wastrels, knaves, scoundrels, and pariahs slithered out the other. Go rip open a bag of trash on the east, or "right," side: name-brand products. Rip open a bag on the west: yellow no-name packaging, Black Cat cigarette butts, bottles of Wildcat lager— which legend has is concocted from vat dregs re-carbonized and sold stone cheap. Sterno Dell's on the westside: a wooded bowl strewn with mattress skeletons where rubbydubs slept the summer months. That is until one shambles dozed off with his cooker lit and burnt it to an unhealthy blackness. Had you been hovering above the fire you would have seen wild animals fleeing all robed in flame. A sight not unlike solar flares releasing from a sun's superheated corona.

Not a town without charm. An escarpment fringes the southeastern edge; the millennia trickle through its steep cliffs. The lake's sailboat-studded green shading to glassy gold lit by a harvest moon. The people within its limits are good stock. If anything, they meet the challenges life throws at them too quickly. Marriage and parenthood arrive and with them the cessation of so many wild ambitions. Some call this an unbeautiful place containing a few quite beautiful people. Others say this is an oddly beautiful place containing a few right bastards.

A spot in Shorthills park overlooks town, near the flame-gutted remains of an El Camino set afire at a rowdy bush party. Were you to stand on this overlook while encroaching darkness flattens the sunlight into a thin red artery between the apartment towers, you could feel the immensity of those lives being lived. The windows of those towers lit thumbprints punched out of the dark. Smoke from GM smokestacks atomizes above the housing projects where lawns go brown each summer. People dancing: in bars, the Ukranian Hall on Louth street, Club Roma near the ball diamonds, teenagers at basement parties—future mechanics dancing cheek-to-cheek with future accountants, plumbers with lawyers, lives elastic with potential. Fucking tenderly, fucking brutally, fucking to bring new life into the fold or satisfy animal drives, entreaties shrieked, empty promises tendered, headboards rattled. Dying: breaking through a stock car's windshield at the Merritville Speedway, a man's body propelled straight as a ballistic torpedo and the shattering Saf-T-Glass a million bloodied starlings startled into flight, the white stripe down his racing suit making him look a lightning bolt forked from the vehicle's interior with a helmetful of red pulp held in place by a shattered jawbone. All those lives thumping at you. One massive thundering heartbeat.

Blood follows blood.

A professional fistfighter's expression. Testifying

to the fact that some cuts absorbed during a fight are so deep or critically placed upon a combatant's face, blood cannot be stopped.

Some believe a skull is a skull is a skull. Yet many of your species have an undeniable sharpness of bone. Chins, cheeks, ridges where brow meets socket of eye. Others, thin skin. Others, a fierce heartbeat to stampede blood through the veins. If your bones are so sharp the pressure of a blow causes your tissues to tear apart over them the way a melon halves itself when dropped upon an axe's blade, or if your skin is stretched tight as drumskin and splits apart easily—as old cutmen say, "his flesh opens with the frequency of elevator doors"—or your heart pounds like a tackhammer to bulge your every vein: if this is you, your blood will run into your eyes, mouth, pooling in your sinus cavities until all you taste, smell, all you know is blood.

Blood follows blood other ways. Offspring follows progenitor. Blood knotted through bodies becomes the red webs binding you. Imagine a net swept over the sea bottom dredging up a frenzy of creation: crab and eel and shark and seahorse and whale caught up in a thrashing teardrop of life. So much life pressed skin on skin on skin.

You are barrels packed to bursting. Barrelsful of frailty, of beauty, of regret, passion, sorrow, envy, horror, guilt, hope, rage and love and pain. Barrelsful of everything it is to be afflicted with your peculiar condition.

So come now, the souls of Sarah Court invite you, and please—open them up.

BLACK WATER

RIVERMAN & SON

It hurts so bad that I cannot save him, protect him,
keep him out of harm's way, shield him from pain.
What good are fathers if not for these things?
—Thomas Lynch, "The Way We Are"

Four hundred. Suicides, failed daredevils, booze-soaked ruins. Four hundred bodies I've dragged out that river.

They start two hundred yards higher, where it narrows between Goat Island and Table Rock. Craning their necks north they'd spy that huge green head fronting Frankenstein's House of Horrors up Clifton Hill—though back in the '70s when Knieval copycats tossed themselves over regular as clockwork, their eyes would be drawn to mist gathering at the head of the Falls while they floated in their giant lobster pot or other idiot contraption.

Rapidly coming to grips with the foolhardiness of their endeavour.

I catch them with hook and rope and a Husky X9 winch. I can only say how they look falling into my care. Simple answer's bad. Crass one's discombobulated. Truth is it's a hard description to approach. The human body's durable. Idiotically so. The Big Drop shows you all durabilities have limits.

First time you motor out you're asking, *How bad can it be*? That question has a way of coming off as a dare to the Almighty.

Most of us cross a body, it's in a coffin. Frozen in pleasing position. What I drag out of that river is death in the raw. Unadorned yet in its way utterly natural, in that nature holds many strange shapes. Men bent at angles failing to match the angles of our understanding. Pressure's a sonofabitch. Trapped in chambers hammered out over millennia, a body churns like a ragdoll in a cement mixer. Mortician who handles Plungers—his pet euphemism—has mannequin limbs the colours of all creation. An incomplete head equals a closed casket. No ifs, ands, or buts.

Once I took my boy Colin on a training run. Two of us in a johnboat on the zinced waters of the Niagara. Up top the cataract was my neighbour, Fletcher Burger, with a ballistic latex Resussy-Annie doll stitched to a pair of weighed legs. Colin cupped a handful of water. Rubbed his fingers over his teeth. Earlier that week his mother had collapsed in the shower. Stuff metastasizing to her bones. She'd begun sinking into herself. I'd knelt fully clothed in the tub. Water pelting down. Covering her breasts best as I was able. For his sake. Hers, too.

"Water goes deep enough, it's always black," I told him. "Sun can't penetrate. Colour spectrum fails. At eighty feet it's total blackness. The sun gives our skin colour. The deepest sea fish get no sun. You can see right into their guts."

Fletcher hurled the doll. I dragged in its torso. Legs I never did find. One of its eyes burst. The insides crawled the shatter-lines in black threads, like when your digital watchface cracks.

"Happens to us, too," I said. "Often worse."

Colin prodded the doll's head with his sneaker. The liquid black of its eye rolled down its rubber cheek. Even back then he didn't feel the odds applied to him.

My name is Wesley Bryant Hill. My grandfather was the Riverman. My father, too. That's the way life unfolds in the territories of my birth.

The boy walks into the strip club as Dracula.

Ordinarily I steer clear of fleshpits. Sadsacks ordering five-dollar steaks—who eats five-dollar meat anywhere tap water runs you ten?—old mares in costume panties with the spanglies falling off, raincoat types with basset faces, DJ playing "Don't Stop Believing" when it's clear everyone has. That gathered humanity disintegrating under a disco ball.

I'm here on account of Diznee. Roberta to her mother. Evicted from her night slot by girls bussed in from Quebec—"Nothing against the Kaybeckers," she says, "but they don't got horny stiffs in Montreal?"—she toils the midday grind at Private Eyes. We share an apartment block. I babysit her boy, Cody. Black-white. What do you call that? Mulatto. Good kid. I'm here to collect my babysitting monies when I spot Boy-Dracula. Chubby, mop-headed, in a black cape. Clive the afternoon barkeep asks what he'll have. A gal old enough to be this kid's auntie slithers naked round a brass pole.

"Clive!"

"One of the girls' kids." He serves the boy a glass of maraschino cherries. "Right?" The boy cocks his head as a dog will. "Oh, jeepers," goes Clive.

I tell the kid he shouldn't be here.

"This is where ladies . . . dance."

"Wizzout zeyr pants," he says in this Nosferatu voice.

Take him onto Bunting road. Sunlight beating on the hoods of Camaros and pickups.

"What's with the cape?"

"I yam a wampire."

20

"You don't say. How'd you get here?"

"Zee buzz."

The bus-riding vampire's name is Dylan.

"How come you aren't shrivelling up in the sun?"

"I yam a magical wampire."

I'll wager this act gets him beat up a fair load. Walk to a payphone beside Mattress Depot. He calls someone to pick him up. Cross to Mac's Milk. One Coke and one "Vampire Tonic": chocolate milk to us non-bloodsuckers. Dylan insists on paying. His fiver has pinpricks run down it.

"So, there a missus Vampire?"

"Sadie," he says in a regular kid voice. "She's sort of my girlfriend."

"A looker?"

"She's got piglet tails."

"I think that's pigtails. Plan on bringing her to visit your Ma and Pa in Transylvania?"

A powder blue Ford pulls in. The driver's Abigail Burger. From Sarah Court. Fletcher's daughter. I believe she recognizes me but as we fail to acknowledge this, the moment passes and we shake as two strangers. One hell of a grip.

"Any idea how much trouble a kid can get into with only a bus pass?" she says. "I sew five-dollar bills into the lining of his pants so he's not penniless."

"What's this about him being a vampire?"

"Dad lets him watch monster movies."

"Mom doesn't approve?"

"Oh, I'm not his mother."

I say goodbye. Head home. The sky's composed of overlapping orange- to blood-coloured curtains when my own son pulls into the complex lot. Driving a shark-grey Olds. Flames lick off the wheel wells. Haven't seen him in two years and three before that. My apartment's a shambles. Grab Lucky Lager bottles and sleeve them in the nearest two-four case. Colin's fist hammers the door.

"Since when do you lock it, Daddio?"

As if he visited weekly and this is a fresh wrinkle. I'm sixty. Colin was born when I was twenty-five. The mathematics bear out in the creases of his face and the calcified humps of his knuckles. His left cheek's caved inwards below his eye. Happened years back when he jumped eleven busses at the Merritville Speedway, misjudged the landing and crushed his skull off the bars. His helmet split in half—helmets are designed to split under pressure; otherwise, you slip it off and inside's red goo—as his body ragdolled over the front tire. He survived, as he's survived the flaming rings of death and sundry smashups he calls a career. Hair flecked with white. Nothing like your son's hair coming in grey to make you feel fossilized. Blue eyes, his mother's, gone pale round the edges. Leather jacket with "Brink Of, Inc" stenciled on the back. Ragged cracks like tiny mouths at the elbows.

He's got a young guy in tow. Look of an Upper Canadian boarding school preppie. Jeans with scorpions embroidered down each leg. Dreadlocked hair. Puppydoggin' Colin's heels. My son draws me into a rough hug. His fingers trace my spine clinically.

"This is Parkhurst," he says. "He's writing my biography."

The kid biographer smiles. You'd think we'd shared a moment.

"What's that doing out, Dad?"

That is a sand-cast West Highland Terrier. Its head got busted off by vandals but I epoxied it back on. Colin's mother collected Westie paraphernalia. We had a live one but he went young of liver failure and convinced my wife she was snakebitten as a pet owner. Her accumulation had been slow and it was only afterwards, sitting in a house full of effigies, that I realized how ardent a collector she'd been.

"Pretty morbid," says Colin.

The cancer ate away her sense of things. Last few months she lived in a terminal dreamworld: drugs, mainly, plus the disease chewing into the wires of her brain. She wasn't wholly my wife. She'd damn me for thinking otherwise. During this time, she—

"Mom treated that dog like it was real," Colin tells Parkhurst. "Fed it biscuits. Don't know why you'd want it around."

My son's generation has a manner of plain-speaking that comes off as casual brutality. Why do I keep it? It maintains a vision. Not of my wife feeding a sculpture because her brain was so corrupted she couldn't tell it from a real dog. It's that she tried to nurture anything at all. Out of all the hours spent with her in good health, why would he conjure the scene of his mother feeding a sculpted dog?

"You want me to throw a towel over it?"

"A man does as he likes in his own home."

"Gee, you're a prince amongst men."

Colin looks raggedy and he looks dog tired. Sad, I'd say—not pitiful: even mummified in bandages in this or that hospital, the boy's never been that—but depressed. I *could* cover it . . . why should I? Where's he been? Dog could damnwell stay.

"How did you find me?"

"We stopped in for an eye-opener at the Queenston Motel. There was Fletcher Burger propping up a stool. Poor guy's looking like ten pounds of shit in a five-pound bag."

He glances at Parkhurst to ensure he's transcribed this morsel of wit.

"What brings you?"

"Can't I visit my Pops?"

Already sick of the tension. Wish I had a beer but balk at drinking in front of my kid and besides, I'm pretty sure they're all drank up. He shifts on his rump and, with reticence or the nearest to it my son might ever draw, says: "I'm going over."

Sarah Court, where Colin grew up, kids had pet squirrels.

My neurosurgeon neighbour Frank Saberhagen cut down a tree. A clutch of baby squirrels tumbled out. The doctor's corgi devoured a few before Clara Russell's sheepdog rescued the remainder. Our kids took them in. The hardware store had a run on heatlamps.

Semi-domesticated squirrels roamed the court. A virulent strain of cestoda, a parasitic flatworm, infested their guts. Saberhagen saw his son Nick clawing his keister and organized for the Inoculation Wagon. To make sure our kids were infected we had to bring samples.

Neighbours idling on the sidewalk with tupperware containers or ice cream tubs containing our offsprings' turds. Everybody shamefaced except Saberhagen, who took evident pride in his son's heroic sample. Wasn't flashing it around or anything so crass but you could tell. Everyone felt sorry for his son Nick, who went on to become a boxer but not a very good one.

The Inoculation Wagon: room enough for Colin, myself, a nurse. Colin hopped on the butcher-papered bench. Shivered. Two kinds of shivers: the fear-shiver and the shiver of anticipation. First time I'd ever marked a clear distinction.

"This is Verminox," the nurse told Colin.

"What's it do?"

"It's a bit of a disease. We inject you with a teeny-tiny bit, your body fights it. The worms can't fight. They die."

"Gonna make me sick?"

"A little sick so you won't get a lot sick."

Colin rucked his sleeve up. Fascinated he'd be infected. The nurse gave me a look. But it was heartening to see my boy cleansed of fear. All the other pansy kids blubbering as my son practically *jumped* onto that hogsticker.

Later I recognized parents should be thankful their kid is like everyone else's in the most critical ways. Pricked with a needle, they cry.

"A prototype, Pops."

"Prototype? It's a plastic oil drum."

"I got people working on a better one."

Ball's Falls is located off old highway 24 in the shadow of the escarpment. The sun slants through clifftop pines highlighting the schist trickling through the rockface. Only vehicle in the lot is a delivery van. SWEETS FOR THE SWEET on its flank. Bark on silver birches peeling like the skin of blistered feet.

Colin boots the drum down the drywash where a waterwheel churns the creek. Parkhurst has pillows stolen from the Four Diamonds motel where they've been shacked up. Next to the KOA campground so when funds run short it will be a painless transition. Colin's earned a chunk over the years: those TV specials in the '90s, action dolls, video games. Tells me he's been working the state fair circuit lately. Jumping junked cars in razed Iowa cornfields. Junked cars in Idaho potato patches.

"You got scientists building you another drum?" I ask. "What, it's going to have non-motel pillows for superior cushioning?"

"I got people, Pops."

"Don't call me that. Pops. Like I'm running a malt shop."

"You'll see it."

"Who says?"

I'll see it. Take this morning: said I wouldn't come but here I am. My refusal wouldn't stop it happening. What if he busts a leg? Pulverizes his spine? Parkhurst bawling into his ratty mop of hair. The real thumbscrews part is that Colin knows he's putting me in a bind.

He boots the drum down a gulch littered with

sunbleached paper cups. We reach the shallows near the head of the falls. Water clear over the flat shale bottom. Minnows dart and settle. A fifty-foot drop into a deep rock amphitheater. My son strips to his skivs. Goddammit, it's autumn. What's the purpose in him going over as he entered this world? Wearing ballhugger Y-fronts—a banana hammock, I guess you'd have to call it—presenting the shrivelled definition of his privates. Gawking at my kid's frightened turtle of a wiener. Hell's the matter with me?

"It's not watertight," he tells me. "Why ride home with wet clothes?"

My son, the pragmatic daredevil. Settling into the drum, he sighs. Can't tell if it's voluntary or if the compression of those old hurts forces it out.

Muffled laughter as the drum bobs into the current. Follow it upcreek, skipping over rocks with a galloping heart until it bottoms out at the head of the falls. Water booms over the creek-neck but Colin's hooting like a wild bastard. I find a strong branch. Goddamn, sixty years old and aiming to tip my half-naked son over a waterfall in an oil drum. The sun's at an angle where I see him through the blue plastic: an embryo inside an egg held up to a flame.

Water sprays. Parkhurst's overbalanced with one

boot submerged in the creek. The stone he's thrown is sand-coloured, huge, and sharp. It could have easily punctured the drum.

"What to Christ were you thinking?"

Parkhurst offers the docile smile of a moron. A surge sweeps the drum over. I hightail it down steps erected by the Ontario Tourism Board. The drum floats near the basin's shore. Lid popped off. Colin crawling out like some zombie from its grave. Soaked skivs hanging off his rawbone ass. Water-thinned blood trickling out both nostrils. Smiling but that's no sign of anything.

"Give me your hand."

He crawls out under his own steam. On the high side of the basin a deer watches in a poplar stand. Tiny red spider mites teem around each of its eyes, so many as to give the impression it's weeping blood. Colin's shivering. Nobody thought to bring a blanket.

Back in the truck I get the heater pumping. Parkhurst I banish to the bed.

"I want you there."

"I'm retired."

"So un-retire, Daddio."

Heat's making me sluggish. Flask's in the glovebox but it's too early for that sort of a pick-me-up in the company of my kid.

"A hell of a thing to ask, sonnio."

He's genuinely baffled. "All's you got to do is fish me out."

A reporter once asked: "When's the last time you saw your son scared?"

I said that must have been at his circumcision. It was taken as a joke.

One time he had a baby tooth hanging by a strip of sinew. He tied it to a length of dental floss, attached the trailing end a doorknob, tore it out. That night he locked himself in the bathroom and tore out four more. Came out looking like a Gatineau junior hockey league goon. He wrapped his teeth in tinfoil for the fairy. My wife figured a fiver ought to cover it.

Another time on a Cub Scout camping trip. My neighbour Frank Saberhagen was scoutmaster, myself a chaperone. Nighttime round the fire. Boys tossing pine cones on the flames to hear sap hiss.

"The Nepalese army trained the most fearsome warriors in the world," Saberhagen went. "The Gurkhas. Make the Marines look like a pack of ninnies. They got this knife, the kherkis, so long and wickedly sharp victims see their own neck spurting blood as they die. What nobody knows is a planeload of Gurkhas crashed on this site years ago."

For a man who'd sworn the Hippocratic oath, Frank was unusually irresponsible.

"Who knows if they're still alive? What the Gurkhas do is sneak into camp at night and feel your boots. If they're laced over-under-over, they identify you as a friend. But if they're laced straight across, they pull out their big ole kherkis and"—drawing a thumb across his throat—"you see your own bloody neck stump as you die."

Afterwards I upbraided Saberhagen. He denied any wrongdoing.

"The Ghurkas are real, Wes. Go look it up."

The boys all re-laced their shoes over-under-over. I assumed Colin had done likewise until I saw his boots outside his tent the following morning. Laced straight across.

Somewhere inside myself I knew he'd been up all night, Swiss Army knife clutched in one hand, listening for the *scrunch-scrunch* of feet on dead leaves.

I'm in the truck with Colin's biographer, Parkhurst. Shorthills provincial park. Sulphur Springs road. A weekly circuit. Fletcher Burger has been tagging along since his troubles but he didn't pick up when I rang this morning. Parkhurst overheard and asked to tag along. I'd prefer to share my truck with Typhoid Mary.

Colin's crashing on my couch. Parkhurst curled at his feet like an Irish setter. Colin's working my phone to drum up media. A "strong maybe" from a cub reporter at the *Globe and Mail*. Wondrous he'd consider committing to the two-hour drive to witness my son heave himself off the face of the earth. My involvement's being hyped.

"Yeah, yeah. Been at it thirty years," Colin's saying to anyone who'll listen. "His dad before and his dad before that. He'll be there to drag whatever's left out . . ."

The sun slits through roadside poplars. Feel of cocktail swords stabbing my corneas. Scan for bodies: tough on corduroy roads as they get squashed between raw timbers and all's you can identify them by is the crushed eggshell of their skulls. Parkhurst smiling that sunny mongoloid's smile. A face pocked with old acne scars looking like a bag of suet pecked at by hungry jays. By no means charitable but some men invite uncharitable descriptions. Snap on the radio. If it's quiet enough I might hear the kid's thoughts, which I envision as sounding much like a boom microphone set inside a tub of mealworms.

Other night I drag myself out of bed in the wee witching hours. Lumbago playing havoc with my spine. Went to the fridge for a barley pop. There was Parkhurst standing over my son. When I asked what he was doing he gave me his doleful empty-headed look.

"Thought he'd stop breathing, or . . ."

A smashed septum made Colin snore loud as a leaf-blower. It hit me what the kid said. Not *stopped* breathing—as in, he was worried. *Stop* breathing—as in, he wanted to witness the dying breath exit his lungs.

If a man makes his living courting death, is it any surprise he should acquire as companion a human maggot waiting to feast on the inevitable?

"Colin said you went to university," he said now.

"Jot that down in your notebook, did you? I majored in geology."

"So why don't you teach it, or . . ."

He's one of those annoying nitwits who never finishes a sentence.

"My wife got pregnant. Needed a job. I became an employee of the Parks Commission."

"Good money, or is it like . . ."

"I could walk into a Big Bee, buy a scratch-off ticket, get three cherries and instantly make more than I've ever made doing this. I weld, mainly."

"Funny the way it'll go."

"Yep, it's a regular rib-ticklin' riot. My split sides are always aching."

"I know how that goes, or sorta like . . ."

Moron. I check up by a thatch of duckweed. A possum had bumbled onto the road to avoid black flies. Most get clipped by a fender and thrown clear but this one got run over square. Hind end squashed. Muzzle stuck with cockleburrs.

"Tourist Thoroughfare Maintenance" the Parks Commission designates it, gussying up what is simply road-kill duty. The grim sight of Mr. Possum here, or Mr. Racoon or Ms. Badger or Monsieur Skunk— any critter who goes jelly-kneed when pinned by arc-sodium headlights—is a guaranteed vacation-spoiler. Call me the merry maid of the roads.

I reach a shovel out the bed. Parkhurst's kneeling a foot from the creature. He fails to note the term "playing possum" was coined after observing such behaviour.

"Hold a mirror under its snout," I tell him. "Fogs up you'll know it's alive. The fact it'll have torn your throat to ribbons will be your second hint."

He finds a stick. Stabs the possum's flanks. The animal rears up over its own squandered wreckage. Crazed hissing noises. Its crack-glazed eyes make me think of the Christmas tree ornaments Colin made in grade school. Glass globes with tissue paper paraffined over top. I found them years later, shrunken tissue peeled back from the glass in veins. The fucking kid pokes it again. Bringing my boot down, I snap his stick. His face may've found its way into the beast's wheelhouse—jam it in a Cuisinart for similar results—if I hadn't shouldered him aside.

"We wanted to see if it was alive. One poke beyond is being an asshole."

The kill-box is the size of a laundry hamper. Lightweight aluminum. Drill holes let the fumes go. A slot-and-grove mechanism for bigger animals so's you can finagle their heads inside. Set the possum in whole. Lock it down. Uncoil the hose. Fasten one end over the tailpipe. Screw the trailing end onto the connecting tube feeding the box. Slide onto the driver's seat. Goose the gas. Carbon dioxide pumps in. Black slivers—possum claws—poke through the drill-holes roped in smoke.

Colin would send his mother and I news clippings. One showed his body laid out as an anatomical graph. Skinless, as rendered by some magazine's crackerjack graphics department.

The Wreckage of Daredevil Colin "Brink Of" Hill.

Numbered arrows pointed to the bone-breaks and contusions and pulped cartilage and shorn tendons and detached retinas and assorted devastation. So many goddamn arrows.

1. Brink Of tore his left kneecap off in a motocross fiasco at the Tallahassee Motor Oval.

2. Brink Of knocked out seven teeth smashing though a plate-glass window as Charles Bronson's

stunt double in *Death Wish V: The Face of Death*.

Another time I got a package in the mail. A video game unit with his game: *Daredevil*. He'd been showing up on late-night talkshows. A TV stunt spectacular where he'd recreated Evil Knieval's Snake River Gorge jump. I called him.

"Daddio!"

"Where are you?"

"Partying in Los Angeles!"

I visualized the standard LA pool with underwater lights shimmering the surface, the same pools over the Hollywood Hills so if you were to observe from on high the landscape would resemble a luminous coral fan. Bareassed girls, starlets as they were known, swimming carefree but not truly, needing their nakedness to be appreciated and the party given a whimsical theme: Christmas in July; Holiday Under the Sea. My son far away from the stink of the killbox and the GM fabrication plant where radial tire moulds are injection-moulded with molten vulcanized rubber: that first nostrilful of air entering Canadian Tire intensified twentyfold. Far away from the rusted skies over the dry docks where men bent the blue of acetylene torches to braise hulls of ships whose prows would cleave the sea places we never dreamt of going. When the whistle blew we showered silently, white holes showing through wetted hair where stray sparks burnt down to our scalps. Colin achieved escape velocity. Who could ever hold that against him?

"Try it, Dad. Try the game."

I picked up the joystick. A digital version of Colin tooled along on a motorbike. His voice came out the speakers:

"Yee-*haaaaaw!* C'mon, chicken-guts, give 'er some gas!"

The bike went up a ramp, landed badly, tossed Colin over the handlebars. He skipped along in a broke-boned jig. A tiny ambulance sped across the screen. GAME OVER.

"Ragdoll physics," Colin said. "How they get me flipping and flapping. Lifelike! A hit in Japan; they love me over th—"

His phone cut out. Or I hung up. I don't properly recall.

The gal, all of twenty, she's up on the parquet stage grinding her bits on a brass pole.

Pageboy hairdo, jet-black and futuristic like an android's haircut. Giving us goons that witchy-woman stare they must teach at the stripper academy. Lithe and firm-delted. Could've been a gymnast or figure skater . . . my mind shouldn't have gone down that route because I'm imagining her mother dropping her off at the rink with a pair of pink skates hung over her shoulders. Eating a

Pop Tart. Now she's up there in the buff doing the higgeldy-piggeldy.

My son's idea. He's been making nice with my neighbour, Diznee. Two of them passing goo-goo eyes. While I don't fancy sitting with Parkhurst along pervert's row at a ta-ta bar, well, here you'll find me. The jugged beer's got a kinetic glow under the black lights. Eerie, like quaffing toxic sludge.

Colin hits the toilet and on his way back sits at another table with Nicholas Saberhagen, the ex-boxer and Frank's son, and a man he introduces as his client. Colin's talking about his stunt tomorrow. Nick says he'll bring his own son. Apparently Nick works for American Express. He'd recently returned from a Russian oil spill where he'd seen a shark washed up on the coast. His client—this odd old duck with a face netted in wrinkles as if he'd slept with it pressed against a roll of chicken wire—tells a story.

"This was in southern Italy," he starts, "by the sea. On a twisting cobbled alley going up, up, up. Behind me came a truck pulling a trailer. I pressed myself against the alley wall to let it pass. The trailer held a shark. A long, sleek, torsional creature. Enormous! The skin round its eyes was wrinkly as an elephant's. It stunk of blood and the sea. Its gill-slits were dilated and past their red flutterings was the wink of teeth. Next the screech of tires and—I swear on my life!—

the shark flipped out of the trailer to slide, thrashing and viciously alive, back down the street. A living absurdity: the world's finest predator skidding down a cobbled alley. It careened into a wall and slid on a sideways course, jaws snapping. Momentum carried it down to a stone wall lined with trash sacks, which it gnashed to shreds as the fishermen in the truck ran with gaffing hooks and knives to finish the job. This beautiful shark thrashing in sacks of trash, hide stuck with potato peelings and junk leaflets. A stone's throw from the sea."

I get rooked into paying the whole bill. Colin sold it as an act of deep nobility. Please, good sirrah, let me ante up for this gargantuan strip club bill! Jack-rolled by my own flesh and blood. Won't be able to afford my phlebitis pills when the prescription runs dry but que sera, sera and thank God for socialized healthcare!

The three of us barrel into a cab. It cuts down Bunting onto the QEW to Niagara Falls. The Falls lit up green, red, and blue by strobelights. White water kicking out into a greater darkness. A banner reads: *"Brink Of," World's Greatest Stuntman!* We continue along the river past the hydroelectric plant.

"Stop," Colin says. "Stop here."

The cab pulls into Marineland. This discount SeaWorld owned by an old Czech who achieved local fame by strangling an animal rights activist who dramatically chained himself to the entrance gates. Parkhurst's passed out drunk. We lean him against a tree. Looks as if he's been shot and arranged *in situ* by a mafia bagman.

Along the back edge of the parking lot a flap of chainlink peels away from the fence. I shoulder underneath. My booze-lubed joints don't note much until a stab at the base of my spine tells me I'll feel it tomorrow.

"What are we doing, Colin? Seriously."

He hugs me. First he's done so in I don't know how long. Try not to read anything into it, him so fickle with these intimacies and myself with no desire to be sucked into his orbit—knowing it can happen, *bam*, that fast—but it feels so damn good.

The amphitheater tiers cast shadows round the tank. Curves of white belly as killer whales glide past the glass. A pair of whales landlocked in the middle of Ontario. Thousands of miles to the nearest ocean. Years back the third, Niska, chewed off a trainer's leg. Were it me and were I aware of how unnatural my life had been made, yeah, I might bite that feeding hand.

Colin takes my wrist. Turns it over.

"That scab's been on your wrist since I got here. Isn't crusty the way a scab should be. A little red oil slick. You seen a doctor?"

"It's a hemoglobin deficiency. I should heal like a thirty-year-old?"

"I see it and a weird twinge runs under my balls. Same way I felt with Mom."

I fail to scab up. On the planet my son occupies, orbiting a sun whose warmth he alone can feel, this is reasonable cause for abandonment. We see the same woman so differently. He remembers her collapsed in the bathtub skeletonized by cancer. I still see her in that same tub after we'd married. Soaking when I'd come in to shave. She asked if I'd like to get in so I stripped right there on the tiles, lickety split, slid in with her. That fabulous lack of friction held by bodies in water. I'm not saying my son lacks empathy. I'm saying it must be hard for him to conceive of his mother and I as holding variable states of being.

Colin's leg twitches. I set a hand on his thigh.

"Come on, now. Please. Don't."

I clutch his sleeve but it's a meaningless, almost motiveless gesture. Colin hops a wooden gate up stairs curling round the tank. Over a bridge spanning the pool onto the show stage. Kicks his boots off, peels his shirt over his head. Chest clad in roping scars and dented where part of his pectoral muscle was torn off. Unbuttons his flies then raises his arms to make an arrow of himself. He screams— "*Yeeeeearrrrgh!*"—and dives.

Rings spread where he goes in. I picture an orca's jaws chomping him in half for no other reason than he's there to be bitten and no animal should be expected to behave otherwise. He surfaces. A whale breeches a foot from him. Colin touches its innertube skin. A giddy hoot. The whale vents mackerel-smelling breath through its blowhole. No cameras or reporters. Only my son expressing the odd way he is made.

Some creatures live as stars do: burn hard and hot, feeding on those nearby but primarily upon themselves. Their lives an inferno and them happiest in that heat. Eating away at themselves until all that remains is appetite. What can I ask of him: that he burn a little less bright? For him that would be a death every bit as final as the one we've all got coming. My son will go out burning at such degrees I've never known. He will die in flames.

Boys in Saint Catharines do this thing come their first teenage summer.

The stump of a train trestle juts over Twelve Mile creek. Boys leap off it. Grandfather, father, me: we all made the jump. If you hit nineteen and for lack of intellect or gumption can't spin out of those childhood orbits to college or a job outside city limits, well, you'll pass many an adult night drinking Labatt 50 under that same trestle. For a boy the jump acts as the bridge between their small world and the world everyone else inhabits.

Could be I overstate it. Maybe it's just the thing to do on those blistering days when the sun hangs forever and the heat makes you a bit crazy.

Each summer boys come together in packs. Not even friends, necessarily; just boys from the same stretch of blocks who happen to be of that age. They'll pick their way over the train ties, each rail-spike inviting tetanus, to where the trestle bends in a rotted arc. Boys'll talk about how best to do it: legs-first, arms crossed over their chest so they fall as if tipped dead from a coffin. They'll shove at each other but no boy ever pushes another over. Some code of boyhood ethics prevents it. You make the leap on your own. If you don't, you clamber down to the cool grass and put your manhood off another day, week, however long.

Everyone knows you must jump, surface quick—even then you'll come up forty yards from where you leapt—and kick like hell for shore. But if you cramp up or get licked by a ripcurl you'll be sucked into the break where creek meets river, two-hundred yards to either shore. That far out, only the sky and water, a body gets to feeling it's filled with rocks. A boy did drown. But that was long ago.

Colin jumped when he was ten. He and one of Clara Russell's boys. They stole Frank Saberhagen's Cadillac El Dorado and leapt out into the teeth of night. First my wife or I knew of it was the emergency crew at the door handing up our son bedraggled and shivering.

I picture him out there. Scrawny kid hunched on the ties in his underwear—they found his PJs flapping on a nail—moonlight plating his bare chest and the indentation of the Verminox scar on his arm. Night breeze ruffling his hair to bring up goose pimples and the darkness such that the water cannot be seen, only heard, this throaty rush and my son naked to feel the contact high more acutely. Perched on the verge of a blackness so deep it must be like leaping into everlasting night or into death itself.

My son and I sat on the sofa while my wife thanked the rescue team. Colin wrapped in a blanket sipping cocoa. Making *hssss* noises between clenched teeth. I switched on the TV. There he was on the early morning news. A bobbing dot gripped in the black fist of the river. "Boys Snatched from Jaws of Death," read the news ticker. My son cleaved in two: one half on the sofa beside me and the other only coloured dots on a TV screen. One place in peril, the other safe—but even beside me he wasn't safe because some defect in his head worked against any safety he might know. Wrapped warm in a blanket sipping cocoa with miniature marshmallows, physically present, but the other part of him suspended in the ashen halo of a rescue helicopter spotlight, a bullhorn-amplified voice calling out and a rope dangling inches from his face—an expression so serene, lips gone blue—but he failed to reach for it. Smiling so sweetly so close to death. Close enough to taste, if death has a taste. Unless it's life he's been trying to taste all these years. Life at its furthest ambit where the definitions are most powerful.

To hold a child and to know conclusively you've lost him. If there is a more jagged and sickening, more powerless feeling in this world I do not know of it.

"You're grounded. A whole month."

"Sounds fair, Daddy."

Across the Falls, U.S. side, you'll find the Love Canal district. In 1942, Hooker Chemical corporation buried 22,000 tons of toxic waste. Later the site was covered with four feet of clay and re-zoned. Prefab housing for low-income families. On top of hazardous waste everyone knew was there. People so happy to have a roof over their heads they weren't fretted by what lay under their feet. Disease abounded: epilepsy, urinary tract infections, infant deformities. The notion that folks could raise kids a few feet above a reservoir of glowing green cancer didn't wash with middle America. But they didn't get it. That was those people's orbit. A doomed orbit, yes, but inertia kept them locked to it.

SARAH COURT

The streets and byways I've roamed my whole life seem robbed of some crucial quality, too: a quality of ambition, could be, or self-betterment. Hard to pinpoint the sickness when everybody's infected.

I stand at the prow of a johnboat I've not set foot on in years. Fingers on the nautical wheel as it rolls with the current. Overcast today, cumulus clouds scudded above the Falls tinting the water the same gunmetal grey as the boat. Only colour comes from pink fibreglass insulation drifting over the basin. I squint at the motley assemblage of press gathered at the head of the Falls. From where I'm standing they're dots. Mildly bemused, mainly bored dots.

Four hundred bodies pulled out in pieces. They don't all die. At least twenty I've saved. They go over, kicked at by the current until they're spat out. If they've gone blue but there's the ghost of a pulse I'll pump their chests and blow air into their lungs. Sometimes it doesn't do a tinker's damn but other times they barf up a gutful of water and go on living their blessed lives. Some lack any conception of that blessing: stay underwater long enough, well, it's no different than a surgeon taking half your brain. A Niagara lobotomy.

This one time. Colin in the backyard while I barbecued. He tottered up with something in his hands. Uncupped his palms enough so I could see a moth battering his fingers.

"You must let it go," I told him. "Lunar moths have a protective powder on their wings. If that powder gets knocked off, they die. Like you with no skin."

Colin's hands sprung open. The moth spiralled off. A shred of one papery wing stuck to my son's hand. Colin was four years old. Utterly wrecked. Hadn't wanted to hurt the moth. Only hold it for awhile. He ran inside and came back out with a bottle of his Mom's talc powder.

"Where's that moth, Daddy? I can give it its powder back."

My son hasn't an intentionally hurtful bone in his body. The only creature he's ever sought to harm is himself.

I see him a hundred yards back carried in the current. Waving to the tiny crowd not yet battened down. He tucks inside the barrel he's had made—he honestly had people working on it—and the earth sits stunned on its axis. I cycle the motor to cut a path through the pink-flaked water, aiming for the spot where they usually come up if they come up at all and the earth starts spinning as my son hits the head of the cataract and I see him in there curled fetally—swear to *Christ* I see him—lit up in a blaze of his own kindling. So hot his shape is an echo of the sun itself.

"Square it!"

Screaming this over the motor's roar and the

boom of the Falls, hammering the engine full-bore and skipping over the water, spray wetting my face so I can no longer tell if I'm bawling, though it's highly conceivable I am.

"Go on go square that bastard one more time!"

My son melts a path into the day. Burning through like an ember through a page painted every colour of our world. Throttling headlong to catch him and when I reach for him he will take my hand.

I have never seen anything burn so fierce trapped so close to earth.

BLACK POWDER

STARDUST

On the day she ordered a police deputy to shoot my squirrel, Clara "Mama" Russell sat on her bed with a baby and a short-barrelled revolver.

I'd come home from school to discover my pet squirrel, Alvin, shot. He'd gotten into the baby's pram. But Alvin was harmless. The baby wasn't even hers. I banged on her door. Jeffrey, one of her boys, answered. Well-dressed and terribly clean. Another of her boys, Teddy, would later burn our house down.

"Mama's pipe is flowing very black," said Jeffrey.

I pushed past him and found Mama with the baby and the gun. Mama Russell, a solid woman. A human dumptruck. But right then, with her radish eyes and bloody fingernails, she looked like a cheap umbrella blown inside-out by the wind.

"Patience Nanavatti, isn't it? The fireworker's daughter."

"Yes, ma'am."

"Mama."

"Yes, Mama."

A shiny silver six-shooter. I'd never seen a gun. Could have been fake except for how it dimpled the duvet. That way its weight expressed itself. Mama picked it up. She tickled the baby's foot with the gun's silver hammer. Then she set the barrel under her own chin. Brought it to the tip of one ear round the curve of her neck. Had it been a razor she would've slit her own throat.

"What it is to be a parent," she said. "Choices. Each more difficult than the last."

Her eyes snagged on that silver "O" of the barrel as it traced the her upper lip. She seemed perplexed to find it there—in her house, in her hands—and she dropped it.

"Oh! But it isn't loaded."

She never did show me the empty chambers.

"You won't tell anyone. Our secret, Patience. Promise me."

"I promise."

The woman angles through racks of OshKosh B'Gosh bib overalls and Jamboree caterpillar-patterned dresses under a display poster of a bugeyed kid heaving on a giant harmonica. She vanishes behind a bin of picked-over boxer shorts.

Wal-Mart. High-intensity fluorescents, elevator music—presently Belinda Carlisle's "Heaven is a Place on Earth"—the thoughtless seethe as shoppers quest for Windex or paperclips or rotisserie chickens. Spell of consumerism: they find themselves outside with bags of crap viable under these lights but in the sane light of day clearly worthless. *Fuck me,* they must think, *what am I doing with this giant plastic candy cane full of cinnamon hearts?*

Myself, I steal. Whatever fits unobtrusively in my pockets. Batteries up to D-cell. Panties, though a woman with too many panties seems debauched. Dr. Scholl's jelly shoe inserts, even though nothing's the matter with my feet. Not that I'm poor. Only that walking past the sensors—I make sure to rip off the magnetized tags—girdled with ill-gotten loot, I am satiated. Before long the emptiness crawls back. My existence is consumed, in fact, by emptiness avoidance. I'll scan nuptial announcements in the paper, don a fugly crinoline dress, show up at churches to insert myself into photographs. It's an art, fitting unobtrusively into the frame. Time it right and there's you with a shit-eating grin backgrounding an earnest portrait of total strangers. My crinoline dress and goofy grin cropping up in wedding albums all over the Niagara peninsula; couples will flip through years later wondering: *Who the hell's that?*

and say: "She must be from *your* side of the family."

That woman in kidswear is shoplifting. I can smell my own. Normally I'd watch the rent-a-cops descend on her. Instead I return the Energizers to their hook and trail after. Down an aisle of picture frames: the same cute, blonde, pigtailed girl grins out of them all. Passing through women's wear I unhook all the bras on the display mannequins: a horde of armless, legless, nipple-less silver torsos in my wake. Catch my profile in a mirrored support column: green eyes beneath brows that fail to reach the inner edge of my eyes give my face a truck-flattened, wide-set aspect. A combat jacket from the Army Surplus. We frumps are the most easily ignored.

I find her in Housewares fingering crockpots. She can't steal those—tough to convince security you're afflicted with a crockpot-sized stomach tumour—so I figure she'll make for Cosmetics. Stuff her socks with eyeliner pencils. She's really down at the hoof. An air of unconcern about her looks. Except there's no calculation to it, the way some people go about slovenly as a half-assed statement. No more interest in her appearance than your average bag lady.

She pulls a U-ey at Fabrics. I lose her amidst un-ravelling bolts of merino wool. I do my best impression of a neurotic shopping for pinking shears—"These ones have the comfort-grip handles," I whisper. "These are endorsed by Martha Stewart"—until she exits the public toilets.

Wal-Mart's toilets. Same Wal-Mart halogens, same Wal-Mart paint: eggshell white with a greenish under-hue. The colour of an egg with a stillborn chick inside. Water slicked over the tiles. Had she tried to flush a tampon—a boxful?

A puffy lump wedged down the lone bowl. My-coloured: I mean to say, the colour of skin. The fact it's in a toilet prevents my understanding. A baby in a crapper fails to conform to any known reality so remains as unbelievable as satellite footage of that same baby orbiting Saturn. Face down, arms pinned in the guts of the bowl where the plumbing begins so all I see is a wad, not distinguishably human, clogging things.

I reach into the toilet to grip the body and turn it, *her*, face up. Skin stained 2,000 Flushes blue. I accidentally bonk her head on the lid and hope to Christ I didn't hit her fontanelle and squash something—her sense of smell? zest for life?—permanently.

I cradle her, dripping, to the diaper change station. Root my index finger through her mouth fearing the insane bitch stuffed her throat full of toilet paper. Close my lips over her mouth and nose. I might've inhaled her entire head if it wasn't so bulbous, that being the style of baby heads. Blow too hard and I'll rupture her lungs. So I'm blowing as if to inflate a fleshed-out plum.

Not a cough, sigh, or puke and all this is now barrelling toward a senseless end. Trying to pour life into a permanently stopped vessel—had to head the list of Worst Human Experiences. Top five, guaranteed. My fingerprints all over this beautiful dead body.

"Breathe." Thumb-pumping her sternum. "You stupid little bitch, *breathe*."

A gutful of warm toilet water. This wee infant girl's bawling.

I was told my mother died birthing me. You could say I killed her, though this is the only course nature can unfortunately take. My father survived, but you could say his heart did not. It went hard as pig leather in his chest, with no capacity for much else but me. And Alvin, as it would turn out.

Philip Nanavatti, my father, built fireworks. An archaic livelihood, same as a cobbler. His work funded by cigarette companies who organized a competition, Symphony of Fire, where fireworkers from across the globe set off volleys from rafts floating on Lake Ontario. He was more wizard than artisan. Much of this had to do with what he created. A cobbler mends shoes, a pair of which is owned by everyone and exist permanently beneath our eyes; through natural processes of alignment, the cobbler comes to be seen the same. Fireworks are totally unnecessary. The cobbler is earthbound. The fireworker's domain is the heavens.

He looked the part of wizard, albeit a modern-day variety. A threadbare man who cultivated a beard out of expediency and the rising cost of razor blades. His favourite article of clothing a macrame poncho bought on a Pueblo reserve, which he wore in his drafty basement workroom. Drywall hung with tools whose outlines he traced in black marker. Unlike other handymen whose toolboxes contained spanners and drillbits and lugnuts, my father's contained pill bottles—he bought them wholesale from a medi-supply company—full of powders, pellets, shards, clusters, and gems all carefully labelled. Sodium D-Line. Potassium Perchlorate. Rice Starch. The indentation of safety goggles permanently impressed into the flesh round his eyes, the way spectacle-wearers have nose-pad grooves on their noses.

My father once found a box of flashcubes at a garage sale. A joyous discovery, it turned out. We returned home with haste, to the basement, where he put the cubes in a vice and drilled a hole through the paper-thin glass.

"Everything on earth is made up of four

elements," he told me. "Carbon, hydrogen, oxygen, nitrogen. All living things are carbon-based. There is a static number of carbon atoms on our planet. No more or less today than a trillion years ago. Things are born, live, expire, break down to component elements. Those carbon atoms go on to be part of new life. Like plasticine: mould a dog, smush it up, mould a cat. The bulk of matter never changes. Only the creations."

He had me fetch an egg from the icebox. He poked a hole in it to drain white and yolk. He mixed coloured magnesium with the flashbulb powder and funnelled it into the egg. Wadding, a fuse, sealed with a bead of paraffin wax.

"You and I are cobbled together out of carbon cells that were once other things entirely. You may have a trilobite's tail in your elbow, pet. A cell from Attila the Hun in your eye. Your tonsils could have a brontosaurus nail in them."

"Where did we come from?"

"The simplest answer is the stuff making up all life is hydrogen, whose atoms come from the fusion process taking place at the centre of suns. So I suppose you can say we come from stellar waste." He touched the tip of his tongue to a canine tooth. "Or from stardust. Better?"

"Better."

"Stardust, then."

The park near our house had shuffleboard courts. White sandblasted stone. Dad centred the egg on the court and waved me back to the jungle gym. He lit the fuse and ran with hands tucked over his head: gait of a soldier running down a foxhole.

"A carbonized imprint," he said after the detonation. "Magical, isn't it?"

The shuffleboard court was framed with colours, shapes, patterns or their raw inklings. A solar system in miniature: every manifestation of life, insect and beast and plant and forms long extinct or as yet undiscovered helixing into each other, nameless in their complexities. Limbs and stalks, broken angles, conchial whorls, geographic forms that struck as unnatural only as they existed beyond my understanding. The arch of a swan's neck thinned into an umbilical cord shot through with emerald threads spidering into beetle-legged strands which in turn shattered into violently-coloured orbits. Such designs must exist, invisible, all about us. When the powder in that egg ignited, powerful chemical magnets drew them out of the air to imprint them, recklessly, on the stone.

Who else but a wizard could conjure a sight like that?

Lieutenant Daniel Mulligan is attractive if horse-toothed. He smiles in a manner that—were his lips to skin back to reveal the pink beds his teeth are buried in—might be wolfish. A horse-toothed wolf?

A corkboard-panelled room at the Niagara Regional Police headquarters. Terrazzo tiles scuffed with shoe skidmarks. It's not difficult to envision them being made by a stave-gutted plainclothesman pivoting on his brogan to smash a telephone book into a poor perp's skull. Lt. Mulligan picks at a wart on his index finger. Distressingly, it resembles a nipple. A finger-nipple. A . . . fipple? When I think of his hands upon my body—as I've been doing since he came in—I now picture spongy growths like toadstools popping up every place he's touched.

"The woman. Tell us what she looked like."

"Us?"

"The constabulary working this case."

"I'm a case?"

Mulligan smiles.

"You're a good Samaritan. Yes?"

He sets a folder on the table. *Patience Nanavatti* on a label affixed to its tab. Cleat-shod music-box ballerinas spin pirouettes up my spine.

"My permanent record?"

He flips it open. "Says here you peed your pants in grade five gym. Kidding. That whole 'permanent record' stuff, it's bullsh—malarkey. If everyone left that kind of paper trail, paper-pushers would get biceps big as grapefruits shoving it around." His laugh indicates the paper-pushers of his acquaintance are shrivelled of arm. "You're nervous."

"Trying to remember if I peed my pants in grade five."

"That's not germane to the investigation."

He directs my attention to a wall-mounted TV. "Security tapes. Took awhile to get clearance—big conglomerates."

Footage: iron greys wash into gauzier greys. Spots of polar whiteness. Humanoid shapes move herky-jerk: the world's most tedious nickelodeon show. The woman is a dark, jagged, lumpen apparition ghosting through the frame.

"That's her."

"Right, we've ascertained as much. What we're interested in, Ms. Nanavatti—"

"Patience. Please."

"Details, Patience. The description you gave the onsite officer . . . you told him"—reading directly from the page—"*the perpetrator seemed to be enveloped in malaise*. He's also transcribed your claim she didn't have an evil heart."

"She was confused. Or ill." Tapping my skull. "You know . . ."

"Descriptions such as 'having the eyes of a hunted animal' aren't valuable from an investigative standpoint."

"She looked . . . like she could use a friend?"

Mulligan rubs his forehead as if a toothy determined *something* were trying to tunnel out. His pleading expression softens the contours of his face. More handsome than the last guy I dated. An in-demand sessional musician, he said. He performed the guitar riff that plays over the Seven-day Forecast on the Weather Channel. He couldn't come inside me. Retarded ejaculation; I looked it up. A phobia based on insecurity. Fear of losing control. Or of infection, which seemed more likely: he told me he'd slept with a groupie "on tour," afterwards spotting a pubic louse drowned in the bus toilet. A tiny banjo with pincers, he said. We worked on it. We'd have sex and when he was close I'd get out of bed and stand in a corner so he could masturbate. Next I sat in bed while he jerked off. We worked all the way up to him spurting on my tummy. Soon after finishing inside me the first time—he wore two condoms—he moved to Portland to join a jam band.

"Are you an artist, Patience?" Mulligan asks. "What is it you do for a living?"

I hand him a glossy leaflet out of my purse. A naked woman, red-haired and busty. Pink stars over her nipples. A large pink star over her crotch. *EZWhores-For-Fone! 1-976-SLUT (UK: 976-SLAG)! The Original Phone Sex Maniacs! Fetish Cellar! Sissy Training!*

Imagine attending a dinner party at an acquaintance's home and using the washroom but instead of the bathroom door you mistakenly open the door to a closet full of mannequin parts. The look on your face at that moment is the same look Lt. Mulligan wears right now.

"I'm only an operator," I tell him. "I facilitate caller interactions."

He slips the leaflet into his blazer pocket. "Ah."

"The woman had brown eyes." Brown is the most common shade and nothing about the woman was remarkable. "Dark brown."

He scribbles this down. I ask what's going to happen to her.

"We have to locate her first."

"I don't mean her."

"Yes, right. Baby's at the General Hospital. Tests, that kind of thing."

"Can I see her? It may jog something."

"I'll check."

"Will you go out for a cup of coffee?" Compelled to clarify: "With me?"

"My wife would not approve of me sharing coffees with strange women."

I'd seen his wedding ring. Many people are married. Not all happily so.

Great fireworks displays," my father said, "should expand within a viewer's mind."

The Mushrooming Imprint. My father's phrase. It describes the effect any disciplined fireworks engineer should strive for. All displays leave a stamp upon the sky: only gasses in their dissipation, as unremarkable as fumes exiting a tailpipe. *The Mushrooming Imprint* was created when viewers closed their eyes as the lingering afterimage evolved. You could go a lifetime, eighty or ninety firsts of July, never seeing *The Mushrooming Imprint*.

My father's signature firework was 'Bioluminescence.'

"Some creatures produce their own light, Patience. It's called 'cold light,' as it produces no heat. The anglerfish has a glowing bell dangling off the front of its face on a pole of skin, like a man holding a lantern before him in a storm. Smaller fish are enticed into attacking the bell and the anglerfish"—he brought his palms sharply together—"chomp! Deepsea fish cannot exist in sunlight. If you one netted one and dragged it to the surface, its skin would turn to jelly and slide right through your fingers."

"Bioluminescence" began by affixing pellets of nitrate fertilizer to monofilament fishing line using a dab of superglue. My father tied these to wooden dowels suspended in a refrigerator box containing a dog's breakfast of camphors and chlorides, the concentrations of which were guarded even from me. The box sat in our basement—"The Fermentation"— and when its seams were cracked the powders had drawn up to coat the pellets. Gumball-sized with patinas invidious to their creation. Some were riots of colour with rips of magenta and gold. Others dusty under camphorous wraps. They went into honeypots packed with black powder.

Each ball, wearing dozens of chemical coats, blasted skyward on a tight trajectory. They bounced off one another; each collision peeled a coat. Every carom and ricochet sent the spectacle higher as it burnt brighter. The balls had a brief life span as combustion and contact peeled them down to their fertilizer cores, which burst with a faraway sound not unlike milk-doused Rice Krispies.

Closing your eyes—as spectators did, instinctively—you would see *The Mushrooming Imprint*. Think of warm breath on a winter windowpane: tendrils of radiating frost, each unique to the breather.

My father was a genius. Narrow of scope, but nevertheless.

I asked my father how creatures came to exist at the bottom of the sea. He said over trillions of years weaker specimens got pushed down deep. Relegated to blackest waters.

"Darwinism, pet. Big eats small. Nature has its hierarchy. They didn't end up there of their choice. Who could want to live in the dark?"

Yet the colossal squid hunts the darkest ocean channels and will attack sperm whales, sharks, even orcas. Prehistoric Megalodon, ten times the size of a great white shark, is believed to still exist in volcanic trenches along the sea bed. As a child it was the darkness between fireworks that enthralled me. The ongoing dark of an unlit sky. Even today I'll wake in the still hours of night to stare pie-eyed into the darkest corner of my room. Dimensionless black like a hunger. Some organisms are happiest at bonecracking depths, guided by lights of their own kindling.

"Ms. Nanavatti? Patience Nanavatti?"

"This is she."

"Donald Kerr. From Wal-Mart. The legal end of the boat."

I picture him hogfaced in a southernfried lawyer getup. Those white suits that incorporate the sweat of their wearers to set the works aglitter like a stretch of sun-dappled shoreline.

"We're calling to see how you've been since your . . . little incident."

"We're calling?"

"I mean to say, we, the legal team. May I first of all say, kudos! Were it not for your calm in the eye of the typhoon, a young life would have been snuffed. A toilet. Dear *God.* Happens every day, Ms. Nanavatti; that's the horrifying truth. Babies left in Arby's dumpsters and worse. The other day one poor dear was found in a crack den—you're familiar with crack, Ms. Nanavatti? The inexpensive derivative of *cocaine*?—in a crack den, Ms. Nanavatti, behind the *radiator*, Ms. Nanavatti. Good Lord," he says, as if in horrified realization at the past fifty words to exit his mouth. "Mainly women commit these acts. As I've noticed in researching the incident you were involved in. The hero of! I mean not to impugn your sex; yours is the better of mine, as anyone associated with reprobate behaviour will attest. You try to make sense of it, Ms. Nanavatti. I mean myself, a man, a father. Beggars reason. An ongoing struggle between mother and child? The mother's way of saying, *I bore you into this world, chum, and I can as easily take you out*?"

I smile. Not at the grisly bent of Donald Kerr's mind, but at the fact a company of Wal-Mart's stature has retained such a colossal wingnut as legal council.

"I never thought of it that way."

"Who would? Crazyperson talk! This job'll do that to the best of us—not to claim I ever was. Have you children, Ms. Nanavatti?"

"Not as yet."

"Flummoxed to hear it. Scalded, electrocuted, burnt to bones. Horrifying to do to anyone, let alone an infant. Donald," he scolds himself, an old dog beyond better breeding. "Again, I apologize.

Some at this firm believe I ought to retire, Ms. Nanavatti. Rumblings I've become an eyesore and embarrassment."

"Are you calling in reference to a problem?"

"Oh-ho-ho, heavens no! It's only . . . have you much familiarity with the law, Ms. Nanavatti? Law*suits*? Citizens of our great land have it into their heads they're karmically entitled to gross financial recuperation for every petty inconvenience. It's a finger-pointing, me-first, I-was-wronged-so-gimme-gimme legal system. Give a jackal a bite of meat and it'll come ripping for your jugular!"

He apologized for this second outburst. I was beginning to like Donald Kerr.

"Ms. Nanavatti, you may recall that dizzy old grandma—sorry, sorry; everybody's got a grandma—that dotty old darling who dumped McDonald's coffee in her lap. A cool mil for a first-degree burn? Buy plenty of calamine lotion. Marinate in the muck. Okay, maybe her coffee was a touch hot. What's the alternative? Serve it cold? Nonsense! Consider your—our—situation in this light. A baby nearly dies in a washroom. Not any old washroom: the most successful retail chain in the free world. Not flukily or through folly of its own devising. Maliciously. What can my client do? Video cameras in their bathrooms? Fah! Customers will worry about seeing themselves on those Girls-Caught-Peeing websites.

No bathrooms, then? Let shoppers tinkle into the pockets of winter coats? Building codes dictate sanitary washrooms in retail outlets. It's one itty-bitty word, *safe*, at issue. Are the bathrooms safe? Insofar as there is nothing innately dangerous about them. Wal-Mart's hardware section isn't innately dangerous until someone grabs a hammer and brains somebody in Electronics. Nothing innately dangerous about coffee, either. Still, one clumsy dingbat made *mucho* hay off a cup of coffee. There's always that nickel to be shaved." Donald Kerr laughs a sporting laugh. "Bleed the beast but leave enough to keep the heart pumping to bleed it a little more!"

"I'd better have my people call your people," I tell him, and hang up.

Afterwards I decide to take a walk. The sky is threatening so: galoshes and an umbrella. After two blocks the clouds withdraw. Sunlight paints the neighbourhood. My feet, trapped in military-surplus rainboots, are sweating furiously. Mormon kids from Glenridge Academy pedal by on bicycles: boys and girls dressed the same, riding the same sized bikes with matching white helmets following their headmistress. Ducklings waddling after their mother.

At the elementary school children are out on recess. Pierced upon the chainlink fence are pop cans and pudding cups. A girl with a mouthful of orange-pulp-clung braces holds out sticks to three friends.

"Whoever gets the shortest stick we'll hate for the rest of the day."

Were a man standing here as I am, rainboots and an umbrella on a cloudless day staring intently over a schoolyard, you'd think he was a molester. But onlookers would peg me as deranged or more likely, wistful. *She wants a child*. I'm fairly certain I could be a molester.

My gaze is drawn to a fat boy in a black cape. Sitting alone on a teeter-totter. The sight strikes me as emblematic of futility possibly cosmic in scope. He's eating candy shaken from a brightly coloured box. Nerds. I haven't eaten Nerds in decades. Abruptly I wish to taste the world as a child.

At the supermarket I stride past a bin of multicoloured spuds—*BOUTIQUE POTATOES ½ PRICE!*—to the candy aisle. Scan for floorwalkers before prying the lid off a tub of gummy worms. Oh! Too bloody sweet. How do kids eat this garbage?

On to the baby aisle. I may look motherly in that my surroundings support that viewpoint. By placing me against a forest backdrop I'd look outdoorsy. Or in a rubber room: bonkers. Lord, all the diapers! Ultra-slim: what sort of parent is so paranoid about their baby's girth they need to buy low-profile turd-collectors? Super-absorbent with moisture-lock gussets. These ones claim to be completely redesigned. How does one *completely* redesign a diaper without Mother Nature first redesigning the human excretory system?

Baby food. Strained Bananas and Prunes catches my eye. It was all my father ate his last months. He said it hurt him to eat. I thought he meant hurt his teeth or belly, but the act inflicted more of a philosophical pain. Fuel for a motor that idiotically kept running. Mashed fruit: our first and last spoonfuls. The first from our parents and the last from our children.

"Perhaps you'll have a child," my father said towards the end, "and I will become part of them. A carbon atom in his eye or a vessel of her heart."

"That's stupid. Don't talk that way."

"It's a loop. Continuous."

"And everything and everyone must be on this blessed loop? What about . . . televangelists?"

"Yes, pet." His chuckle dissolved into a hacking fit. "Even them."

It isn't stupid. It's the most unselfish theory of the afterlife I know of: instead of your spirit floating intact upon a cloud, you particalize into millions of fresh lives.

A jar of Blueberry Tapioca goes into my pocket. Wax Beans and Vegetable. Fruit Medley. At home I arrange them in a pyramid on the table. The answering machine flashes.

Lieutenant Mulligan from the NRP. It's been approved for you to view the baby. . . .

I had a pet squirrel. I wanted to name him Alvin, after the cartoon character. My father preferred Ming Fa, after a fireworks guru from feudal China.

Alvin entered our lives in the jaws of Excelsior, Mama Russell's sweet-tempered sheepdog. She deposited the red, squealing, saliva-slick blob on our lawn.

At the house of our neighbour, Frank Saberhagen, there once stood a pine tree. The tree failed to jibe with Saberhagen's post-divorce aesthetic: he'd ripped out the sod, salted the earth, and carpeted his yard with shaved white schist imported from Egypt. The pine was plagued with bark weevils. Needles gone brown. Only the doctor's macabre taste kept it alive.

A brain surgeon who'd assisted on the groundbreaking Labradum Procedure at Johns Hopkins, Saberhagen evidently found it cathartic to set aside the scalpel in favour of the double-bitted axe. A fluid tornado of a man with the tight-packed frame of a circus acrobat, he'd stood shirtless, axe in hand, boots gritting on the schist comprising his front yard—a horticultural perversity rendering him *persona non grata* in the neighbourhood—taking crazed strokes at the tree. For all his deftness in the operating theatre, Saberhagen was a bungler when it came to lumberjacking. The axe blade ricocheted off the trunk. Pine cones pelted his head.

"Give 'er hell, Quincy!" called his neighbour, Fletcher Burger. Saberhagen's nickname was based on the coroner played by Jack Klugman in the series of the same name, the morbid suggestion being Saberhagen was such a poor surgeon his professional dossier included as many corpses as the fictional coroner.

Observing the flailings of his owner was Moxie: a vile-tempered corgi Saberhagen had been forced to accept during his divorce proceedings. Whereas in many divorces custody of a pet is viciously quarrelled over, the Saberhagens' quarrel was over who would be obliged to shuffle the dog off its mortal coil. The ex-Mrs. Saberhagen—who at a block party was heard stating that her then-hubby possessed "All the personal charm of a deathwatch beetle," and went on to characterize him as "giving about as much back to the world as a drainpipe"—was victorious. The flatulent, oily-coated, grumpy old dog became Frank's tortuous burden.

Moxie was deeply disagreeable. He constantly escaped Saberhagen's yard by digging under the fence. Nobody would pet him on account of (a) the corgi's furious digging occasioned some breed of canine skin disorder manifesting in a greasy hide that stunk of rotting fruit and (b) Moxie snapped at anyone who petted him, anyway, providing less incentive to perform what was already a revolting kindness. Cross-eyed and splenetic, Moxie pissed on marigolds and harassed birds at their baths. Saberhagen no longer responded when his pager flashed: *Neighbour called. Dog loose again.*

Saberhagen eventually delivered the pine's deathblow. The tree split up its trunk and toppled. Moxie was splayed on the porch with Nick, Saberhagen's son. Cross-eyed as he was, the corgi did note the clutch of baby squirrels tipped from their nest. He bounded off the porch to gleefully gulp down three or four.

Their frightful dying squeals compelled Excelsior to leap off Mama Russell's porch into Saberhagen's yard. Crazed on squirrel meat, Moxie lunged for the much larger sheepdog's throat. Excelsior seized the corgi by his scruff and whipsawed her head to fling Moxie a good ten feet. The dog's ungraceful trajectory took him over the tree; he hit harshly and rolled as tumbleweeds do.

Excelsior rooted through the branches to recover the remaining squirrels. That all four fit safely in the pouches on either side of her teeth was the first oddity. The second was that she dropped them on four different lawns. One she left at the Hills. One she left at Mama Russell's house, where it was taken in by her "boy," Jeffrey. One for Abigail Burger. Alvin given to me.

"The momma squirrel won't take it back now," my father said. "Your scent's on it. It's tainted. The mother might eat it. Mothers can be like that. In the animal kingdom."

We packed a shoebox with cotton batten and set Alvin beneath a gooseneck lamp. I was concerned this may scald him: his pink skin put me in mind of the flesh under a fresh-picked scab. His paws so much like tiny human hands. I wished he would open his eyes so I might intuit what he wanted. But when his eyes did open they were inexpressive black bulbs.

Each day Alvin remained alive, often barely so, I took as a breed of miracle. My father filled an eyedropper with cornstarch-thickened milk and fed him. He'd squirt hypoallergenic soap into his palm, set Alvin in the bowl of his hand to clean him with gentleness bordering on reverence.

"So fragile. Bones like sugar."

A covering of black fur filled over Alvin's body. His tail, a nippley nubbin, came in bushy. He never grew quite as big as a squirrel should.

One afternoon he dashed out the patio door. My father pursued—"Alvin! Come to your senses!"— and, spying him in the crotch of the backyard elm, jabbed a banana on the end of a stick as an enticement. When the squirrel refused, Dad mooned by the window, yet he soon turned philosophical. Not an abandonment, he reasoned, but the animal's natural predilection.

"Squirrels live in trees. Gather nuts. As they've always done."

"Sorry I left the patio door open, Dad."

"Never mind, pet. Recall the old saying: 'If you love something, let it go.'"

Overjoyed as my father was when Alvin returned that night, he resolved to let an animal be an animal. Mornings Alvin bolted out his squirrel-door—a miniature doggy door my father installed—to dash across the fencelines attaching yard to yard. Plaguing, in the inimitable manner of squirrels, the local canine population. Even Excelsior chased Alvin, who chattered cheekily from a high bough while the poor sheepdog howled.

Later, Alvin was shot dead with a revolver.

Mama Russell took in troubled children. Her "boys," they were known. Teddy and Jeffrey spent years in her care. Others who broke curfew or broke into neighbours' houses were sent away. At the time of Alvin's death, Social Services remanded an infant into Mama's custody until a foster family could be secured. Mama named him Carter, though she had no right. Afternoons she paraded baby Carter round the court in a pram. Alvin, naturally curious, stole into the pram. I pieced this together afterwards.

Mama swatted at Alvin, who scrambled up a tree. Mama called the police. A cruiser was dispatched. A deputy not long on duty unloaded on Alvin with his service revolver. Centre of mass, as they teach at the academy.

A squirrel weighing that of a bar of soap. Annihilated. My first attempt at parenthood culminated with a squirrel so blown apart there wasn't much to bury.

"You mustn't give your heart to wild things," my father said that night. "Or take on burdens of care more than you need to."

"But aren't I a burden?"

"I had no choice with you, pet. And was glad not to. But." Spoken with finality. "But."

Take the hospital elevator to the pediatric ward. The evening shift nurse—body garrulous in heft but her face having none of it—eyes me in my military surplus parka. REYNOLDS stamped in black on the breast pocket.

"A fine thing, what you did," she says, after I identify myself. "Lucky you were there."

The compliment comes off backhanded: as if my managing to rescue the baby was as unbelievable as my having landed a harrier jump-jet on a cocktail napkin. The nurse glides past darkened delivery rooms on soft-soled shoes silent as a razor blade through a bowl of water. A mesh-inlaid mirror runs the length of the nursery. Inside I am struck by the smell of new life.

We're all rotting. Your body hits a peak at eighteen, maybe, and that perfect bodily zenith lasts how long? A day, or a few hours of that day? Next, descent and decay. Strains and aches and dimming sight. Stuff yourself with carcinogens because you've surrendered to the inevitability of collapse. You get winded climbing a flight of stairs. Following that, lumps and lesions to ice your heart. The Big C? Hold the whole tortured works together another fifty years and you're granted the merciful stillness of the grave.

But the nursery is stuffed full of showroom-model humans. Brand-spanking new, factory-fresh rolled off the assembly line. Impregnated with that new-baby smell. Assaulted by pound upon pound of sprightly, helpless baby-meat, I fleetingly wish I was some breed of vampire. A youth vampire. Flap round the nursery on talcum-powdered wings poking my head into hermetically-sanitized tubs to hoover the youthful essence out of these helpless things. Partake of their luscious and nourishing, sinfully *yummy* esprit. Drain these beautiful babes until I was a child again and my organs no longer on the rot, cherubic as I dash away shed of my too-big clothes. I'd flee barefoot from a nursery full of withered crepe-paper baby husks.

"So small," I say, peering at my little toilet baby. "Was she . . ."

"A preemie?" The nurse shakes her head. "Only malnourished. Think of a plant under a porch: it'll grow down there in the dark and damp. Just not so well."

"May I have some time alone?"

"Make it quiet time. If one wakes, they all wake."

The baby's name card affixed to the tub: JANE DOE #2. I section her sleeping face in search of the woman who'd tried to murder her. But that woman exists in my memory only as a tangle of emotional drives. Her face is my own face. The face of everyone I've even known. She made a premeditated choice to dump this life in a retail chain toilet. Abdicate her responsibilities in such vicious fashion. How had she seen her life changing? Your own defenseless child— how deep must you core into any heart to find that mammoth well of expedience?

Unbutton my coat. Cradled in stirrups of my own creation—oversize suspenders accommodating a cardboard papoose—is a doll I'd stolen from a toy store.

Teddy, another of Mama Russell's boys, set fire to my father's workshop and burnt to death in our basement. Dad was mailing a package. I was in my bedroom with Abigail Burger, Fletcher Burger's daughter.

Teddy was a pygmy pyromaniac with burn scars on his arms pink as pulled taffy. He wore boxy black glasses with melted armatures. He'd soak ant hills in lighter fluid and set them ablaze. He said things like: "My penis is two and a third inches long" or "Anacondas have one twelve-foot-long lung" or "My mama had a nerve disorder. And Poppa is a sailor." He was known to eat his elbow and knee scabs. Cut holes in his trouser pockets so he could squeeze his testicles. Mama had Teddy wear linen gloves so he wouldn't break the skin as he throttled them. He shimmied through our basement window while Abigail and I ran our squirrels through a maze of shoe boxes and toilet paper rolls.

Abby was my only real friend. Her father, Fletcher, had the bombastic and overbearing demeanour of an East German gymnastics coach. Forever dragging her off on bike rides or nature hikes that unfolded more like the Bataan death march. Of orangutang proportions, he was often seen in a sweatsuit with a digital stopwatch strung round his neck.

"Abby!" he'd call. "Bike ride!"

"I don't want to ride my bike."

"Who's that talking? Is it Flabby Abby?"

"I'm not flabby."

"You will be, my dear, if you don't ride your bike."

Fletcher was fanatical about his daughter's fitness. Abby became a champion powerlifter. Her father credited much of her success to his "Energizer Bowls": brown rice, broccoli, and amino acids concocted in massive batches and stored in a chest freezer in the garage. Abby said the last few bowls sat in the freezer so long they tasted like "a doomed Arctic expedition."

The explosion shuddered the entire house. Volcanic wind blew up the ventilation ducts. Spumes of burning dust. Abby and I went to the window. The lawn sparkled with glass. Flames climbed the siding from blown-apart casements. Our squirrels scrambled down the downspout. We followed suit. Abby fell and snapped her wrist. A hole burnt through the roof as it collapsed into the foundation.

Teddy's carbonized skeleton was later doused by firemen. Hands heat-welded to my father's steel workbench. Skull pushed back on his spinal column from the force of the blast.

Insurance covered the rebuilding costs but my father assumed the neighbours blamed him. We moved away from Sarah Court, resettling way across town. Not long after the fire, my father told me I was adopted.

"Patience, sit there on the couch. A bit of a bomb I'll be dropping."

Less a bomb than a grenade lobbed between us—a grenade he'd feared would shatter my psyche, sense of self, my whatever else. It occasioned in me nothing but curiosity.

Where was I adopted?

"An institution north of here. I wasn't an ideal candidate but a solid citizen."

How did I end up there?

"Nobody saw the need to tell me. People do take on burdens that overmaster them."

Why take me in?

"You needed adopting. I was in a position to do so."

Did it ever scare you—being a father?

"There should be a training guide for new fathers. Either your head's screwed on tight and gets unscrewed, or you come into it a wreck and fatherhood is a centralizing circumstance to an even greater crackup. Fatherhood destroys some men."

He offered to help track my parents down. I'd no urge to find them. My father was Philip Nanavatti: this fact as cleanly connected to me as each finger at the end of each hand. The circle closed upon itself and I was content within its circumference. That I may still have a mother was no different than discovering I had an extra organ. A tiny sac or bladder that contributed nothing to my health nor brought about any sickness. A surgeon could excise it, yes, but since it was benign and I could quite happily exist with it somewhere within me, why bother?

"Your mother was not a bad person, pet."

I never thought of her as bad. My mother is any one of a billion women in as many conditions. In prison or a boardroom or an oil sheik's harem. A housewife in Paramus, New Jersey. A roller derby queen going by the name of Cinnamon Kiss in Poughkeepsie. A cipher, as the woman who stuffed baby Jane into a toilet was a cipher.

My mother died birthing me.

The only worrisome quality to not knowing your parents is you don't truly know yourself. You never know what you are capable of, as you cannot see your roots. The skews of their braiding. What they touch, or fail to.

It's that time of evening where the sun rests at that particular point in the sky: hitting your eyes directly, sunlight robs the world of dimension. Buildings become black cut-outs hammered flat by the refraction of the sun. A shape darts onto the road. I swerve, no thump, missing it.

Jane Doe sits in a car seat facing away from the dashboard. Otherwise if I crashed, accidentally or on purpose, the passenger-side airbag would deploy to crush the little-bitty bones of her face. I hit the QEW highway, going east. A squad car rushes past in the opposite lane. The highway wends past Niagara Falls to the Fort Erie border. It suddenly occurs to me that my mental state is not up to explaining Jane to the border guards.

I return to St. Catharines and park at the Big Bee convenience store near the bus depot. I pull in beside a minivan, unbuckle baby Jane, and enter the store. I microwave pablum in one of the baby bottles I'd bought. Another customer scans a low shelf with his back to me. I spy a pack of fireworks next to sacks of expired dog kibble. The microwave dings. I dab pablum on my wrist. Outside a man hops into the minivan and peels off. I angle the bottle so Jane's lips clasp round the nipple. Press her warm body to my chest.

Tufford Manor is set off Queenston street. With its bevelled wrought iron gates inset with seraphim, its faux-granite facade shielded by second-growth willows, you'd be forgiven for mistaking it for an upscale condo complex. Until you noted the proliferation of walkers and wheelchairs and oxygen canisters. Orderlies with the air of bored cattle wranglers.

The one behind the desk is a large black man. Above the starched white collar of his uniform, his head seems to float disembodied, in the style of a magician's trick.

"Patience," he says.

"Nice to see you, Clive."

A man so ancient it is conceivable he'd seen his first military engagement during the Boer War staggers into the lobby in his sleeping flannels. His body's all shrivelled up like a turtle that crawled under a radiator.

"Where'd you sneak off to?" Clive spots the box of wooden matches tucked under the old man's arm. "Give them here, Mister Lonnigan."

The old man, Lonnigan, stashes the matches behind his back. They poke past his hipbone.

"Don't make a nuisance," Clive says, gently wresting them away.

"You sadistic bull Negro."

"What have I told you about that trash?"

"Big as a bull, sadistic, and you're a Negro." Lonnigan pronounces it *Negra*. "Where am I lying?"

"You speak to wound. The preferred nomenclature is African Canadian."

Lonnigan's jaw juts. "When are you gonna fix my record player?"

"It's been bust since they rolled you in."

"You said you'd help."

"Tomorrow," says Clive. "Go on, now, give me peace."

"Visiting hours are over," Lonnigan says to me.

"Why fret every little thing, Mister L? Lighten up. You'll live longer," I say.

"Here's a nudie club bartender telling me how to live. I lived plenty enough."

"Nine-tenths of the time he's demented," Clive says to me. "But there's that other tenth."

Clive folds his arms across his chest. A puzzled but not aggressive gesture.

My father died seven months ago. His body's interred up the road. His room presently occupied by someone else.

"I saw these fireworks and thought of Dad."

"Long ways off the First of July, Patience."

"Bad idea?"

Clive unknits his arms. "Long as we aim them over the golf course I can't see the harm."

The courtyard: clean-swept and hemmed on three sides by balconied terraces. Clive wheels Lonnigan out. A patchwork blanket is draped over the old man's legs.

"Mr. L chummed around with your father," says Clive.

"Didn't know you were his relation," Lonnigan says. "That your baby?"

Lonnigan appears to have forgotten we all start out so small. Jane grasps his index finger in her tiny fist.

"The grip on him. Be a ballplayer."

"He's a she."

"I'll be damned."

Clive wrestles a stone flowerpot into the centre of the courtyard. Windows brighten about us. I angle a roman candle east over the golf course.

"We need matches."

"How about it, Mr. L?" says Clive. "You got some matches for the little lady?"

"Skunk. You rotten skunk."

"I smoke," Lonnigan says after Clive's gone inside for some. He cups his neck while he talks, as if to keep in fingertip contact with his heartbeat. "Cherrywood briar. Got the tobacco but they won't let me lay my hands on matches. My doc's a wet-behind-the-ears little sonofabitch shaver. Bastard still wears dental braces. Taking my marching orders from a, a, a—a brace-face. Pipe but no matches. Like to give a man a gun but no bullets. Don't grow old, is my advice to you." He gives this same warning to Jane in a high baby voice: "Don't . . . grow . . . old."

Clive returns with a Zippo. Coloured balls of fire arc over telephone poles at the courtyard's edge. Lonnigan's eyes close. Eyelids thin as tissue paper wormed with red capillaries.

"When we were kids," he says, "we'd find bullets in the fields. Battles had been fought there, you see. We'd take our spades"—he clarifies—"I mean spades as in shovels. Not that we had slaves the colour of Clive here who did our digging."

"I'm sure Patience appreciates your meaning, Mister L."

". . . took our spades and dug up whatever the soldiers left behind or died carrying. Crates of 30-30 slugs. We'd pry the slug-heads off, tap the powder onto a slip of parchment, twist it into a sachet and light the bugger. That was our fireworks."

Screaming Devil, Volcano, Hearts of Fire. Residents occur on their balconies. Me, an old man, Clive, a child whose life I'd first saved and now stolen. If it isn't quite the picture I'd framed in my head . . . had there ever been that picture?

"Fire hazard," calls a fear-stricken voice from one of the surrounding balconies. "Fire hazard!"

"Calm down, missus Horvath," says Clive. "Nothing but fireworks, and see? Landing on the golf course."

"Fire haaaaaaaaaaazard!"

"Large Marge. She's big as a barge." When I ask Lonnigan if that's who had voiced her concern, he chuckles. "No. That's the other Marge yelling."

Clive lights the Burning Schoolhouse. Cathartic for some. I never hated school. The baby's weight against me. Exhale of her lungs.

Close my eyes. Against the canvas of my lids

the schoolhouse burns on. Fresh trajectories and possibilities. Each one of my own summoning.

BLACK BOX

THE ORGANIST

You might configure my existence as a string of air disasters. Commercial jetliners scud-missiled to smithereens in foreign airspace. Botched water landings where the exits crimp shut: eels and sharks dart past the porthole windows like an inside-out aquarium until pressure cracks Plexiglas and the sea rushes in. Lover, husband, father. All ruinous, all fatal. Except I survive. My life a pile of flaming wrecks I somehow stride clear of.

A black box is recovered from each crash site. My own voice catalogues events, idiotic and selfish, principal to each fiasco. It isn't the voice of a man nearing his own excruciating death, face torn up in flames with shards of a shattered instrument panel deep-driven into it. It's the penitent voice of a man addressing his God.

CRAIG DAVIDSON

The houseboat's an Orca Weekender. Its sixty horsepower Evinrude belches lung-blackening smoke. I stripped linens off every bed and piled them in a sultan-like mound on the one where I sleep. Compass, marine radio, microwave, TV: baby's tricked out. Whatever wasn't clamped down I threw overboard. Yawing near shore I blasted every emergency flare at the trees in hopes dead leaves might catch fire. That was yesterday morning when lint-like fog hung over the silvered water until the sun chased it upshore to linger between the trees like low-lying smoke. Raw-beautied county, this far north.

I stole the boat from a hairy-fisted rental agent who overused the word "doggone." As in: "This is the best doggone houseboat in my doggone fleet." As in: "Talk about your doggone fine houseboating weather!" After the umpteenth "doggone" I said to myself: I'm stealing this fucking spaz's doggone property. Handles like a bear. Aim it like a ballistic missile—*precise*—and hold that course or else you're doomed.

What jackass steals a houseboat? A jackass such as myself, evidently. Idiotic as hotwiring a car to drive at speeds not exceeding four knots down the same unending stretch of road. Inlets crook like arthritic thumbs and riverside towns sporadically carve themselves out of the barrens but I am locked upon this waterway.

It's the second vehicle I've stolen. The first was a minivan left running outside a Big Bee store in the city of my birth. Freakishly clean. CDs alphabetized. Bright yellow hockey tape wrapped at '10' and '2' positions on the wheel. So enervated did I become within its confines that I stopped at a ramshackle fried chicken shack hours past Toronto. Manning its counter the ungainliest teenager I'd ever clapped eyes on. This shocked expression you'd find on a man kicked awake in his sleep. On his head sat a paper chicken hat so saturated with sweat and grease its head drooped to peck the gawky sonofabitch in his forehead.

"Welcome to the Chubby Chicken."

The kid blew at his hat same way you'd blow a lock of hair out your eyes. The chicken head popped up, came down, pecked the kid in his head. *Ah, Jesus,* I thought drinking in his dreadful spectre. *This is too fucking sad.* I have been overly sensitive lately, granted, but this cow-eyed cupcake in his soggy chicken hat in the airless middle of Buttfuck Nowhere summoned within me that breed of quasi-abstract sadness where spiritual malaise digs in roots. I mean, not to make too big a deal.

I purchased a family bucket and paid with my credit card. Gave the mopey bastard a hundred dollar tip. Hey, big spender! Such largesse from a man who scant months ago pawed through a box of old birthday cards hoping an overlooked sawbuck might fall out.

I ate the entire bucket. Pure gluttony. Choking down the seventh drumstick the realization dawned that these were modes of behaviour a man would adopt upon the discovery he has a week to live. Once it ceased to matter whether he overate, drank his face off, snorted Borax. Healthy living is an undertaking only men with futures bother with.

Full disclosure: I always wanted a boy.

Shall I put on display the greasy-crawly scraps of my psyche? You won't like me. I don't really give a damn. I want to be understood within the parameters of what I am: a hardcore bastard. A rotten piece of work.

So, honest goods: a boy. Ask a hundred expectant first-time fathers: boy or girl? Ninety-nine will tell you boy. The one who doesn't is giving you the breeze. The imprint of one Fletcher Burger would chalk itself more clearly upon the slate of a boy's mind so I wished for one. But as wishes are fickle, any even-minded wisher should be satisfied with half measures. Which I got: a ten-fingered, ten-toed baby girl.

My marriage was in shambles by then. My wife

caught me sniffing the seat of my jeans to see whether they were clean enough to wear again and refused to kiss me for a week. She'd buy too many bananas and when they blackened throw them in the freezer to bake banana bread that never materialized. "Is it me," I'd go, "or is our freezer full of frozen gorilla fingers?" She stockpiled my foibles in a mental armoury and frequently launched tactical strikes. Blind-siding me with how I begrudged buying my own daughter baby gifts. "She's happiest playing with a crumpled ball of newsprint!" Arguments often ended with her saying: "I never worry about Fletcher Burger's happiness. Someone's always watching out for Fletcher Burger's happiness." Pointing a finger at me. It did anger and disgrace me—I recall weeping over it in a Dollar Store, the most dispiriting and pitiful of retail outlets—that I couldn't love my wife in the manner that, as a husband, I likely should have. The way she probably deserved. Weeping while picking through 99¢ canisters of discontinued, highly flammable silly string. Two of which I bought as stocking stuffers.

We'd relied on that baby to salvage whatever was broken. Yet we knew the only way that could happen was if our kid was born malformed, encephalitic, with a hole in its heart. A *Lorenzo's Oil* scenario to ennoble us through shared suffering. But as Abby was perfectly healthy and neither of us suffered from Münchausen syndrome to make us dissolve rat poison into her pablum, well, that infant life preserver we'd hoped would rescue us from the misery of one another may as well have been tossed off the deck of the Titanic. Fuck it all, anyway. Men and women are fundamentally different creatures. DNA helixes, desires, plumbing, hysteria levels. What fool stuffs a mongoose and a viper into a gunny sack, tosses the sack in a raging river, and harbours hope of a pleasant outcome?

Then Abigail was born . . . staring at her blood-scummed face I knew I'd do anything for her. Never such ache for my wife. On our marital altar all I'd been thinking was: *I will let you down.* Yet I can no longer recall Abby's face with exactitude. They say when a person dies you often lose the image of them; your memories degrade at the pace of that body interred. She isn't dead. Still, I cannot frame her face. Her profile made of sand, continually erased by a steady wind gusting through my head.

The setting sun is a swollen ball backgrounding shore pines as I crank the wheel starboard to butt a dock girded with hacked-apart radial tires. WELCOME TO BOBCAYGEON reads a sign above the marina fuel pumps. Summer rentals all battened down. Locals look startled in their habitat: slugs at the heart of a lettuce head. Catch sight of myself in a shop window. A winnowed aspect to my face. You'd think its angles had been scored using a dentist's drill.

The bar's enclosed by a wrought-iron fence. Girls too young to be legal sit on the patio with a jug of radiant green cocktail resembling engine coolant. Inside it's quiet enough to hear the *suck-suck* of sorrows in their drowning. The assembled rubbydubs' faces look fashioned from slum-grade tin. Pitted, discoloured, robbed of whatever dignity flesh possesses robing men of substance. Fuck me if I don't fit right in. The draft beer glows unhealthily. Quaffing the blood of an irradiated god.

Blood. Bones. Organs.

Imagine your breastbone cracked apart. Organs gouged from knits of silverskin. Price tags clipped to each. How much is a gently used gallbladder worth? Liver and pancreas and heart and kidneys attached to threads extending thousands of miles. Design of those commercial airline maps tucked into seatbacks: a fountain of red threads departing The International Airport of You. Those threads are mercilessly winched and your parts skip-roll-bounce on tethers, sucked through incision lips into new habitats, plugged into varied veinwork, pumped with foreign bloods. Your skin and bones rolled up like a moth-eaten carpet. Can a body shatter into some greater good? Are some men worth more in pieces? Again, I say: Fuck it. I'll do as much damage as I can. This hilarious scene in my mind: my blood-slicked organs in vats and when the faceless butchers get to my liver—the crown jewel!—it's naught but a blasted wineskin riddled with ulcers and while by rights I should be dead I rise up in a triumphant jerk to shriek:

"You bought a *LEMON!* Caveat emptor, motherfuckers!"

Drain my beer and order the next with a bourbon chaser. I'll get so stinking pissed you could douse me in kerosene and strike a match: I'll burn in bliss. Some forensics team will be amazed to discover a resin of boiled bourbon has epoxied my spinal knobs together.

I'm three sheets to the wind—erstwhile goal: nine sheets or full-body paralysis—when one of the girls swans in. Vision of pulchritude! Minx! Wood nymph! Pixie! That green goo has stained her tongue the colour of a freeze-dried frog. She's so perfect she belongs in a music box. You forget skin possesses marvellous tension when teenage-fresh. My own feels moored on strips of ancient velcro and if a few more hooks come free my face will slide right off, bunching up in my neck like an un-elasticized tubesock to present my rye-stained skull.

"Don't hate me because I'm beautiful," I tell her solemnly. She brands me a "freak." So, I've been reduced to weathering insults from this hip sophisticate who likely believes pink bubble gum to be the ideal pairing for a bottle of six-dollar Chardonnay.

"You can't come in here with that," says the bartender.

That: a pitbull. Off-white with a bridled coat tufting at the rolls of its neck. Heeled beside the man who is presumably its owner. Trousers torn up his calves showcase the baguettes of his legs. A friendly face but his teeth jut on tangents like a handful of dice rolled into his gums: *Come on, lucky seh-vaans!* One eye's so discoloured it looks like a plum kicked into his socket.

"She won't whiz on the floor."

Bartender says: "Health code violation."

"No offence, but this whole place is some kind of violation."

"Takes a dump, you clean it up."

"Bottle of Jamieson's and a pint glass."

The bartender obeys. The guy presses the ice-chilled pint to his battered eye and faces me.

"Well, how bad is it?"

"The first I've seen you. No basis for comparison."

He sets a bowl of cocktail peanuts on the floor. The sound of tiny bones snapping as the pitbull chows down.

"He looks tough."

"He's a she. Matilda. Matty. I'm James. Owner."

"Fletcher. She bite?"

"A little."

Matilda sniffs my topsiders. I pet her anvil-heavy head—like petting an Indian rubber ball. No water in the tendons beneath that stretching of hide. Each defined muscle a ball of copper wire. Ears bitten off. She licks my fingers. Tongue hard as strop leather.

"You've fought her."

"Birds fly. Rabbits fuck. Pitties fight."

"And you—fighting?"

"Mighta been."

"You win?"

"Basest human nature. Who ever wins?"

James pinches a stray peanut between his fingers. Eases open his swollen eyelid. It rests cradled in the pocket of purple flesh.

"My wife's hubby decked me."

"She's got a couple of you on the go?"

"Ex-wife, okay. The new hubby socked me. Busted his hand. Ha! Ha! A surgeon. Dumb bastard makes a living with his hands."

"What provoked that?"

"When we split I said keep the dogs." The peanut pops free. Matilda eats it. "I didn't have the bottle for a pissing match. But I love that bitch"—indicating the pitbull—"and let her be taken away. I knew they had a cottage somewhere-hereabouts. Practically a mansion, on a lake. I pitched my tent off in the bushes."

"You robbed them?"

"My property." Meaning Matilda. "How's that robbery?"

"The stipulations of my divorce are pretty ironclad."

"Are we talking laws? Jurisprudence? No—karmic fairness. That dog and me are wedded above any law. Anyway, when they showed up, my ex leashed Matilda in the yard. Went to do whatever she does with Doc Hotlips. Screw on a bearskin rug. I grabbed Matilda. She's barking her head off. Next it's Hotlips steamrolling at me. I took a swing. He painted me. All she wrote."

"The whole fight?"

"When I come to he's apologizing. My eyes were really watering from the punch—could've *looked* I was crying. Off me and Matty ran. They're yelling kidnapper and what-have-you. I need a drink."

James and I slouch down the alcoholic's ladder. James shows me Matilda's trick: he balances a peanut on her snout and at his command—"Giddyup!"—she pops the nut up to snatch it out of midair.

We roll out of the bar into a star-cooled night. The road dead-ends at the dock. For whatever reason James and I are holding hands. This blissful look paints his face. The realization comes that I like him quite a bit. Self-love, partially, that reflexive fondness a man feels for another whose beggared circumstances mirror his own.

"Nice boat," he says. "I had a motorhome. That baby was repossessed."

James swings his hand, attached to my arm, as if we are on a playdate. Matilda paws down the gangplank. Wind blows off the liftlocks, ruffling our thinning hair.

Black Box: Wife

This flight was buggered from takeoff. Headsets broken. Beef stroganoff poisoned with botulism. An albatross got sucked into the right fuselage. Some other bird—flamingo? charred pink feathers—sucked into the left. We're going down. Mayday, mayday! . . . screw it.

When we dated she made it known I must earn her. A breathing kewpie doll. I learned to tango. Bought a '78 Cougar with flake-metal finish. Was the first to say, "I love you." Once I'd won her, everything that was hard in her went to goo and I hated it and we married. She'd howl when we fucked—I mean, firing on all cylinders. Sounding like a stray cat yowling on a winter's night. Has chemical castration been undersold?

She drove a school bus when we first wed. Cash was tight. My young bride behind the wheel of a big yellow bus, jouncing down the road on leaf springs that make school buses less conveyance than amusement park ride. So young, strong, and gorgeous, whereas school buses were usually driven by bat-faced hags with names like Carla. But as the years wore on it became a way to wound her. When arguments got heated I'd find myself screaming: "You were a fucking *bus driver*!"

The steering wheel—what do they call it on planes? a yoke?—just busted off in my hands. A shitload of shrieking in the cabin. Gunshots.

My grandfather sang my grandmother's name in the shower after she died. They quarrelled, publicly, often at Christmastime, but lived sixty years together until she died of liver cancer and he followed from cancer of a different sort. While still alive he sang out her name, a trilling call like a bird's. He missed her more than he could bear and called her name without knowing.

My wife and I could share a roof sixty years, she could die, I'd grieve—but would I ever sing?

The emblematic event signalling the derailment of my marriage, the precise instant the train skipped the tracks to hurtle headlong into a ravine, was when my wife attempted to fellate me while I slept.

Shocking she even bothered. Under her gaze my member had become a poisoned salt lick ringed with dead deer or worse: as if through some means of anatomical gymnastics my asshole had cartwheeled round to my crotch. Not to mention I was dead asleep. Oblivious, unconsenting. What if I had rucked up her nightie and gone down on her like a thief in the night? Her timing was flawed. I could have been in the grip of a nautical nightmare. The sensation may have knitted with those stark terrors. A hungry sea-leech sucking out my blood and vigours? My leg lashed out instinctively. I awoke to my future ex-wife at the foot of the bed. A goose egg on her forehead.

Our divorce was highly amicable. My wife could have challenged for sole custody despite my being in those halcyon days a functional member of society. I relocated to Sarah Court. Quaint, family-friendly. Myself clinging to the outdated notion I was ever that sort of man.

At the risk of sounding like a drill sergeant, the sooner you structure your child's life to befit future growth, the better. I rose to anger hearing my girl recount the litany of lackadaisical activities she was now permitted in her mother's custody.

"I dug yesterday."

"Dug for what, Abigail?"

"Treasure?"

"My dear, there's no treasure in your mother's backyard. You'll dig up a lump of petrified doggy doo. You'd enjoy discovering that? Let's go for a bike ride."

"Can I have an ice-cream sandwich?"

"Your mother lets you eat ice-cream sandwiches all day? Have an apple. Nature's candy. Can't have you turning into a Flabby Abby, can we?"

"What's a flabby?"

"Flabby's fat. Fat Abby. Big Fat Abigail."

I never dreamed my daughter might compete as a strength athlete. "Female bodybuilder" conjured images of mustachioed Olympians from coldwater republics galumphing through the Iron Curtain with mysterious bulges in their weightlifting costumes. But Abby was freakishly strong.

This discovery had been made in my next-door neighbour's backyard. A surgeon, Frank Saberhagen, whose serpentine decline kept pace with my own. Everything between us became a competition so it was no surprise we'd race each other down the drainhole. Our first conversation had been emblematic of our confrontational fellowship. I'd spied rolls of uncovered, browning sod in the backseat of his Cadillac El Dorado and chummily asked what his purpose was. "Oh, wouldn't *you* like to know," was his reply. Our troubled friendship was forged upon that rocky foundation. I never did discover what he did with that sod.

This particular afternoon we were drinking "Flatliners," the good doctor's signature concoction, while his son Nicholas roughhoused with Abby.

"Up the tree, Nick."

Saberhagen forced his son—who would go on to be an amateur boxer good enough to get plastered by future pros while never earning a dime for his pains—to climb the maple daily. Supposedly it developed his fast-twitch muscle fibres.

"Dad, come on."

"Don't give me that, buckaroo."

"None too sturdy, doc. Had it sprayed for Dutch Elm?"

"What are you," he asked me, "a tree surgeon?" He swayed to his feet and kicked the maple as if it were the tire of a car whose purchase he was considering. "*Solid.*"

"Your father is a stubborn man, Nicholas."

"What's wrong with my taking an interest in your improvement?" Saberhagen asked his son. "Mr. Burger is clearly uninterested in his daughter's."

"Why—because I refuse to send my firstborn up your arboreal deathtrap?"

"The tree's a metaphor. Life is challenging but what can you do? Watch others climb to success, forever peering up at the treads of more ambitious shoes? Life requires gumption. Good old-fashioned balls."

A dig at my Abby. Cursed to trudge through life bereft of said apparatuses.

"You slug. Abby can do anything Nick can."

Saberhagen scoffed. "She's got a pudding belly."

Her mother's fault. Those goddamn ice-cream sandwiches! I'll admit too many Flatliners had cut my mental age into halves, or in all likelihood quarters. We somehow found ourselves in his garage where Frank welcomed us to the First Annual Saberhagen Pentathlon.

"Saberhagen Pentathlon? Why not Burger-Saberhagen?"

"My garage," he reasoned.

Our debate was derailed by the appearance of Clara Russell, in a wheelchair, at the base of Frank's driveway. Awhile back one of her "boys" had hotwired Saberhagen's Cadillac, along with Wes Hill's boy Colin. I remained in the garage while Frank chatted. Mama's sheepdog barked. Frank's corgi kicked up a ruckus behind the garage door.

"Welcome," Frank said upon his return, "to the Saberhagen-Burger pentathlon. First event: vertical jump."

He proclaimed a busted rake the "Measuring Stick" and, holding it at a drunken loft above his head, urged Nicholas to jump and touch it.

"Hold straight, Frank. It's hanging all crooked-ass."

Saberhagen set his Flatliner down and used both hands. Nick came up short.

"Abby's turn."

"You get two tries," he said. "No-no, wait—three."

"Making up the rules as we go, Quincy?"

"Three tries, Fletch. Olympic rules."

On the second attempt Saberhagen bent his knees so Nick could touch.

"Foul! Running rigged contests here at casa de Saberhagen?"

"If I bent my knees," he filibustered, "I'm not saying I did, but *if*—we can all agree to it being an honest error. I've got fluid buildup on my left knee."

Nick made a fair touch. I reached for the Measuring Stick. Saberhagen balked.

"I'll hold for Abby, why not?"

"She's my daughter. Fathers hold for their kid."

You'd have thought my request was in contravention of the nonexistent rulebook.

"Look, Fletch, now seriously: I'm two inches taller."

"Your elbows were all crooked-ass."

"*Like hell* they were crooked-ass."

Eventually he gave over the stick. Abigail missed her first attempt.

"Put your legs into it, Abby." Another miss. "For

heaven's sake. Jell-O in those legs? Tuck your shirt in"—the bastard was right: she did have a little pudding belly—" and touch . . . the . . . *stick*."

A third miss. Quincy whooped it up. I wanted to twist his head off like a bottlecap.

"That's what I'm talking about," he told his son. "Old-fashioned balls."

"Butter churns," I seethed, "and horehound candies are old-fashioned. Am I to take it that, what, your son's got a pair of *steam-driven* testicles?"

A belly laugh from Saberhagen. Too late I realized he'd accomplished his main, if not sole, ambition of that afternoon: pissing me off.

"Next," he said, "feats of strength."

In a corner of the garage was a stack of paint cans labelled *Bongo Jazz*. The hue of afflicted organ meat. To be inside Saberhagen's house was to inhabit a diseased pancreas. We settled on paint can hammer curls. Nick staked himself to an early lead.

"Twenty-three, twenty-four," counted Saberhagen. "Look at Hercules go!"

Abby's biceps muscle was a hard lump under her sleeve. "How long do I have to go, Dad?"

"Longer than him."

"Daddy," Nick said, "my arm's hurting."

"Don't call me Daddy, please."

Abby's fingers whitened round the paint can wire. Only her circulation temporarily cut off. Nick dropped his can. Twisty veins radiated from his elbow joint. Abby showed no signs of flagging. Arms raised, I jogged a victory lap of the garage.

"Quit carrying on like she's Sybil Danning," said Frank.

Best part of waking up in a strange bed is how you lay emptied of personal history. Literally forget who you are. Then, spiderlike, your brain gathers every trapping of your miserable history and entombs it in your skull. You're you again.

James slept in the bunk below mine curled up like a potato bug. I'm unsure why I've invited him aboard, other than my inability to face the coming days alone. He shares DNA strands in keeping with Saberhagen and myself. At a certain age a man welcomes into his life those who are dimmer or more intense reflections of his self. That way, the views he holds are seldom challenged.

We spend the day on the Trent-Severn Waterway. I cut the motor with the sun at its peak. Cones of midges coil off the water. James strips and dives in. Matilda follows. They come onboard covered in snotlike algae. It dries to a green transparency they variously lick or peel off.

Of all my features, my eyes are nicest. They can be transplanted, which I wasn't aware of until recently. Keratoplasty, it's called. Only the corneas.

Topmost layer peeled off like skin off a grape, scar tissue and ocular bloodclots removed, donor cornea stitched to the recipient's eye with surgical thread one-sixteenth the thickness of human hair. The International Eye Bank's donor cornea wait list is years long. Eye Bank sounds so terrifically creepy, doesn't it? A supercooled vault where disembodied eyeballs float in jars. But not so. As eyes rot same as any living tissue there is no physical bank, per se.

A setting sun red as new blood. The tops of shore pines resemble teeth on a bucksaw as we approach Fenelon Falls. We dock and head into town. Nothing's open except the local chapter of the Legion. A stag and doe scheduled. We're bidden entry by a veteran in a sailor's cap with a face like a bowl of knuckles.

"No pets," he tells James.

"But this dog saw duty in Afghanistan."

The vet's features soften significantly.

We sit on orange plastic chairs beneath a mangy moose head with a half-smoked cigar crammed in its mouth. The premises are occupied by runny-eyed lumbermen, many of whom look to have been dragged from under a thicket somewhere. Hairs the colour of week-old piss sprout from every orifice on their faces. James and I bang back shots of Johnny Red with the self-medicating air of alcoholics searching for a level spot on the beam. Sprinkled amongst the backwoods gnomes and tricksters are veterans smoking home-rolled cigs which burn so quickly it's like watching fuses burn down into the wizened powderkegs of their faces.

A woman sits nearby. Young-ish and familiar, if distantly so, neither beautiful nor plain, and with a baby. Ungodly out-of-place amidst the cigar smoke and shipwrecked vets.

"Cute kid," James says. "Yours?"

"Cute dog. Yours?"

They fall into conversation. I feel strung-out and edgy. I hear everyone's fingernails growing. Inappropriate salsa music pipes up. A woman dances. So girthy in her white shirt and tan trousers that from the back she resembles a vanilla soft-serve cone. Her technique makes it appear as if an invisible entity has yanked down her pants and is presently pummelling her to the lungs, kidney, and liver. Steamy dance stylings hold a commonality with killer bees: both are more destructive the farther they migrate away from their equatorial birthplaces.

When the next woman arrives, every eyeball settles on her.

"Chivas Regal, barkeep!" Sounds like: *Shave-ass Raygull.*

She enters with the ultimate *fuck me* walk. A strut, more like, a stalking strut that in every hip-shift, every swivel and jive, says: *I know much about the carnal acts and you better believe it—I'm fucking goooooood.* To say she's beautiful would be to lie. She has a harelip and the surgical repair's been botched; Saberhagen would howl to see such butchery. But by God, she is purely magnetic. This erotic beartrap of a woman. Big. Nordic-valkyrie big. Stately pipestems like hers you tend to describe in equine terms; I could picture her snapping a fetlock treading in a gopher hole at full gallop. I'd bet folding money she's a mudder. Her fella stands a respectful distance apart. Rangy and bowlegged in stovepipe jeans. The sad bastard brings to mind visions of a sucking axe gash never let alone to heal.

She sits nearby. Downs her first drink at a gulp and sends the boyfriend off for another *Shave-ass.*

"Who the hell're you?"

I'm amazed this woman registers me as anything other than flesh-toned wallpaper.

"Call me Mr. Burger."

She smiles in a peculiar way. An arrowhead-shaped tongue darts over her lips. It strikes me as a gesture she uses often, suggestive of all manner of undefined intimacies.

"Mister Burger?"

"You're too young to use my grown-up name."

This woman could destroy me. This woman's hot white teeth could strip the skin from my bones. Dismantle me piece by piece. She could have me begging for that honour. To throw yourself at her is to throw yourself off a skyscraper. Screaming all the way down. Teeth driven into your skull like tent pegs into clay.

"Call me Sunshine. What are you doing here?"

"Paying my respects to the betrothed."

"Well, the betrothed's got no idea who in blue fuck you are."

"You? Hitched to that tall drink of water?"

"The culmination of my every hope and dream."

Her hubby-to-be's axe-wound of a face registers pitiful gratefulness that this woman would condescend to entwine her life with his. Sunshine downs her second drink. The ice's refraction magnifies the scar slit down her upper lip. Her fiancee's name is Rodney.

"I had a dog named Rodney," says James.

"He's my little dog," Sunshine goes. "My wittle Wodney." She chucks him under the chin with the edge of her glass. "When hims a bad doggums, hims sleeps in da doghouse."

Rodney smiles like a man in a tiger cage. Lovestruck sap. His every molecule made of galling attributes: servitude, resignation, bootlicking. As a man I want to slap him around out of pure heartsick revulsion.

Doctor Burger's cure for the whole maudlin scene? Booze. An oil tanker's worth. I line up shots of navy rum to fill my prescription. Prognosis: stunningly positive! Rodney's hand pumps shot glasses into his face with the mechanics of an oil derrick. He tries to kiss Sunshine. She gets her elbow up. His lips meet the knob.

"You're a slobbery drunk, darlin'. What's the use getting all lovey-dovey now, champ? Why not save it for when it could be of value?" Stated to nobody in particular: "A wet noodle in the sack, this one. Like to bed down with a hunnert-fifty pounds of cooked spaghetti stuffed in tube socks. Keep thinking the cops'll bust down the door and arrest me for what's-it? Sleeping with dead things . . . ?"

"Necrophilia?" James offers.

"Yeah!" Her laugh is so profoundly crazed you could imagine it echoing down the austere halls of a funny farm. "On the money!"

How exhausting it must be for Sunshine. Stomping Rodney's self esteem at clockwork intervals. Rodney's skull half-squashed from her foot. But then some men yearn to die curled up in a boot-print.

A fuse blows inside my head and when the juice flows again I'm in a pickup between Sunshine driving and Rodney riding shotgun. The *Shave-ass Raygull* spilled over Sunshine's jeans makes it look she's pissed herself. This close she smells of mentholated cigarettes and Noxema. Crazily alluring. Reaching between my legs to downshift, she gives my crotch a cheery honk. Her poor prehensile tail of a fiancée turns from the moon-plated river to face us.

"Nice having you at our party, Fletcher. Sincerely. We made a new friend."

"Bless your pea-pickin' heart," says Sunshine. "You're too fuckin' corn-pone to live."

"Never claimed to be perfect."

Rodney's spine must have marinated in battery acid. Strange wonder his ribcage doesn't sag to his hipbone. Sunshine swings into a gravelled half-moon facing the water. We spill out laughing—Jesus, at what? I'm about ready to slip a dry cleaning bag over my head. I gulp air coming off the river in hopes of oxygenating my rum-soaked cells. I am seriously hallucination-hammered. Sunshine staggers down to the water.

"Got to tinkle, boysy-woysies!"

Rodney's bellied over the truck fender. His body comes by such positions naturally. Not a single unbroken posture. A cannonball on a chain hooked to his forehead.

Sunshine returns topless. Standing at the lip of the berm with her head cocked. Just . . . y'know, *BAM*. All there.

"Look at yous two. Standing there with your teeth in your mouth."

A body so young taken in by the eyes of a man old as me . . . lechery only another word for jealousy.

I want to eat her skin. She hoists herself onto the hood. Undoes the topmost button on her jeans.

"Put your hands all over me, Fletcher. A real man's hands, for once."

She's crazy. Not in any diagnosable way. Not so much that she'll bring harm to anybody but herself and those who hie too closely. My hands on her would only be an encouragement of that lunacy but what was my onus of burden? Me, with the lifespan of a fruit fly.

"Sunny, baby. You make loving you hell."

"I'm just sitting, Rod. If this man's hands happen upon my body, well, it's not me causing that collision, now is it?"

The heat of the engine block warms the hood where I set my hand. Moonlight plays upon the water. A vein of white fire snaking through things.

"Go ahead and fuck me." She pulls the take of their stag and doe from her jeans. "We'll leave this scratch-ass town. Escape." *Ex-cape.* "Just us two."

Is she purposely degrading herself with those crumpled fives and tens? Her jeans melt down to her ankles. When a woman really wants to shed her clothes it is an act of bodily voodoo. Lips shiny with blackberry Chapstick. She draws down the lip of her panties. I see the definitions of her intimates same way you spot a mouse at the mouth of its hole: by the wet glints of teeth and eye.

I say: "You doing anything about your little sexpot of a fiancée, here, Rodney?"

"He's my dickless little dog."

Rodney moans like a sick animal. My hand traces Sunshine's neck. The panicked thrum of her heartbeat in my fingertips. This expression of fear and disgust skims over her face—fleeting, but it's all there in that. Sunshine laid open like one of those Dali women with the chest of drawers where her guts should be. My rummaging hands inside. I've been wrong from the get-go: believing Rodney lives in wretchedness when in truth he exists in a state of ongoing ecstasy.

"You don't want me. You couldn't possibly."

"Sure," she say. "Sure I do."

They love one another. You can glimpse such twisted configurations and acknowledge yes, it is still love. A brutal and excruciating manifestation but unmistakably so. Love as a sickness.

"Fuck me, Fletcher. Take me away."

"I won't."

"What's the matter with me?"

Turning from her, I offer: "You're cute enough."

"I wouldn't mind," says Rodney.

Sunshine claws a hand around my hips. That I'm not erect infuriates her.

"*Two* dickless wonders!"

"I could fuck you, Sunshine, but I couldn't kiss

you." I'm a brutal human specimen. "Not with your lip like that."

Retrospectively speaking, I shouldn't have said this with my back turned.

"Pussyeating dickface mother*fucker*!"

She leaps onto my back. One mitt's sunk into my hair while the other lances stiff shots into the vein-bunched curve of my throat. The shock of it is quasi-paralyzing: the way you'd feel inadvertently catching your mother naked through an open bedroom door. An idiotic sense of masculinity compels me to make like she isn't hurting me when in fact it hurts *vastly*.

"Rodney. Please . . . control your woman."

By whipping side-to-side I manage to buck her off. She strips off a plug of scalp. I stagger toward the river with blood trickling down my neck.

Zany bitch!

"Stick your pecker in her, y'old buckethead!"

"She's gonna be your wife," I tell Rodney. "Do your own grunt work!"

At the lip of the berm Sunshine kicks me in the spine. The spectre of getting an eye poked out petrifies me. Clamp my eyelids tight. Hurts like hell but I laugh a sad bastard's dirge rolling blindly down. Must have sounded I was mortally injured because when I check up on the lee side their truck motor is gunning into silence.

I haul myself out of the bracken. Tear a clump of

moss ringing an elm tree. Press it to my scalp. Kick through frosted dandelions, snapping their little bald heads off. Frozen berries hang on a branch and I eat a handful and they hurt my teeth. I zone out, bleeding. The perpetual movement of the cosmos pushes the moon across a star-salted sky.

My houseboat rounds the horn of the river.

"*Fleeeetcherrrr!*"

"Over here! Here!"

The engine cuts. A flashlight beam pins me.

"I ran into those two you left with. Asked where the heck were you. They said check the fucking river! Can you make it out?"

"I can try."

The river laps against the torn spot in my scalp. Snapping turtles and steel-mouthed walleye quest at my toes. James hauls me onboard and sits me in the galley kitchen. Drapes me in a metallic emergency blanket. Next he removes my shirt and socks. Matilda lays across my bare feet. I feel her belly nipples against my skin.

"That's one nasty hematoma on your head," James says.

SARAH COURT

Black Box: Compassionate
Human Being

We're going down. I saw it coming. Takeoff smooth, clear skies, but twenty years into this flight my arms got tired. It felt pointless. I let go of the yoke.

So much of being considered a good person is decent planning. A steel-trap memory. So much is: "So-and-so's birthday is coming. Better send a card." Make these token efforts and everyone says you're a good person. You're not necessarily. You may occupy some Outer Sulawesi of the soul, but you keep a well-organized day-timer. Real tests of goodness ignite out of nothingness and stick it to you bluntly: are you the person you think you are? The door swings two ways. Swings a hundred million ways. In those moments you come to know yourself. Can you exist within that reckoning?

Out the starboard window one wing snaps off. Trailing wiring and spitting sparks it falls through the sky, through a sea of puffy cumulus clouds. Anyway, who cares? The freight bay is full of sandbags.

The group: "Over-and-Out." Called a "group" to imply we were pleased as punch to gather every second Thursday. Our only regret it couldn't be weekly, or thrice weekly, or daily or two times a day. Parents helping parents. What a crock. Over and out. Get it? Support groups have punny names. Craniofacial Abnormalities: About Face. Sickle Cell Anemia: Reaping Hope. Ours was a catchall for parents "over"-something: overzealous, overbearing, overcompetitive. I had no choice but to attend. I'd slit my own throat with earlier actions at a provincial powerlifting meet.

After discovering Abby's unusual strength I'd embarked on a systematic plan to make her a champion lifter. I bought Joe Weider dumbbells at Consumer's Distributors. Set up a gym in my old rumpus room. Enrolled her in the Superior Physique Association: a female weightlifting fraternity founded by Doris Barrilleaux, a hyper-developed hausfrau from Canton, Ohio.

I arranged for muscle-responsiveness tests. Abby possesses some seriously enlarged vascular bundles. The cellular walls of her arteries were elastic. Improved circulation equals increased blood flow. Superior protein absorption. *Bigger muscles*. Muscle tissue is cellularly complex: the muscle of your biceps, for example, consists of different cellular strata. First the parallel arrays of tubelike muscle fibres bundled together like crayons in a box. Each fibre is made up of smaller sub-units, myofibrils, stacked neatly one atop the other like plates on a shelf. Inside the myofibrils reside the working parts, heavy lifters called sarcomeres, arranged in a lineup like beads on an abacus. Look closely at championship powerlifters: it's like iodized salt has been sprinkled over every muscle group.

The day her bone density test results arrived I hightailed it to Saberhagen's house.

"Abby scored a -0.1 on the Bone Mineral Density test. What's that mean?"

"Means she's got dense bones," Frank said. "To match her dad's skull."

"I knew it." As if we Burgers were famous for our bone density and it was only natural this trait should find its pinnacle in my daughter. "*Dense.*"

Massive blood-pumping bundles, solid spinal stem, lode-bearing joints, bones dense as titanium. Can I be blamed for thinking she was ideally suited?

Now, get it straight: powerlifting, not bodybuilding. The Olympic sport, not the freakshow. I'm disgusted by those steroid-enlarged gals with patio flagstones where their boobs should be and their HGH-swollen faces so out of whack even the best maxillofacial surgeon couldn't make them look womanly again, telling you "But I'm still a *lady*," in their Barry White voices. So full of toxins they'd set off a fallout meter. Steroids: an idiotic lifestyle, what with the shrunken nuts and prostatitis. They can turn a gal's clitoris as big and hard as a baby's thumb!

I entered Abby in regional meets. She demolished her own sex. The Ontario Power-lifting Association agreed to let her compete in the male 14–18 class. The meet was held in a Hamilton gym inhabited by strapping male bodies.

"Dogs, the lot of them," I told her. "They got heartworm. You'll pulverize."

Truth told, I was taken aback at the proliferation of prepubescent beefcakery. I wanted to run around with plastic cups: "Piss tests. Piss tests for all!" I sauntered up to the biggest kid, all of seventeen yet so prodigiously venous he appeared to be covered in livid spiderwebs.

"My daughter's kicking your ass. Bet you folding money."

His father, a buzz-cut bohunk with a Hamilton FD shirt stretched across his chest, pricked up his ears.

"You're flabby as all get out," I went on. "Look at her dorsal definition. Like peering into a barrel of snakes, isn't it?"

"S'matter with you?" his father went.

"This kid's a bum." I kept my tone pleasant. "What do you feed him, tubs of Oleo?"

"You're not helping," Abby told me.

"I'm simply allowing this man to prepare the collection of overgrown blood platelets he calls a son for an emasculating ass-kicking."

A judge overheard the commotion. "Back to your competitor, sir."

"I got every right being here."

"If you don't leave this vicinity—"

"This is my *job*. Don't you tell me how to do my job. You don't see me coming down to the public toilets to knock the can of Ajax out of your hands, do you?"

We were eliminated from competition. Abby nailed it as "a real bonehead manoeuvre." My ex got wind. Rumblings of a revision of custody rights. My lawyer advised a token of penitence would smooth things. So, the group: "Over and Out."

Sole tonic to my misery was I didn't have to endure it alone. Frank Saberhagen—whose ex-wife levied charges he was pushing Nick too hard to become a third-tier pugilist—was pressured into attendance. And Clara Russell was there, even though her "boys" weren't hers by blood.

Our meetings were otherwise populated by decaying alpha males. Gym teachers in sweat suits with teeth marks dug into the plastic whistles dangling round their necks. Business suits with men inside whose skin was so tight-flexed you feared their scalps would tear open to reveal the twitching nests of their id. That breed of intellectually and/or emotionally impoverished male whose pickup truck hitches sport oversized, rubberized novelty scrotal sacks. We were overseen by Dr. Dave, a "Behaviour Coach." Six-five, one-seventy: his body resembled wet bedsheets hung from a flagpole. Add to this the overeager demeanour of a drivetime DJ. Like he'd signed a contract mandating he be inoffensively funny.

"Welcome to Over and Out," he began each meeting. "Let's help each other get 'over' the hump, so you can get 'out' of your boxes of destructive habitual behaviour."

We stood at a plywood lectern parading our parental sins in hopes of exculpation. Quincy— who insisted on being called Doctor Frank—was a hambone.

"Why should I, *we*, be pilloried for promoting our offspring's betterment through a regimen of physical discipline and structure?" went his typical monologue. "The same structure promoted by my father and his father, which made me the man I am today. A healer of men."

"Times change," said Dr. Dave. "Society and, ha-ha, expectations also, Mr. Saberhagen."

"Doctor Frank, please."

"You cannot rob a child of choice. Autonomy."

"Let them choose to be what: carnival roustabouts? Years ago my son wanted to be a tap dancer. What was my option?"

"My boys can be whatever they want."

This from Clara Russell. She sat with one of her charges, Jeffrey, a little turd who stole eggs out of the robin's nest in my oak tree. Unwed and technically childless, Russell shared her home with a rotating herd of youthful fruitcakes and some poor old bastard she made a habit of kicking out, quite publicly, every year or so.

"Dancers," she persisted, "or bricklayers—"

"Or little arsonists or kleptomaniacs, obviously," Saberhagen said.

"You'll let that stand, Dr. Dave?" said Clara. "Isn't this a supportive haven?"

"Everyone, ha-ha, let's take a step back. . . ."

"My boys have behavioural anomalies and unnatural fixations, sir." Russell was an imposing woman. Paul Bunyan in a smock. "Can't wave a magic wand and fix them."

"Listen, Dave," Frank went on, ignoring her. "I love my son."

"Unconditional, Dr. Saberhagen—can you say your love is that?"

"Whose ever is?"

After meetings, most of us loafed about smoking, gnashing wads of gum, or grinding the weave of our sweaters against nicotine patches. Always a mobile party kit in somebody's trunk. We drank and decompressed. It mainly took the form of jibes at Dr. Dave, who we all agreed was about as useful as a set of tonsils.

The usual post-group clan: three fathers and one mother, Nadia, whose gymnast daughters tore ACL ligaments in separate pommel horse calamities. Saberhagen and I nicknamed her "Nadia Commen-Nazi." The third father was Dale Mulligan: a slab of free-range masonry with the primeval face of the Piltdown Man. That, or a block of clay punched into a rude semblance of humanity by a mildly artistic gorilla. He taught Phys Ed at Laura Secord, an "arts" school where students interpretive-danced their way to course credit. His son was the football team's running back. You'd think the sun shone directly out the kid's ass.

"My boy, Danny," Dale prattled on one night, "racked up a hundred-twenty yards on the ground in scrimmage. Took a few tackler's arms as trophies."

I was uninspired at the boy's ability to tear through a defensive line of landscape painters. Shortly afterwards the aforementioned apple of Mulligan's eye arrived to pick his father up.

"My daughter's stronger than him," I heard myself say.

"You out of your sonofabitchin' mind, Fletcher?"

"Dale, please. He's got the build of a snow pear."

By the time Abby arrived to pick me up, Dale and I were nipple-to-nipple, bumping chests as men do when each feels he's been affronted yet neither is ready to plant a fist in his antagonist's nose. Not *quite*. At Abby's arrival I strode to the bike rack. Rusted bars, solid steel, welded at right angles.

"Okay, Mulligan. Dead lift. Your boy, my girl."

"I'm not lifting anything," said Abby.

"Just a few lifts. Look at him."

"Go fall in a hole, Dad. I'm picking you up. That's it."

"Abs. This guy thinks he can beat you."

"You think you can beat me?" she asked Dale's son, Danny Mulligan.

"I don't even know what we're talking about," Danny said, mystified.

"How about," said Quincy, "the two dads lift? Hey, Abby—your old man puts his shoulder to the millstone?"

"What does that prove, Frank?"

"Tell you what it proves if you don't, Fletch: you're a grade-A chickenshit." Quincy tucked his hands under his armpits and flapped. "Bro-bro-broooock."

Dale Mulligan had already installed himself at the bike rack. No heroic way to extricate myself, so after deep-knee bends and some isometric stretching I spat on my palms. Gripped the rack. I could *do* this, baby! Feet set, hammies flexed, I straightened my spine and loosed a convulsive grunt—*YE GODS!* A firecracker exploded between my fifth and sixth vertebrae. I came to on my back. The motherloving pain! Spine ripped out, soaked in jellied gasoline, lit, the white-hot knobs sewn back inside. A paraplegic. I'd be blowing into a straw to move the hubs of my wheelchair. My droppings evacuated into sterile plastic bags. Crippled . . . by a bike rack!

"Oh, fuck my life!"

Quincy knelt. Ran a finger up my spine. "You tweaked a disc. Nothing earth-shattering."

"Can't believe you did that," Abby said.

Was it wrong to cherish the fear in her voice?

The post-therapy group swiftly disbanded. Quincy offered to help drive me home.

"You viper. I'd as soon take a lift from the Malibu Strangler."

Abby drove slow: partially because she was freshly licensed and partially because any jolt would cause me great ache. Once home I sent her inside for a beer. She returned with tallboys. We popped the tabs and drank.

"What?" she said. "I've had beer."

"You damnwell have not around me."

We clinked cans.

"Hungry? Energizer Bowls in the freezer."

"Pass. Group's working wonders, by the way."

Our eyes met in the rearview mirror. I don't know when, exactly, I hit the understanding that my mother and father had been responsible for rearing me and were thus somewhat reliable but still, they were only human and entitled to their own screwups. I'm reasonably sure Abby hit it right that instant.

"Who was that boy?"

"Who, Danny Mulligan?"

"Danny. Daniel."

"He goes to Laura Secord. That place is an incubator for fairies."

"You don't have to be a jerk every day of your life. Take a day off. He's cute."

"Danny Mulligan. Cute. These two absolutes fail to sit comfortably within my universe."

"He looked at me. My boobs."

"The scumbag. Did he, really?"

"Better than the horndogs at the gym going on about my pectoral definition."

"Please, Abs."

A vein throbbed down her neck. Beautiful, my daughter, but physically solid. Workhorse legs. All those veins. "What do you feed her," Saberhagen once joked, "cotton candy spun out of Dianabol?" The culture of her sport was one where female powerlifters were met derisively: my daughter was a stunt, like a foxy boxer. It bothered Abby her thighs rubbed together walking. That her abdominal muscles were so prominent they resembled a turtle's belly. That the dress she wore to commencement made her look, in her own self-appraisal, like "a linebacker in drag." But each sculpted protuberance was evidence of our training regimen. The tensile integrity muscle attains amongst the very best athletes gives it this pocked look. When there's only enough fat separating flesh from tendon that you won't die of hypothermia on a mild spring day. Individual fibres present themselves as defined waves. Tendons rumble like gathering thunder over a body.

You're rumbling, I'll say when she's in top form. *Rumbling and raging.*

She's a goddamn beautiful lifter. I'll load the bar with six forty-five pound plates plus the bar: a 315 squat. She chalks her hands—calloused as a dockworker's—grips the crosshatched bar and swings herself beneath that weight. Legs flared wide: a pair of baby spruces. Jerking the bar off its pegs she'll go down, thighs perpendicular to the floor. Veins spiderwebbing from the rounds of her shoulders. A serious case of the butterflies as her quadriceps jump and dance. Eyes rotating to the ceiling she *explodes* with a lung-shattering scream. Primal. A lioness. One time she blew a blood vessel in her eye. Powering out of her crouch, bar bowed over her shoulders with all that weight. Blood surged into her eyeball. The pressure on the vein wall was so fierce it tore. Abby didn't even feel it. Alarmed, I took her face in my hands. I was so terrified. She said: "I'm okay, Dad. Calm down."

"Abs, if you never lift another weight . . . that'd be okay."

"Right. You'd be busted up."

"It makes me happy we're doing something together. That's all. We could go fishing. You like fishing? I hate it. But anything else. Okay?"

"Yup. Okay."

"I want to know you're happy."

"I know."

"So. Tell me."

"I'm happy."

Did any kid comprehend the love of a parent? Frightening in its rawness. An excised kidney: naked, unprotected and lewd. It sprang from failure and regret which only sharpened the edge. Fanatical, protective, rooted in an understanding the world's a broken place filled with broken individuals. The fact your child was a part of that ruined tapestry was a kind of miracle.

The parasite Saberhagen pulled into his driveway. He and Nick trotted across the yard. Nick had a black eye but Frank's poor son always sported a blackened eye, busted nose, facial sutures, or the like.

"You go to hell," I told Frank.

Saberhagen appealed to Abby. "Did we handcuff him to that rack?"

"You did the chicken thing," she reminded him. "Chicken-chicken brock-brock."

Saberhagen opened the rear door and sat behind me. "Nick, you and Abby grab more barley pops."

"Why don't you?" said Nick.

"Someone's fixing to chow down on the brown bag special, son o' mine."

They went. Frank tapped my shoulder. Pinched between his fingers: a pill. I swallowed it. Adjusted the rearview to frame his face.

"We've known each other years. Broken bread together. Why do that to me?"

"Sort of do it to ourselves, wouldn't you say? Don't be a drama queen."

"Go fuck your hat."

"Not wearing one. As you can plainly see."

The kids came back with more icy tallboys. Cool wind blew through the windows. Saberhagen's pill— fabulous! My body may slide into the footwell, my bones soft as poached eggs. Bryan Adams's "Summer of '69" played on 97.7 Htz FM.

"Love this tune, Fletch. Pump it."

"Oh, go home."

Saberhagen shouldered the door open, swooned onto the driveway, nearly fell, steadied himself then strode before the hood. Abby snapped on the high beams.

"Rock out, Mr. S!"

"You bet your bippy!"

Saberhagen squinted weevil-eyed into the headlamps before embarking on an energetic and truly abysmal faux-rock performance. He brandished an air guitar that to judge by his hand spacing was the size of a classical base: fret-fingers above his head, strumming fingers down at his thighs. Hips gyrating, fingers spasming: he could have been experiencing an epileptic attack.

"Those were the best days of my laaay-fe!" Frank sang. *"Baw-baw-baw-ba-ba-baw! Yeah!"*

He reeled off the classic cock-rock staples. The Pigeon Neck. The High-leg Kick. The Lewd Crotch-thrust. The Pursed-lips-chest-out Rocker Strut. The Angry Schoolmarm. He then threw in moves in no way appropriate to the song: The Water Sprinkler, The Running Man and The Robot.

"I guess nothing can last forever, forever—naaaaaw!"

"You're not cool!" I shouted, though I had to admit the man did a damned fine Robot.

Abby and Nick joined Frank. Abby gave him one of those mock-tortured-slash-ecstatic your-axe-playing-is-rocking-me-so-*hard* faces. Frank launched into a face-melter guitar riff. He went down on one knee like James Brown. Nick peeled off his shirt and draped it over his father's shoulders. Frank threw it off with a flourish and kicked out one leg as his performance reached its crescendo.

"*Those were the best days of mah liiiiife!*"

The three of them collapsed on the hood, howling. Abby thrust devil's horns into the sky.

"You're beautiful, Saint Catharines! Goodnight!"

The afternoon following my encounter with Sunshine, the houseboat drifts north. Steel sky. Poplars with metallic bark. The whole world aluminum-plated. Whippoorwills ride updrafts above the boat, their reflections statically pinned to the river's surface. We're making three knots against the current. I ask James about the woman from last night.

"I got her number," he says. "She loves dogs. Who knows? I'll get off at Coboconk."

A little town upriver. I ask what's in Coboconk. A moneymaking opportunity, I'm told.

"I know I give the impression of being a pretty squared-away guy, Fletcher."

". . . yuh-huh."

"It's a smokescreen. Know how I make ends meet? A phone titillation provider."

"Phone sex?"

"We providers prefer 'titillation.'"

"That has to be weird."

"You play characters," James assures me. "Biker Badass. Out-of-Work Model. Southern Dandy." He puts on a nelly voice: "I douh decleah, this heat's plum wiltin' mah britches."

We reach Coboconk by nightfall and tie to an empty dock. The town unrolls along a single road. Chains of bug-tarred bulbs strung down each side of the street hooked to tarnished steel poles are the only lights. James uses the lone payphone, while I wait with Matilda.

"He'll send a car around. Meet you back at the boat?"

"I can come. It's safe?"

"Won't enjoy yourself, but if you want."

The car—a Cadillac, new but not flashy—rolls up. The driver's a kid with stinking dreadlocks piled atop his skull. The open ungracious face of a moron.

We drive until we hit a dirt turnoff. Starlight bends over a lake. Cottages, some no bigger than ice-fishing huts. The Caddy pulls into a horseshoe-shaped driveway in the shadow of a monolithic log cabin built by a man who must lack all conception of irony.

The driver leads us into an antediluvian sitting room dominated by a stone fireplace. Raw-cut pine walls. No pictures, rugs, indications of a woman's touch. An eighty-gallon fish tank but not a single fish. James and I sit on the calfskin couch. Matilda licks the salted leather. There's a bowl of cashews on the coffee table.

"So, which of you is James?"

The man's wearing a lumberjack vest and a pair of corduroys so oft-washed the grooves have worn off. Or migrated to his face: his cheeks and forehead are worked with startlingly straight creases that run laterally, resembling the grain of cypress wood. A pleat of skin with the look of a chicken's coxcomb is folded down over his left eye. James introduces us.

"Fletcher, a pleasure. That must be Matilda." He points to James's swollen eye. My scabbed scalp. "Boys look like you've been through a war." So jovial it's hard to believe he gives a damn. "I'm Starling. Your driver's my biographer, Parkhurst. I picked him up someplace."

As if Parkhurst were a tapeworm Starling drank in a glass of Nicaraguan tapwater. Which may not be far off: the kid, Parkhurst, strikes me as the type who'd happily use an old lady as a human shield during a gunfight.

"A fine bitch," Starling says of Matilda. "I love dogs. What sort of rotten bastard doesn't? Loyal, forgiving. Run themselves to death to please you. I knew this one bitch, Trudy. Bulldog. She birthed a litter but her pups were taken away. Trudy forgot they were hers. Placed in her care again, she ignored them. When they mewled for her nipples she hounded them off. Yet if her owner was gone for years, that dog would remember. You could rub a pair of his old trousers on her nose and she'd yowl and slobber. Didn't give a damn about her own kith but old trousers got her yelping."

Saliva accumulated at the edges of Starling's mouth; every time his lips moved looked like a Ziploc bag coming open. His skin loosely moored to his skull as if to disguise a more fearful face lurking underneath. A Russian doll: faces inside faces inside faces.

"What is it you do?" I ask him.

"I'm The Middle, Fletcher."

"You don't say."

"I do say. You know that old wheeze about the butterfly flapping its wings in Asia followed by a tidal wave swamping Florida? Sure there's that butterfly and sure, there's that wave—I mean to say there's the person who wants a thing done and there's that thing getting done—but effect doesn't meet cause and A doesn't meet C without The Middle. Point B. Moi."

And he says no more.

Starling leads us into a cool scentless night as they often are this far north. James and Matilda, myself, Starling in a camelhair coat. Moonlight falls across a flat-roofed shack enclosed by chicken wire. A huge white dog exits. Matilda squats on her haunches. Licks her hindquarters.

"This is a joke," James says. "Right?"

"That's an Akita," Starling tells him. "Japanese fighting dog."

"I know what it is. A puffed-up husky. We can't roll them."

"The man I bought it from called it a quarrelsome breed. I feed it chicken blood."

"And I'm a dogman, not a butcher." James is fuming. "We met in an online *pitbull* forum. You've got a fucking sledder here. Akita versus any pitbull, let alone a dead gamer like Matty . . . it's Mike Tyson fighting a five-year-old. Matilda will crunch that poor thing's skull like a crouton."

"Oh, I very much doubt that. Shall we see?"

"Are you psycho? Look, I'll show you."

James approaches the chicken wire with Matilda. The Akita yowls: a sexually aggressive sound. Rips at the fence with its teeth. Ropes of drool dangle from the wire. The dogs' noses touch through the fence. Matilda's lips curl: a black-gummed riptide displaying the pegs of her canines. She doesn't growl. Barely moves. The Akita twists upon its flanks. Gnaws its own ass. Turns and crawls inside its doghouse. Flat on its belly. Whimpering.

"What am I supposed to do with a cur?" says Starling, heartbroken.

"Akitas are good hunt dogs."

"My life's too complex for a dog."

Back inside we have a drink. James and Starling are bummed. The dogfight was to be wagered upon. I'm glad they're gutted. The booze beelines to my bladder.

The cabin's toilet is brushed steel and tiny. An airplane latrine. On the toilet tank sits an old issue of *Dog Fancier* bookmarked with a memorandum from one Donald Kerr, solicitor. *That little thing we discussed* . . . reads the subject heading.

I shake off. Zip up. A darkened room stands opposite the bathroom. Empty but for a box. Glass-walled, eight feet tall: a magician's box, the kind you fill with water for shackled escapes. Inside rests what looks like an enormous kidney bean. Except it quivers and in this way is more of a Mexican jumping bean. I'd once given such a bean to Abby. I told her the *Cydia* moth lays an egg inside the bean. The larvae eats away the inside. When the bean warms in your palm the pupal-stage moth quivers to make the bean hop.

Starling's smiling when I return.

"You've got a bloody nose, Fletcher."

My thumb comes away from my nostrils with a bead of blood on it.

"Show me again," says Starling, who couldn't care less about my nose.

James sets a cashew on the tip of Matilda's

snout. "Giddyup!" Matilda pops the nut into the air. Swallows it.

Starling claps. "Bloody marvellous. Could she do it ten times in a row?"

"All night."

"Ten times. Without missing." Starling studies James. "Why don't we make a bet on it?"

"Bet sounds fine. Big bet, fine."

"Okay, okay, I'll make you a very good bet. I'm a rich man. A sporting man. The Cadillac that picked you up. Like it?"

"It's nice." James leans back and he laughs. "I don't have anything like that."

"Get that fine bitch of yours to do her trick ten times in a row and it's yours. You'd like a Caddy, wouldn't you?"

"I'd like it, sure. A Caddy. Who wouldn't?"

"We make this bet, then. I put up my car."

"And I put up?"

"I wouldn't ask you to bet what you cannot afford."

"You can't have my dog."

"Some insignificant thing whose parting would not leave you too bereft."

"What, then?"

"How about, say . . . your thumb."

"What do you mean?"

"I mean I chop it off."

"That's insane," I say.

"James tells me he needs money," says Starling. "He can sell the car."

James considers it. He passes from consid-eration to acceptance far too swiftly for my liking.

"Otherwise I'm here for nothing. Matilda can't fight a sledder." James drinks his drink and says: "Matty does her trick ten times running and I get the car. If she misses even once I lose my thumb. She's never missed. Which hand?"

"Your right. Which one's dominant?" Starling waves it off. "Left, right."

"So, left thumb?"

"That's the deal. Left thumb."

"I can get it reattached. How about my pinkie?"

"No, thumb."

"Index finger."

"Thumb."

"What year is the car?"

"Last year's model. Parkhurst! Keys."

Parkhurst materializes and hands over the keys. Starling sets them beside the cashews.

"Middle finger."

"Fine. But I keep it. No re-attachments."

"I don't recall ever having much use for the middle finger of my left hand." James massages the folds of Matilda's mouth. "It's a super bet."

"Let's strap your hand down," says Starling.

"Parkhurst. Fetch nails, string, and a chopping knife."

Starling's biographer returns with hammer, nails, butcher twine and a campfire hatchet. Starling hammers nails into the edge of the coffee table four inches apart. Cheap ten-penny nails with metal burrs clung to the nailheads. He tests them for firmness with his fingers.

"Put your hand in here. Middle finger out."

Starling winds twine over James's wrist, across his knuckles and around the nails. James's fingernail whitens. Starling hefts the hatchet: new, shiny, with a foam-grip handle. James seems unperturbed with the blade hovering above his outstretched finger.

"Begin," says Starling.

James sets a cashew on Matilda's nose. The curve of the nut shapes itself to the dog's snout. Matilda goes cross-eyed focusing upon it.

"Giddyup!"

The nut disappears down her gullet.

"Good girl."

James sets another nut on Matilda's snout. Starling holds the hatchet level to his ear.

"Giddyup! Two. Good girl."

"Three."

"Four."

"Five."

"Six."

Matilda's a machine. James works her through the procedure steadily. Cashew on snout, pause, "Giddyup!"

"Seven!"

"Eight!"

One end of the ninth cashew is broken off, leaving an imperfect edge. Later I'll wonder why James chose it when the bowl was full of perfectly good ones.

"Giddyup!"

The sound it makes glancing off Matilda's teeth is the tinny *wynk* of a shanked golf ball. The sound that comes out of James's mouth is not a scream so much as a breathless hiss. Starling raises the hatchet above his head. It all happens rather quickly.

Matilda leaps onto James's back. Uses him as a springboard. The cashew bowl's upended, nuts spraying in a fan. Matilda's jaws clamp fast to Starling's shoulder.

"Yeeeeeeeeeeeee!"

This is the sound that exits the broken hole of Starling's mouth. Matilda's jaws are nearly hyper-extended, upper teeth sunk into the wrinkled flesh of his deltoid. Starling shakes at the mercy of a creature one-third his weight but every ounce of it working muscle. Momentum carries them to the floor. Matilda's skull impacting hardwood sounds like a bowling ball dropped on a dance floor. She forfeits her grip, flips over, digs her teeth into the fresh punctures. Starling's eye rolls back in some kind of horrible dream-state. The hatchet flails wildly and its blade hacks into Matilda's beer-cask side.

James drags the coffee table—his hand's still trussed up—over to her. His feet crunch on cashews. I help him tear free of the twine. He grips the top and bottom halves of Matilda's jaw.

"Drop it. *Drop.*"

Matilda forfeits her grip. James kisses her nose.

We help Starling onto the sofa. Parkhurst is AWOL. Starling's skin stinks of busted-open batteries as adrenaline dumps out every pore. His shirt's torn open. Blood bubbles through the puncture wounds and comes off him in strings. Odd knittings of skin bracket his armpit and where his shoulder meets his neck.

I find a first aid kit in the medicine chest. Starling's nearly stopped bleeding by the time I return. The trauma isn't nearly so bad as it appeared. The car keys are on the floor. I slip them into my pocket.

"That was unex . . . pected," Starling gasps.

"I'll call you an ambulance."

"No ambulance."

"You need a doctor."

With his good arm Starling digs a cellphone out of his pocket. Speed dials number one.

"Come now."

He hangs up.

"I have an employee who . . . handles this sort of . . . thing."

Matilda has crawled into the darkest part of the room. When James calls she creeps to him on her belly, grovelling the way dogs do when they believe they've behaved poorly. The clipped stub of her tail wags weakly. The hatchet wound is shockingly wide and it shocks me more, somehow, to see Matilda— less flesh and bone than bloodless fibres coalesced into the familiar shape of a dog—hurt this way. The shining off-pink ligaments banding her rib cage whiten as they flex.

James picks her up. "Fuck me. She's light as a feather."

I tell him to wait outside. The flap of skin covering Starling's eye has folded back. Pale and membranous as the inside of an eyelid. The eye underneath has no cornea, iris, or pigment.

"Will you be alright?"

He manages a grisly smile.

"Bugs, Fletcher. A million slipper-footed space bugs. Walls of my guts. Cores of my bones. Churning, Fletcher. Softest churning you can imagine."

"I have to go."

"So go. But don't take . . . my car. You didn't . . . win."

"Fuck off," I tell him solemnly. "I'm taking it."

I fishtail the Caddy down the dirt road. Moths drawn to the phosphorous glow of the headlamps smash on the windscreen. Matilda's shovel-shaped head pokes from a mummification of towels. Her eyelids are ringed with blood.

"I can't bury another dog, Fletcher," James says.

Black Box: Daughter

The emergency crash slides deploy ten thousand feet above sea level: slick yellow tongues sucked into the engines, which explode in twin fireballs. Shrapnel punches through the fuselage. The hiss of decompression as air inside the cabin is drawn outside. Pinhole contrails stain the blue sky.

This one time, when Abigail was a kid. The playground at the school round the corner from Sarah Court. Sunday: parents airing their kids out after church. Abby on the swingset. This churchgoing man set himself in my sightline. Calling in an abrasive baritone to his own child:

"Down the slide! Down the slide!"

I couldn't see my daughter past this man in his church suit. I wanted to kill him. An animalistic response. You don't stand between papa bear and his cub.

Karma's a mongrel. Its blood isn't pure and it fails to flow in a straight and sensible line. It bites whoever it can and bites randomly. It tallies debts but makes no attempt to match them to the debt-committer. Spend your life totalling black smudges upon your soul thinking in the end they're yours to bear.

Capillaries burst beneath my fingernails. Looks as if I've had them painted candy apple red. My eardrums explode. Instruments shatter at the same instant my jawbone tears free of its hinges. The air's full of silver flecks: my fillings, added to blobs of mercury from split dials. Pressure works around the hubs of my eyes, in back, rupturing the ocular roots. I go down in blackness.

Total muscular failure. The bread-and-butter technique of powerlifting.

The theory behind total muscular failure is simple: max out your poundage until it is impossible to lift without assistance from your spotter. Easy to spot lifters who embrace the technique. They're the ones who've reached familiarity with the "zonk out": passing out during your final rep. Acolytes of total muscular failure trust their spotters implicitly.

The first medal Abby earned was silver in the clean-and-jerk at the Pan Am Games. Bronze initially, until the gold medalist's urinalysis proved she was whacked out of her tree on Anavar.

Around this time Abby had found her first true love. Danny-*freaking*-Mulligan.

He blew his MCL on an end-around sweep the final game his senior season. He enrolled in arts college, grew hippy hair, majored in modern sculpture. Particularly galling was the fact he made a point of buying not only a mattress but also underwear, all used, from the Sally Anne.

"He doesn't care about brands," Abby told me. "A total esthete."

"Sounds filthy. His used bed could have mites."

"They bleach everything before selling it."

"I can't believe it."

"Isn't he fantastic?"

"No, I mean I can't believe there's a place actually selling pre-worn gitch."

Danny invited her to drive cross-country in a VW bus he'd bought at Junkyard Boyz in Welland. I forbid her. We were in up her room. She tore blue ribbons off the walls. Chucked trophies out the window into Saberhagen's backyard. During the commotion I'd grabbed her. She pushed back so hard I went down on my ass. If she'd known how to translate that strength into violence she could have beaten the living shit out of me.

"I quit! I'm through lifting."

Danny and my daughter reached Moose Jaw before the minibus broke down. The trip convinced Abby that Danny's posturings were more affected than esthetic. He later dropped out of college to join the police force. I didn't hound her. If she really wanted to quit, well, what could I say? My thinking— hideous, but I'll say it—went along the lines of Pavlov. My daughter is a rational and complex being. Still. If you've imprinted it deep, sooner or later that creature will ring the bell itself.

"I want to work him out of my skin," was how she put it.

Forget about Danny the way you'd slap a coat of paint on a roomful of sour memories. We buried Danny Mulligan under a fresh coat of muscle. That was many years and several coats ago.

So it went until last September. I've come to divide my daughter into separate entities: pre- and post-September Abbies. She'd sustained a shoulder injury. The shoulder is our most fragile joint structure: a cup-and-socket mechanism as precarious as an egg balanced in a teaspoon. The only curative for a ruptured shoulder is rest. But every muscle possesses a memory. Should you train to a peak and for whatever reason quit, your muscles retain a memory of that peak. Olympic-level athletes surrender, on average, ten percent capacity every week. But muscle remembers.

Her layoff included a Mexican bender with old high school cohorts. She returned with a shocking heft. *Puffed wheat*: my thought as she cleared Customs at Pearson International. This big ole, tanned ole Sugar Crisp. Someplace in Mexico my daughter lost her fire. Along came that September afternoon at the YMCA.

"Bench press, Abs."

Her legs: a pair of cocktail swords. Goddamn the defeatist workings of the human body. She'd rubbed her wrist. I remember all of it. Crystalline.

"Feel that."

A nubbin of cartilage floated free where her wrist met the meat of her palm.

"Olympic trials next month. You're gold-bricking?"

"What did I say? I just said, 'Feel that.'"

Abby dusted her palms with chalk. I slapped on 45s. Abby bench pressed it easily. The old striation of muscle beneath a veneer of vacation-flab. Two more plates. She shook her wrist loose. Clenched and unclenched her fingers.

"It's just tightness, Abs. Loosen up."

On the eighth rep of her following set Abby abruptly hit total muscular failure. At the same time and at the very height of extension Abby's right shoulder and left wrist broke. Her wrist re-broke: she'd first broken it years ago leaping from a house on fire. She zonked out. The sound of my daughter breaking apart—greenstick snap of her wrist, fibrous ripping of her shoulder socket—shocked me on such a purely auditory level that the bar slipped through my hands.

Four forty-five pound plates. A weight bar weighing forty-five pounds. Two safety clips weighing an eighth of a pound each—225¼ pounds fell the distance of a child's footstep onto my daughter. Her windpipe would have been completely crushed had the bar not been checked by her chin, the bone of which broke into several pieces. Her eyes closed, then opened. They say she likely never regained consciousness. Only body-shock trauma. Blood hemorrhaged into both eyeballs.

I heaved the bar off her throat. Dislocated both shoulders doing so. She rolled off the bench. Her skull hit the rubberized weight mat. Her eyes tiny stoplights. Jaw hanging open. A dent on her throat where the bar crushed the cartilage-wrapped tube of her airway. Fingernails ripping at her neck hoping to gouge deep enough to let air in. My broken-wristed, broken-shouldered, broke-chinned, red-eyed daughter crawling on the shockproof mat of the downtown YMCA. I grabbed for her. Abby's hand swung wildly. My nose burst. Blood all over. Every part of her flexed so hard.

When the ambulance arrived an attendant slit

her throat below the crimping. Threaded in a tube.

Our cerebral hemispheres begin to corrode one minute after oxygen is cut. Hypoxic encephalopathy. Cerebral hypoxia. More simply: black holes eating into the fabric of our brains. Wesley Hill, old neighbour and friend: his job was pulling people out of Niagara Falls. If they had been under too long it was no different than pulling turnips out of a garden. A Niagara Lobotomy. Abby's neurologist—not Saberhagen—said Abigail had surrendered sixty percent neural capacity. Blood surging into her ocular cavities bulged and burst the corneal dams. She's blind.

A week afterward purple bruises blotched my shoulders where they'd been pulled out of joint. The local rag painted me a monster. Dredged up Over and Out. My ex-wife secured a temporary restraining order that, following token legal wranglings, would become permanent. I cried easily at things of no importance.

That evening I found Saberhagen on his back porch shooting at squirrels with a pellet gun. Working on a Flatliner. A booze-puffed texture to his face. He'd been relieved of duties as neurosurgeon at the General. His scalpel had slipped a fraction. When the blade is inside a patient's head, a slip is catastrophic. A patient may forfeit his childhood or sense of direction. Saberhagen, participant in the famous Labradum Procedure at Johns Hopkins, was disbarred from the operating theatre.

I said: "Why shoot the poor things?"

"Eating seeds I laid out for the birds. I'm not running a squirrel soup kitchen. How are you faring?"

"Guess I want to die, Frank."

"If that happened to my kid I guess I'd want to, too."

He went inside to fix us drinks. When he sat again, he said: "The very definition of freak accident. I'm sorry."

"For what?"

"A hell of a thing to happen, is all. Abby's such a good gal."

The evening shadows grew teeth. Frank said:

"Remember that kid who burnt down the fireworker's house?"

"Philip Nanavatti. The kid's name was . . ."

"Teddy. Wasn't a bad kid. Just fucked up. In animals, there's what's called a biological imperative. What they're hardwired to do. We're the same except that little bit smarter. We're not too smart as a species. Just enough to screw ourselves up. That kid, Teddy . . . burning things was his biological imperative. I was there when firefighters drug out what was left. A carbonized skeleton but Fletch, I swear: that boy died happy. Abby jumps out the window. Breaks her wrist . . . we do it, too. Break things. Ruin ourselves then ruin everything around us. Those closest we ruin worst. Ninety-nine percent is good intentions, I think. We want good things for others. To do good ourselves."

Charter members of the Bad Fathers Club, the two of us. Men with matching polarities—we habitual if accidental brutalizers—amplify what's worst in ourselves. Seeing it reflected in each other somehow justified it. All these years me thinking I wasn't so bad and my only evidence being my neighbour, the surgeon, was cut from the same cloth.

"Could she be fixed, Frank?"

"Her brain can't."

"Eyes?"

"If you had a donor."

"Ever done eye surgery?"

"Eyes are the newspaper route of the surgical world."

"Could you do Abby's?"

"The Eye Bank's wait list is long as hell."

"What if you had a donor?"

". . . as a matter of skill, yes. I could. Changing sparkplugs. Thing is, I can't. Red tape runs round that sort of procedure."

"It's the two of us speaking."

"Even on a purely conjectural level I'd need to know you were serious. Not only serious about the procedure. About everything. Your frame of mind."

"I've stopped buying green bananas."

Frank searched my face. Finally, he said:

"There's a loose consortium of businesspeople. Most surgeons know of them. For a price, you can get an organ. Only rule: don't ask where it came from. And it doesn't come cheap. Eyes won't be all they'd take, Fletch."

"These people are professionals?"

"Far as I know, you're asking whether the mob is professional."

Nick showed up. He now worked for a credit card company. Recently divorced. His kid, Dylan, was with him. A chubby boy smelling of peanut butter. I put my dukes up for playful shadowboxing. Half-hoping Nick would slug me. He pushed my hands down. Hugged me. His kid being there, I guess. Frank said something mean-spirited but ultimately truthful. I left.

The farmhouse stands off the main road. Several dozen head of cattle sleep in the abutting pasture. James kicks the door open before the car checks up. Staggering around with Matilda in her cowl of bloody towels.

"My dog—my dog's dying!"

Light blooms in a second-story window. A man in sleeping flannels leans out.

"She's been chopped," James tells him. "Bleeding real bad."

"Chopped?"

"Scratched," I tell the guy. "Clawed. Badger or something."

"He said chopped."

"He's out of it. We thought you could help. Or tell us where the nearest vet is."

A second sleep-puffed face, female, materializes.

"How bad is it?"

"She's a tough dog," I tell her. "But deep."

The woman rubs the flat of her palm over her face. "I'm no vet, but I could stitch that dog up. Give me a minute to get decent."

She meets us downstairs. A hard-shouldered woman stepping into a pair of galoshes. Husband taller and thinner with big-knuckled hands. A hunting rifle is crossed over his chest.

"He thinks you guys could be running a home invasion scam," his wife says. "Show up at night with a sick dog, appealing to our tenderest feelings—"

"How do we know that dog's hurt?" the guy says. "Towels soaked in red food colouring."

"Fair enough," I say. "I'm Fletcher. This is James and Matilda."

"Michelle. Matt's the hubby. We do all that work out in the barn."

Frost-clad grass crunches underfoot as we make

our way through cattle whose bodies steam like stewpots in the moon-plated field. I touch one: skin texture of a truck tire. Michelle unlatches the barn door. Lights screwed into high beams fritz and pop. She leads us to a metal gooseneck from which a darkly knotted noose suspends.

"For cows. Drag a bale over so she can reach," Michelle says. "Head through it."

"She won't bite," James says.

"Your say-so doesn't make it any less likely. I'm not getting my face chewed off." She's threading a needle with surgical catgut. "Thinnest gauge I've got. Use it to repair labial tears after cows give birth."

She peels towels away to reveal Matilda's wound. A near-bloodless gash: stiff white lips with a shiny red trench between. The needle works through Matilda's hide. Michelle pulls the incision lips together, loops, ties. She swabs Matilda's hide with rubbing alcohol. Paints the sutures with mercurochrome.

"Good as I can do for her."

Back in their kitchen Matthew digs a gallon tub of ice cream out the freezer. Rinses it, cuts the bottom out with a utility knife, slices halfway up its hull. James works the plastic until it fits round Matilda's throat. Matthew duct-tapes the cone in place. Matilda gives the plastic a desultory lick, chuffs, lays across James's legs.

We want to let them get back to bed but they say it

isn't worth bothering. They'd have to be up shortly. Such are the hours of cattle ranchers.

"Before cattle Matt was a sharecropper," says Michelle.

"What sort of crops?"

"Potatoes," Matt tells me. "Little coloured ones. Boutique potatoes, they're called. Funky colours: purple and orange and bright red. All the rage with top-flight chefs."

"Rages come and rages go," says Michelle. "Why not russets? Mashers, bakers, fryers."

"But they aren't *niche*," Matt says. "We've done better with cattle."

"A wonder you didn't suggest pygmy cows." Michelle kisses the top of his head. "Bright purple pygmy cows."

The hospital room was stark white. Abigail covered in a white sheet.

Her nipples were hard. I tried to fiddle with the thermostat but the box was locked. As my presence was a breach of the restraining order, I couldn't ask for help. I smoothed my hands over the sheets. So glossy they could be made from spun glass. Somebody had trimmed her fingernails. Went too deep on the left pinkie: a rime of dried blood traced the enamel.

The brain is a funny organ and breaks in funny

ways. Saberhagen says a damaged brain is an old car in a junkyard that, every once in awhile, you twist the key and it starts. If this was her forever after and she'd never remember anything of who she'd been—pre-September Abby—I could live with it. But some days the chemicals inside her head would surge, old doors would open and she'd be who she once was for an instant. An instant of complete confusion and rage and in the next she'd know nothing. A lingering sense, only, a taste on the back of the tongue.

A tray sat on the bedside table. Cold minestrone soup. Meatloaf. Lime Jell-O. How long would it sit before being taken away? Would another tray arrive for breakfast? I wanted to find the orderly who'd brought it and throw him down a flight of stairs. Above the tray sat the machines. Beeping, wheezing, heartbeat-spike-emitting machines. If I didn't leave soon I might find myself fiddling with those dials and knobs. With the easy notion of it.

Imagine driving home one night. You hit a girl on her bicycle. That broken tapestry of limbs splayed over your hood. The sound of impact with the windshield—would it sound like so much at all? Twisted handlebars in the grille and the ironclad assurance that the existence you'd followed up until that moment was finished. Every overblown ambition harboured. Each foolish hope nursed.

Now imagine it again. This time it's your own girl. Realizing you'd settled behind that wheel the very night she was born. Guided yourself with terrible precision into that collision. No man can live inside his skin after reaching such an understanding. Even a one-celled organism, a planarian worm, would turn itself inside-out.

I walked down Queenston past a Big Bee convenience near the bus depot. An elderly man in what appeared to be pajamas exited a late-model minivan. He'd left the engine running. I hopped in.

Thus kicked off my short, silly career as vehicle thief.

The highway runs north. James and I can't return to the houseboat. I don't even want to. I'm nearly where I need to be, anyway.

Dawn rises over tailback hills. I drive into the town of Peterborough. A bakery's just opening on the main drag. I go in, buy coffees and rolls hot from the oven. James and I sit on the hood of the Cadillac. Matilda lays on the passenger seat. Cone-wrapped head lolling in the footwell. A pickup passes, its bed full of itinerant workers in snowmobile suits. The bus station lot lights snap off, halogen coils dimming inside their plastic shells as the sun breaks over the squat block of a Woolco store.

"Where now?"

"Back south," James says. "I got a place. Niagara Falls. U.S. side. For tax purposes."

"To do what?"

"I'm thinking—this may sound crazy—about raising earthworms. It's a messy enterprise," he admits, "but they're gold. Not just for fishing: it's the composting wave I'll ride. Easy to start a worm farm. Couple kiddie pools, nightcrawlers, off you go. But you need quality worms. Good bloodlines."

"Worms have those?"

"I've been told so."

"Well . . . I got to go, James."

For whatever reason he's confused. As if he'd expected me to tag along the rest of his life. The sun carries over the low-rise architecture of this central Ontario town. In the Cadillac's windshield stand James and myself, reflected. James with his bruised face, me with my scabby scalp. Matilda stares through the glass. With the cone round her head brightened by the sun she looks like the bulb in a car headlamp.

I catch a cab at the bus terminal. It heads to the destination I'd been given over the phone by a man with a Robert Goulet voice. Lakefield Research Centre. Some kind of metallurgy lab. It takes about an hour. I doze. I give the cabbie everything I've got left on me—everything in my pockets. Cash, half a pack of gum, a Subway Club card one punch-hole shy of a free footlong. He takes it all gratefully enough.

Lakefield is painted that industrial lime shade common in the seventies. Inside are the partially lit hallways, gypsum floors, and whitewashed concrete walls of any elementary school. I walk down halls, finding nobody, nothing but the hum of machinery through the walls. I come upon a chair and man sitting in it. Old, in a janitor's outfit. I tell him who I am and he nods. I follow him down another hallway, up a flight of stairs. The reek of ozone. A green-tiled room. Riveted metal floors. Military cot. I lie upon it and fall into an exhausted sleep and awake to face my butcher.

Starling looks not bad, considering. Bandaged up, everything safety-pinned in place. He sits awkwardly in a wooden chair backgrounded by a man I find familiar. Starling sniffles. The other man wipes his nose with a Kleenex, which he balls and tucks up his sleeve as an old biddy would.

"The man's dog?"

"Tough dog."

"Tough," Starlings agrees.

"So who cuts—you?"

"I'm not a professional," Starling tells me. "Or a gifted amateur. Only The Middle. Your organs are point A. Their destinations point C. They meet through me. We have surgeons. Not, mind you, the best this world has to offer."

"You can cut me to rags and throw my body to the dogs. But my eyes . . ."

"Your daughter," says Starling. "You love her? You must. There will be various handler's fees," he explains. "Other miscellaneous expenses. Whatever's left will be deposited into your account."

I brace my arms on the cot's edge. "How much do you figure I'm worth?"

"Depends how much you're needed. By whom."

"There'll be some kind of . . . gas?"

"We're businesspeople, not animals. Go shower."

A shower room as I remember from high school. Steel colonnades stretching ceiling to floor. Nozzles strung round. I strip down and twist the knob.

She will see life as an eternal ten-year-old. The worst fate in the world? Hardly. That this is the most cowardly plan of action can hardly be denied. History is crowded with fathers who've fled blood debts. I could try to pay back in increments what I stole. In moments and hours and days. Fifty years paying back what is essentially un-repayable. But I'm not that man. Never possessed that strength. Not for one instant in my existence.

It hurts to deny my daughter her rage. Hurts she cannot scream it into my face. Direct the cold barrel of that hatred at me. Melt the flesh off my bones. My deepest frustration finds itself here. Since anyone can be a father, can't they? Half the human race. Takes nothing but to find a woman, tell her you love her—or love her truly, if you have that in you. Fatherhood follows. Yet nothing is so easy. I do love my daughter but this much is true: love is a sickness. Some kind of pathogen existing above all explanation.

A peculiar darkness falls through the casement window—a cold hole opening in the centre of the sun—as droplets fall, silver freckles striking my skin. No noise at all. The water. My heartbeat. That cold widening spot in the sun.

Black Box: Fletcher Burger

The plane is afflicted with vehicular leprosy. Exterior panels flake off, rivets bursting, plates of steel carried off in the jet stream. Grip fast the yoke as it shimmies in my hands. I could let go but to this final end I am selfish. The life you cling to most dearly, worthwhile or not, is your own.

Guilt crushes you into shapes unrecognizable. Hate to sound weak of will but things happen. They happen. And yet I am truly quite sorry.

I pull back on the yoke. The line in the sky

separating earth from sky, that sketchy pastel scrim of blue, gives way to darkness. The plane comes apart. As do I. My hands blacken. Whiteness of knuckle through charred skin. My eyes catch fire in a green flash the way phosphorous flares burn in the colours of their dyeing.

How deeply do any of us know our own selves? Ask yourself. We hold a picture of how we wish to be and pray it goes forever unchallenged. Passing through life never pursuing aspects of our natures with which we'd rather not reckon. Dying strangers to ourselves.

BLACK CARD

NOSFERATU, MY SON

First, let me tell you about my boy. Dylan. Great kid. The greatest.

He's chubby. Chubby-edging-fat. I've always been thin and my wife, ex-wife, she's trim as a willow switch. The charitable genes we inherited reversed polarities in him. Now I don't mind that he's chubby but I don't know what it's like to be chubby so I'm a stranger to his struggles. My dad suggests a dietician. Too Hollywood. A ten-year-old with a dietician. What next—a PR flack?

Other week he found a grocery bag full of used work gloves at a building site. Sweat encrusted. Worn through at the fingertips. The sheer uniformity— gloves! a humongous bagful!—must have intrigued him. Then days ago he came home with a trash sack slung over his shoulder. Chewing on a Snickers. Two questions, son of mine: why did you pick up that charming sack of trash and where'd you get the candy? His answer: he discovered the candy in the sack, which, naturally, was why he picked it up. Its contents: twenty-odd pounds of chocolate. We drove to the site of his gold rush. The home's owner, the manager of Haig Bowl skating rink's concession stand, told me that yes, he'd pitched chocolate bars past their best-before date. They wouldn't *kill* anyone. I let Dylan keep five. A finders fee. On the drive home a sugar rush gave rise to one of my son's parented Deep Thoughts:

"Daddy, would a cloned human being have a soul?"

"Sure, Dill. Why not."

One vivid-as-hell imagination. He's been a stegosaurus, a fusion-engineered-saber-toothed-rattlesnake (with stinging nettle skin), gas vapour from a 1973 Gran Torino, an atomic mummy, both a llama and an alpaca as apparently there's a difference. For days he'll speak in this spur-of-the-moment dialect: "Fitzoey blib-blab hadoo! Wibble-wabble?" His whimsy gave birth to the Phantoids: aliens the size of atoms who colonized a marshmallow he carried in a shoe box. When the marshmallow went stale he told me the Phantoids returned to their home world.

"Wasn't the marshmallow their world?"

"They were on vacation."

"Budget travellers, those Phantoids."

You've got to carefully monitor his stimuli or he'll pick up a contact high that lasts weeks. It can be a bit embarrassing, as when he overheard a private conversation between his mother and I and created a jazzy new superhero: Captain Pap Smear. For a minor eternity he shouted, in *basso profundo* voice, "This sounds like a job for Captain Pap Smear!" and "He seeks out evil and smears it!" Or during his Night Stalker phase, where he deployed his skills at sneaking about—he tiptoes like Baryshnikov!—to catch my wife and I in *flagrante delicto*. He'd popped up at the end of our bed with a cry of "Yeah-*HA!*" but his brow beetled with perplexity so I'd leapt up chuckling "Ho ho ho!", girding my hips with a sheet to escort him back to bed.

Lately he's been a vampire. A manageable fixation. Before that it was No Bone Boy. That incarnation saw him lounging in sloppy poses over sofa arms. Splay-armed on the floor.

"Dinner's on, Dill."

"Sure am hungry, Daddy, but"—big sigh—"no bones."

I'd drag him into the kitchen. Perch him in a chair like a muppet. Head flat on the table.

"Having a no-boned son sucks, huh?"

"Are the doctors working on those space-age titanium bones?"

"Around the clock."

Next he would slide, *sans* bones, onto the linoleum. I mean, my kid is *method*.

The phone call comes at three a.m. Flights booked: Hamilton to JFK onto Russia. From there by charter to the Sea of Okhotsk. I call Abby.

"It's Nick," I whisper. "Sorry, sorry. Alright I bring Dylan over?"

"Mrrrmf-*fah*."

I pop a Black Cat caffeine pill. Grab a pre-packed duffel. On into Dylan's room.

"Dill, gotta get up."

His eyes crack. A stale drool smell wafts off his pillow.

"I'm taking you to Abby's."

"Can't I stay with Mom?"

"Mom's still settling in up in Toronto."

He pulls his planet-patterned covers up, squashing Jupiter upon the curve of his chin.

"No time for this, buckaroo. Either Abby or grandpa."

That does it. I bundle him into the car with his "Emergency Away-From-Home Kit": locomotive to his Lionel train set, a book: *Lizards of the Gobi Desert*, packets of banana-flavoured Carnation Instant Breakfast which he takes blended with one real banana.

I drive Ontario Street past the GM plant and its stargazer's constellation of security lamps. Chase a yellow through the intersection of Louth past the Hotel Dieu hospital. A man sits on an ambulance bumper. Bloody towel pressed to his head smoking a cigarette. St. Paul a cold strip hammered flat between shopfronts. Men in snowmobile suits with frostburnt fingers black as cigar butts. Dylan's touching the inside of his wrist with two fingers.

"What are you up to?"

"Checking my pulse. It's the most reliable indicator of bodily health."

Russia. Goddamn. Okhotsk? Sound you'd make choking on a fishbone. These gigs usually go a day or two. Any longer I'll have to buy local vestments. Waddling about in a bearskin parka, a babushka, one of those furry too-big KGB caps.

Abby musters a groggy smile when we arrive. Boxers and a MET-RX tee shirt. Corded legs and calves a-trickle with veins.

"Hey, troublemaker," she says to Dylan in his one-piece pajamas with padded booties; I think he's too old for them, but the fact they're manufactured in his size makes this hard to argue.

I drive to the airport and check in. Doze with

the pocketed lights of Hamilton burning through the airplane window. Awake to a New York dawn. Layover in JFK. Commuters shuffling under halogens that accord us the look of zombies cooling our heels between takes of a grade-Z horror flick. No jetsetters. Jetlagged middle-of-the-roaders. Economy-classers. Shreds of airline-peanut foil under our fingernails. We, the tribe of semis: semi-handsome, semi-intellectual, semi-successful, semi-leisure class, semi-happy, semi-alive. Half lifers.

I'm in what a headshrinker might call "a fragile state of mind." Not so much I cannot cope, not so much I'd abdicate my responsibilities, but . . . yeah. Fragile. There's this commercial on TV a lot these days. For the Alzheimer's Society. Maybe you've seen it? This old fellow in a house full of lemons. Shelves, the floor, fridge chockablock. He can't remember he'd already bought them, see? Buys more and more. This poor old man in a house full of lemons. Playing solitaire. It wrecks me. Takes precious little, so suddenly. The ass-end of Christopher Cross's "Sailing" on an easy-listening station. The smell of burning leaves. I'm standing there, welling up, asking myself: *What the hell's this all about?*

A pair of leggy foreign girls—German tennis players to take a wild stab—breeze past. Young and somehow more attractive for their harried-ness: a woman-on-the-go quality. Speaking in exotic tongues. Hair done up invitingly. I try on a smile but catch my profile in a chain pizzeria's mirrored facade and the sight—punch-squashed nose, cauliflower ears: reminders of a childhood in the ring—causes the smile to rot on my face. I can't even summon the enthusiasm to play the gay divorcée.

Auf Wiedersehen, ladies.

The next flight finds me stranded between beefy members of the beleaguered proletariat. A breakfast omelette resembles novelty vomit. My stomach curdles over the vast grey Atlantic.

I work for American Express. Caretaker for Centurion holders. The Black Card.

It began as an urban myth: American Express distributed a card with which you could buy anything to the limit of the company's 20.87 billion dollar worth. A decommissioned battleship or gently used space shuttle. But the card never existed. Until one of the bigwigs at head office said, "Why not?" The Centurion is limited to 4,000 clients worldwide. Member fee: $350,000.

You can look at me as a concierge. A perk built into the card's exorbitant fees. Occasionally this reduces me to professional nose-wiper. I'm sent to monitor peculiar purchases. If a client's aiming to buy a cruise missile, I have to say: *nix*.

Clients do fall from Centurion status. In those cases we do as with any deadbeat: cut their card up.

I cut up Michael Jackson's, if you can believe it. He was in Europe. We charted his egress by the locations of each gobsmacking purchase. Three Qing Dynasty vases ($750,000 apiece) at a Glasgow antiques emporium. The 1.5-ton chandelier from the Belfast Grand Opera House auctioned at Sotheby's Helsinki. An attempted purchase of Marienburg castle, a deal nearly shepherded to fruition by Duke Philip von Wuerttemberg—that man knew a pigeon when he saw one—occasioned my dispatch. I tracked Jackson to a hotel room in Budapest. Ushered past muckety-mucks and a diaper-clad chimp before reaching the man himself. Who was a mess. Face falling off the put-upon bones of his skull. "Big fan," I told him awkwardly, snipping his card in half. "My first slow dance was to 'Baby Be Mine.'"

That damn chimp scratched my arms all to hell.

Novosibirsk airport holds the eye-bruising shade of a black market kidney. Red, arterial red, steak-tartare-served-on-a-stop-sign red stretching everywhere. The arcade past Customs consists of four Ms. Pacmans. Three of the four are busted. The man waiting at the luggage carousel—check that, luggage disgorger: scuffed tongue of a conveyor belt drooling suitcases into a metal basin—jabs a squared-off finger at the pocket he assumes I keep my passport in.

"*Shab-ruh-hoegan*. Dis not name you company to give."

"My company's an idiot," I tell him.

That I'd refer to my company as a massive useless singular evidently tickles his Bolshevik funny bone. He smells strongly of pickled something: beets, to guess by the staining of his teeth. He leads me through the airport to a runway where a twin-prop plane awaits. My baggage handler is the pilot. Could be it's this way all over Russia. The doctor who empties your bedpan cuts out your gallbladder, too.

It's late afternoon by the time we touch down on a grassy landing slip. Goats graze over a stone wall. A Lada waits. Unsurprisingly, the pilot's my driver. He guns the four-banger engine.

"Dah. Ve go."

Stone houses, filling stations, churches with onion-bellied spires. Heaved-backed men with skin so hard and whitened it looks like an exoskeleton. It's darkening by the time we reach a bluff overlooking the sea. A bay edged by cliffs. A military-style tent is set up on the beach below. A Jeep. Up the bluff with us: a TV truck. Russky station. The satellite dish on its roof is a rusted toadstool.

"Dah," says my Man Friday. "Joo go."

Egg-sized beach stones rounded smooth with each tide. Dark skeins of kelp. Blackness of water leeching into the sky. I hear frantic peeps. Light burns out of tents' eyelets.

"Saberhagen?"

Conway Finnegan steps through the flaps. A St. Catharines native who hopped a ship to the Saudi oilfields and in the ensuing decades became our town's richest expat. His American Express status took the same upwardly mobile route: green to gold to platinum to Centurion. We'd last met in Delta's first class lounge at Dulles airport. He'd been off to "sort out some monkeyshines with those Halliburton bastages." Even at sixty-odd Conway's huge: a chunk of slob ice broken off the Niagara river miraculously grown legs, arms, and a salt-and-pepper head. One of those guys who, when he hugs you—as he does now—he cradles the back of your head as if you're an infant with a neck too weak to support your skull. Despite this, he looks smaller than my memory of him. Circumstances tend to shrink a man.

"TV truck still up there?" When I tell him it is: "Vultures a-circling."

We hop into the Jeep. Connie drives to the seashore. Flicks on foglamps bolted to the roll bar.

"See it? Volganeft-188. Bearing cargo I paid for and insured."

A metallic tusk juts from the water a few knots out. Moonlight bleeds along the downed ship's hull to make it appear as a curved knife slicing up out of the surf.

"Borne for the western seaboard. Busted apart two-hundred miles from where she was loaded. Four thousand liquid tons of motor oil into the drink. Glug, glug, glug."

Connie's flashlight sweeps the shore. It lingers on tar-scummed life rafts. It takes a moment to accept the flat, eye-shaped objects washing in and out as flounders. The seaside is cobbled with dead fish. Oil-smothered birds. Feathers slicked down they're tinier, the way a dog shrinks when you bathe it. Only the red pinpricks of their eyes aren't black.

"Cleaned a couple best I could," Connie says. "Still, they died. Oil's earmarked for Wal-Mart. Biggest oil-change providers in the hemisphere. I got a buzz from their legal eagle, Donald-someone-or-other. Real nut-buster. Says I better get out here, deal with the mess I'd made."

He crimps one nostril with his thumb. Blows a string of mucous out the other. Back home we call that a gym-teacher's nose blow.

"He said what I ought to do is collect some of the poor things as samples. A charitable educational initiative. Put them in glass boxes of formaldehyde. Give it a preachy name. Our Poisoned Seas. It'll spin, he kept saying. It'll spin!"

Huge fearsome noises rumble up the beach. Connie trains the flashlight. Down the stones, gripped in the oil-thickened surf, is a shark. Easily a thirteen-footer—a rogue, they call lone sharks— threshing on the polished stones. Black, its body all black and while this should have made it more fearsome, a living nightmare, it only looks pitiful.

"Great white," Connie says. "Didn't think they swam this far north."

Its saw-like tail slashes. Its massive, rubber-like mouth flexes. Stones burst between its jaws. Pebbles adhere to the glutinous sheen of its oil-covered skin, making portions of its anatomy look like black bedazzled leather. A second tail, far smaller, protrudes partway from its sternum. The shark must've swum into the shallows to give birth. The metallic fluttering of its gill-slits. Dark arterial blood pouring out as it suffocates.

In the tent we can still hear her dying. All the little sounds of death. The tent: folding table, chairs, hurricane lamp hanging on a loop of jute cord. Bottles of native spirits.

"My father, Seamus" Connie tells me, "had an embolism. Blood pooling in the brain. First morning I'm back home he shreds the newspaper into a bowl and pours milk on it. Then he goes and shakes cornflakes over the table. Trying to do what he'd done for thirty-five years: eat cereal, read the paper. But the circuitry was screwy."

Connie takes a haul off the nearest bottleneck.

"Money wasn't a sticky point—I'd have shipped him to Beth Israel—but I was told Frank Saberhagen, your Dad, was good as any. Part of some big medical thingamabob . . ."

"The Labradum Procedure."

"—right, at—"

"Johns Hopkins."

"Blood from that blown vessel lingered in Dad's head. It . . . turned hard? Went to jelly? Anyway, in the channels of his brain. Weeks in the hospital. Norris wing. As a kid, I thought that place was a . . ."

"Nuthouse."

"You, too?"

"Teachers used to threaten: behave, or I'll ship you to the Norris wing with the crazies. You'd think it was padded cells and straightjackets—"

"—and electroshock therapy, sure. Just rooms, Nick. Ordinary hospital rooms."

Wind howls in off the sea and hisses through the eyelets. My first trip to the Soviet Union. What would I carry home? Busted Reagan-era video games. Beet-stained teeth. A shark's gills sharp as the steel teeth on a circular saw. Conway Finnegan so shrunk inside his skin he had the look of a sick Shar-pei.

"Sorry to drag you out," he tells me. "American Express was happy enough to dispatch you. Your father, mine. We're town boys. I'm just the son of a welder from St. Kitt's, Nick."

I close my eyes. Behind my eyelids fins and beaks, wings and tails break up from the dark. Two boys from southern Ontario perched on the other end of the world at the edge of an oil-black sea.

"How's your father, Connie?" I ask.

"Cemetery off Queenston. By the liftlocks. Yours?"

"Still kicking."

Secondly, I'll to tell you about my wife. Ex.

What I miss is a hand on her hip. On line at the movies or navigating the kitchen while we cooked. An undervalued perk of married life. My hand on her hip, whenever.

Our first kiss she had Sambuca on her tongue. Like sucking on a licorice pastille. Making out in my father's Camry with "C'Mon and Ride It" by Quad City DJs on the radio. One of many life events on which I'd gladly take a do-over. These disassociated memories I carry forward. These memories, I imagine, are the ones I'll die with. Back then I was still rooting through my father's *GQs*, ripping out the scented cologne ads, rubbing them on my neck.

Also training to fight the curtain-jerker on a card at the Tonowanda VFW. My opponent: Ox "Eighteen" Wheeler. Irish so far as I'd been told but he walked to the ring in a serape and sombrero accompanied by a mariachi guitarist strumming "Prisonero De Tus Brazos." Yes, seriously, and yes, I lost. Ox headbutted me in the first round. The pressure of our heads colliding caused veins in my forehead to burst. Those veins spraying blood like fire hoses under my skin occasioned two plum-sized mouses to form above my eyes. By the sixth round they were so massive I couldn't see much: like peering out of a basement window. My father said I'd looked like a goat with clipped horns. He slit them afterwards. Blood pissed out of my face halfway across the locker room, splashing the robe of a flyweight warming up. The scars now meet in a shallow 'V' above my eyebrows.

The adrenaline overload of sparring for the Wheeler fight made me immoderately, ungovernably horny. More so even than your run-of-the-mill nineteen-year-old. Dad blamed it on an overstimulated hypothalamus gland. "I tell guys with ED to join a boxing club," he'd say. "A round of sparring beats that little blue pill all to hell." Oversexed boxer + rebellious daughter of landed gentry = hormonal fireworks. Eleven months: the span separating our eyes meeting across a crowded campus bar to Dylan's birth. To cop a lyric from a song getting radio play around then: "We were only freshmen."

I was KO'd by an overmuscled bear from Coldwater, Michigan on a card sponsored by the railway switchmen's union the week my to-be wife announced she was preggers. The sting my father felt at my losing to a guy he trumpeted as "The Coldwater Crumpet" was inflamed by the fact we'd be keeping the baby. We arranged a quickie civil union at the courthouse. Our mothers' hearts broken: they who'd pined for rose petals, centrepieces, and perhaps to pin some inexact debt on us for arranging it.

My wife: cute, athletic, a field hockey defence-man. The physics of childbirth terrified her. Her "vaginal integrity" would be ruined by a new life steamrolling out. At Lamaze class our instructor, an elderly wide-hipped lesbian ("A dyke with child-bearing hips," my father had said; "Irony, thou art a coy mistress!") asked us men to picture passing a cherry stone through our urethral tube. "If I could birth our baby that way, I would," I'd said to my wife during one quarrel. "Even if it widened my urethral tube so bad it ended up a . . . a windsock!" I was there in the delivery room. She insisted. My first sight of Dylan: this slick quivering mass extruded from my wife's birth canal. Her labial lips stretched and torn. I'd touched her weeks later, in bed, felt those hairline scabs in the process of healing. To know I'd wreaked that manner of intimate violence upon her. She regained her figure but the skin of her stomach lost tension. She said it looked like a balloon from a New Year's party fallen behind the couch to be found in April, mostly deflated with half a lungful of sad old air inside.

We had typical married couple fights. My wife hailed from a proper English family. One did not use one's utensil as a shovel. Food should be pushed up the underside of a fork. She made Dylan—three years old with the fine motor skills of a spider monkey—roll corn niblets up his fork. Or we'd be having sex, she'd run her fingers through my hair and say: "I liked it better long."

Dad says: "Surveys prove a third of women cheat on their spouse. But if you're honest with yourself, you'll know if she's in that third before it ever happens." *I'm not happy.* She kept repeating this the night she left. After the rationales and rage had burnt us down to the bones of it. *I'm not happy.* What can I change? *Nothing. I'm not happy.* Is there someone else? *No.* But there was by then the idea of someone else. She craved the catharsis of a clean break. To tell the truth, it was foretold in one silly everyday episode.

I'd driven her to the mechanic to pick up our old Aerostar. She drove home behind me. At a stoplight on Martindale I observed her out the rearview mirror. In that moment she became a stranger, and my understanding of her that of a stranger. I saw a lovely woman in a minivan singing along to the radio. Really belting it out. One hand drumming the wheel. Wedding band fracturing the sunlight to spit it off in sparks.

She wasn't my wife, in that moment. Just a beautiful girl who'd married too young and gotten trapped—only she hadn't quite reached that realization.

I catch a redeye into Toronto. A message from Abby awaits me at home.

"Dylan's in trouble at school. You've got a meeting with Iris Trupholme. He's still a vampire."

I'd let Dylan watch *The Lost Boys*. Afterwards he begged me to go to Toys R Us. I outfitted him with a bargain-bin cape and plastic fangs. He's adopted that Lugosian accent where every 'w' becomes a 'v': *I vant to suck jor blood, blah!*

Abby's waiting outside Dylan's classroom with a girl my son's age. She's got those enamel-coloured dental braces that make wearers look as though they have sets of overlapping teeth, like sharks. She's chewing an Eberhard eraser and spitting pink bits on the tiles.

Missus Trupholme, Dylan's teacher: sixtyish,

with a low centre of gravity. Her skull sports a vaporous cloud of frizzy red hair which, if it had a taste, would unarguably be cherry. On her desk is a kid's cellphone. The pink faux-gems are a dead giveaway.

"They're video cameras now," Trupholme says. "Everyone's making their own amateur videos. Next regional meeting it's number one on the bullethead."

She flips it open. Fiddles with buttons. "Kids recording one another. Their age's version of Truth or Dare. Put videos on the Internet. There's a place . . ."

"Youtube," says Abby.

"That one. One shows a grade ten student beating up his Math teacher. The man was months shy of retirement. Phones so small, it's hard to patrol. Cassie!"

The eraser-chewer slinks in. Trupholme says: "How does this work?"

Cassie presses a few buttons. Trupholme says, "Now go on."

"Can I have it back?"

"All signs point to 'no.'"

The girl performs a deep-knee bend, arms hugged round her knees.

"My dad's gonna kill me."

"Tell him it's evidence."

"Swear to *God*, I'll only . . ." Her lip juts. Stuck with crumbs of eraser. "It's my property."

183

"Sue me."

Cassie stomps back into the hall. Trupholme shows us the video on the phone's inch-wide screen. Dylan in corduroys with his vampire cape tied round his throat is standing at the front of the class. Shaky footage shot from halfway under a desk. Trupholme chalks a math problem on the board. Dylan prowls up behind. Rubs against her. She sets both hands on Dylan's shoulders. Moves him gently away. Dylan presses forward, smiling, to rub on her again.

"Oh, God," I say. "That's not Dill at all."

"His first quasi-sexual offence," Trupholme says.

Quasi-sexual. Something breaks in me. She goes on:

"Are either of you familiar with the term 'frotteur'? A person who derives gratification from rubbing. Crowded busses, subway cars: where adult frotteurs operate."

"That's what you think Dylan is? A—a budding frotter?"

"*Frotteur*. Your son's too young to have his sexuality sorted out. That said, Mr. Saberhagen, we're suspending him a week."

"Yes. Fair. What he's done is a bad sign. In a year of bad signs. We should make him clean the playground, too."

"That's not necessary."

"Hell, yes. Physical, demeaning labour."

"I doubt our groundskeeper would be happy to hear that."

Dylan sits on an orange plastic chair in the cafeteria. Vampire cape draped over its back.

"Outside. You're cleaning the schoolyard."

"Vampire Dylan doze not clean."

"Shut up with that. You're suspended a week."

He wipes his nose on the cape. "It was just a joke . . . blah."

The wind gusts round the school's industrial edges. Kid-centric garbage—Fruit Roll-Up sleeves, YOP bottles—skates across autumn grass. Dylan mopes along the fence, cape aflutter, tossing trash haphazardly into the bag.

"That was a dandelion," I call from the swingset. "Since when are they garbage?"

"They're *weeds*!"

His whole life I've played the hardass. When his "terrible twos" habit had been to strike out with his fists: always me holding his pudgy hands. He said "Mom" at eight months; he didn't say "Dada" until he'd reached a year, by which point he'd already said "Car" and "Wow-wow." Instead of putting trash in the bag, he's skewering it on fence barbs. Yogurt cups piked like heads.

"You're supposed to pick it up, not redistribute it," Abby says. To me: "He was on the computer all day."

"Should I suspend his privileges?"

"The only way he interacts, Nick. His own birthday—who shows up? That exchange student, Rigo, and me."

Dylan's poked the bag full of holes to wear as a muumuu.

"All done. Blah!"

"By the tetherball pole: see? Pop can. Hurry up. Boxing tonight," I say. Abby gives me a look. "The basics," I tell her. "We'll fit a gumshield to his mouth." I don't tell her how last time Dylan burst into tears biting down on the warm rubber. "It's good for him."

"Yeah, because it was so good for you."

Old wheeze in the boxing game: *In the ring, truth finds you.* Didn't put in the roadwork? That finds you. Didn't leave enough sweat on the heavy bags? That comes to find you. Not just the work: it's all you are from inside-out. Every little thing, even those you got no defence against. If you're cursed with brittle hands, say, that truth finds you. If you cut easy or your heart's not the equal of the man you square up against. In every punch and feint, broken bone and chipped tooth, every gasp and moan, each time you wish you were someplace else, anywhere but here taking this punishment, in your guts and marrow in every place you thought hidden. Boxing is simple arithmetic. The ones and twos never fail to add. Truth always finds its way back to you.

CRAIG DAVIDSON

Impact Boxing is located in a strip mall on Hartzell next to a knife shop, King of Knives, whose banner reads: *Knives, The Perfect Gift for Knife Lovers!* Beyond lies Sterno Dell. Charred tree skeletons poke from its rain-sodden ash like spears.

Entering the club gives me the same sensation an Olympic swimmer must get slipping on a clammy Speedo for morning laps: uncomfortably familiar. My DNA is soaked into these speed bags, headgear, punch mitts. Atomized remainders cling to sewage pipes spanning the ceiling. Photos of prematurely aged fighters on the walls. My favourite a B&W portrait of Archie Moore, the Mongoose, with this quote: *Nowadays fighters tussle for money. I was fighting when the prize was going to jail.* When I was a kid, two men nursing a blood feud stepped through the ropes to go at it barefisted. One hit the other so hard he face-planted the canvas. While unconscious he sneezed involuntarily; a pressurized hiss as the air driven into his skull vented around his eye sockets. My father said the man had suffered an orbital blowout fracture and was lucky: had he sneezed much harder an eyeball might have ejected itself.

Dad's beaten us here. Following his medical suspension he's taken to drinking at the Queenston Motel, a bar lonely, dispossessed men gravitate to before gravity hauls them off the face of the civilized world altogether.

"Look," he says with a sigh. "It's the Count."

"Good *eee*vening," Dylan greets his grandfather.

In the changeroom Dad unfurls Dylan's handwraps like lizard's tongues. Spreads the fleshy starfish of his grandson's hands to gird them.

Dylan sucks air through his teeth. "Tight."

Dad unwinds his work. He believes Dill's wussiness hovers round the fact he required an operation to correct an undescended testicle. But my father is prone to tendering wild accusations based on picayune evidence—such as the time he spotted me with a grape juice moustache and got into a big kerfuffle with Mom, levying the charge I must be "guzzling the frigging stuff," which according to him was a sign of burgeoning gluttony. I was seven.

The club is sparsely trafficked. A retired bricklayer hammers away at a heavy bag with a watchman's cap tugged tight to his eyes. Young hockey players—goons in training—take wild swings at the bags adjacent. I untangle a skipping rope.

"Try for a minute, Dill."

He can't go ten seconds. As always, I am shocked by his lack of coordination. His feet snarl in the cape. He stomps on the hem and its cord chokes him.

"Swell cape," Dad says. Queenston Motel suds percolate out his pores.

"*Saaank* you," Dylan says in his vampire voice. "Jor blood vill stay in jor veins tonight, old one."

"Yeah? That's swell."

I tug Dylan into a pair of sixteen ouncers. Giant red melons attached to his arms. We stake out a bag beside a poster of a vintage Lennox Lewis with his high-and-tight MC Hammer hairdo. Dylan throws a whiffle-armed one-two. The feeble *blut* of his gloves slapping the bag stirs a deep sorrow in my chest.

"Pretend it's vampire bait."

"Vampire bat?"

"Bait." I shouldn't encourage it, but: "Vampire *bait*."

"Eef it vas wampire bait, I vould do dees!"—and bites the bag.

"Dill. How many people you figure sweated all over that?"

Dylan smacks his lips. "Eet's wary, wary hard to be a wampire deez daze."

He heads to the fountain. Dad's emptying spit troughs: funnels attached to lengths of flexible PVC hose feeding into Oleo buckets in opposing corners of the ring. The cell-phone girl, Cassie, comes in with who I assume must be her father: Danny Mulligan. His romance with Abby broke down in Moose Jaw along with his VW Minibus. He's a cop now and looks it: Moore's suitcoat shiny at the elbows, saddle shoes squashed at the toes like a clown's, horse teeth, a Marine's whitewall haircut shorn close to the scalp. I can already picture him as an old man: high blue veins, buttons of nose-hair. He looks—why do I harbour such unreasonable, mean-spirited, *perverse* thoughts?—like the sort of guy who, mid-fuck, grabs his own ass-cheek with a free hand. That self-conscious hand-push, like he needs help burying it home, coupled with an equally affected back arch. Yeah, he's *that* guy.

"Nick, right?"

"Danny," I greet him. "Yeah, hi."

"It's Dan. My little girl tells me there was some ruckus today at school."

"That's right. Something to do with videos."

Mulligan spread his legs as if readying to perform a hack squat.

"Trupholme took away her phone. I bought that for Cassie's birthday. All her numbers stored in it. Important dates, too."

Important dates. She's ten. What, when the next *Tiger Beat* hits the newsstands?

"I imagine she'll get it back."

"If not?"

"Are you telling me to buy her a new phone?"

"How about we'll talk."

With that, Dan dismisses me. He pulls gloves onto his daughter's fists and leads her to a bag. Cassie summons enough force out of her tiny frame to rattle it on its chain.

"Why not your little gal get in with Dylan?" Dad calls to Mulligan.

"We're game," goes Mulligan, with a shrug.

Dad turns to Dylan. "What d'ya say, Drac?"

Dylan scuffs his shoes at a black streak on the floor.

"I don't vant to heet a girl."

"Not hitting," I say. I hate seeing him cave. "Manoeuvring. You'll be okay."

Headgear squashes his eyes-nose-mouth into the centre of his face. I tuck his cape into the back of his shorts. The silicon gumshield stretches his lips into an involuntary smile.

When the bell rings, my son stares around, confused, perhaps thinking the fire alarm's gone off. Cassie bears in, one gloved fist big as her head glancing off Dylan's shoulder. Mulligan's next to me on the apron. He carries himself in a physically invasive manner. Commandeering airspace. It speaks badly of a man.

Dylan rucks in gamely, gloves hipped and rubbing against Cassie. Latent frotteur behaviour? He stumbles on his heels trying to find me in the lights, smiling at nobody in particular before turning that silly bewildered smile on his opponent as if to say, "We're having fun, right?" Cassie's snorting round her mouthpiece as the headgear constricts her

191

sinuses. She bulls Dylan into a corner and drives her hands into his face before pulling away to slap a glove into Dill's breadbasket. Dylan quivers: a seismic wave up his neck and down his thighs. They joust in the centre of the ring. Dylan's pushing at Cassie's shoulders to keep her unbalanced. I see my son in the west-wall mirror, and the reflected action states more profoundly just how lost he looks, soft and salty and unprotected like a massive quivering eyeball and I'm stepping through the ropes to stop it when Cassie plants a foot and rears so far back at the hips her lead hand nearly touches the back of her knee, coming on with the nastiest overhand right I've ever seen thrown by anyone so young. The sound she makes throwing it the screech of a gull. With the blood knocked temporarily out of his face, Dylan looks like an actor in a Japanese Noh play. He gets plunked on his backside where the ropes meet, spread-legged, skull too heavy for his neck. It dips between his knees to touch the canvas.

Dad's saying: "To your corners!"

I reach into Dylan's mouth. Strings of mucous-thickened drool snap as I pull the mouthpiece out. Vacant-eyed—belted into that groggy space where nothing's fully solidified—he blinks as a berry swells under his left eye. His gloved hands reach at his shorts as if he thinks he's bare-assed and needs to hike them up. I cradle my hands under his bum. Pick him up.

In the changeroom I tug his gloves off. Mulligan comes in to apologize. Genuinely surprised and regretful. He asks is Dylan okay. My son smiles. A sheen of blood on his teeth.

"I'm sorry," Dylan tells me.

"You didn't do anything."

That berry under his eye: you'd think an insect laid eggs. A red ring round his neck where the cape string's choked him. Dylan looks at his hands with the most pitiable expression. Not a fighter, my boy. But he seems aware of it, too, a failure that pains him. He thinks I give a damn. He opens his arms to me and I sense he's terrified I won't hug him back.

"I'm sorry."

"Dill, please. What is it you think you've done?"

On the way home I stop at Mac's Milk to buy him an ice-cream sandwich. When I get back he's flipping through a book I'd tossed in the back seat. *Over-and-Out Parenting*, by Dr. Dave Schneider. "Gobbledegook," I tell him. He's eating Nerds.

"Where'd you get those?"

"The stocker."

"Night stalker?"

"The machine stocker."

Machine Stalker. Robo-stalker. Presumably

bought with the five dollar bills Abby stitches into his trousers. He traces the ice-cream sandwich to his lumpy eye.

"In class we watched this movie about war."

"What war?"

"The one where everything's blown up," he says. "And like, the world gives us everything we need to blow it up. The steel to make planes is dug out of whaddayacall . . . ?"

"Mines."

"Like, the stuff that's inside is the stuff blowing it up." He points to his belly. "What if tiny-tiny aliens landed here—"

"You mean Phantoids?"

"Phantoids are peaceful, Dad . . . and so they hate each other and so get into a humongous war? Dig mines into my stomach. Make planes out of my bones and so, the gas is my blood? Mix the juices and the, uh, so, other stuff on my skin to make bombs? Everything they need to kill each other is *on* me."

He rips the waxed wrapper in neat ribbons. He's fallen into an obsessive habit of taking things apart. Pocket calculators, stereo remotes: anything with diodes, springs, cogs. He asked for a set of jeweller's screwdrivers to facilitate his deconstructions. I'd bought him a decent Timex for Christmas: he used the screwdrivers to gut it. End-stage methamphetamine addicts take gadgets apart with no intention of putting them back together. It accelerates or accentuates their grotty highs. I'm scared my son is exhibiting meth-head behaviours.

I say: "There's a drawing class at the Learning Annex."

"I like drawing."

"That's why I said it, buddy. Maybe that's a little more your speed than boxing."

"So . . . if you want."

"Not what I want. What you want."

"Is it?"

"You tell me."

"Okay, it is."

The naked girl on stage has jet-black hair fitted precisely to the plates of bone composing her skull. Playmobil hair—clip it on and off.

I hate strip clubs. Truly, they leave me grief-stricken. They cater to a pitiful male hopefulness. For the young guys, the hope of sucking tit in the champagne lounge. Older guys, the hope a girl might drop her defences to tell him her real name. Not Puma: Trudy. Not Raven: Paula.

The black card holder's name is Starling. Wide, lashless eyes set far apart on his head give him the look of a trout. As the girl on stage performs a dead-eyed gymnastic manoeuvre, spine bent like the Arc de Triomphe, he tells me he'd recently bought a Japanese dog. While we're talking, a guy I find familiar walks past. Long hair up in a ponytail. Jacket with *Brink Of* embroidered on it.

"Colin," I say. "Colin Hill. Hey!"

He smiles, a celebrity posing for paparazzi. "Man, aren't you . . ."

"Nick Saberhagen. From Sarah Court."

"*Riiiiight.*"

He's here with his father, Wesley, and some kid with dreadlocks. Colin tells us he's going over the Falls tomorrow morning. I recall reading something in the Pennysaver. I tell him I'll be there. And my son. Starling tells a bizarre story about a shark that plunges a dagger into all further conversation. Next he's saying we've got to leave.

Our cab glides down Bunting to Queenston. Tufford Manor and the cemetery where Conway Finnegan's father lies, on over the liftlocks. QEW to the Parkway to River Road running along bluffs of the Niagara. In the basin puntboats—smugglers, jacklighters—run the channel with kerosene lamps bolted to their prows. The smell of baked wheat from the Nabisco factory. We pass the hydroelectric plant. Static electricity skates along my teeth to find the iron fillings and touch off fireworks in my gums.

"I imagine," says Starling, "a fair number drown."

"In this river? It happens."

"Most common cause of brain damage is oxygen

deprivation, Nicholas." I hate that he calls me that, but his membership fee entitles him to call me "dickface," if it so pleases him. "Most common cause of oxygen deprivation is water trauma. A man of average intelligence deprived three and a half minutes—he'll end up with the brain capacity of a colobus monkey. Up to four minutes, a springer spaniel. Truth is, the humans whose company I enjoy most are those most like animals. I spent time in a brain injury ward. One boy suffered massive cerebral hemorrhages due to his mother's narrow birth chute. The most beautiful, open smile. He experienced more moments of pure joy in one day than I'll lay claim to in a lifetime. Most of us would be better off having our heads held underwater a couple minutes. Ever see an unhappy dog, Nicholas?"

"No, sir. Not for very long, anyway."

The taxi pulls into a warehouse. Security spots throw light at odd angles. Starling leads me down a domed hallway. A man sits on a wooden chair beside a door.

"Donald Kerr, you old scallywag."

"No names. I said no—"

"What shall he write on the cheque?" Starling asks, indicating me. "Wal-Mart bagman?"

Donald's got a narrow chicken face. Easy to picture him sitting on a clutch of eggs. A flatteringly tailored suit cannot disguise a physique shapeless as a pile of Goodwill parkas. One hand is cocked high on his second rib: a prissy, girlish posture.

He leads us into the warehouse, which is empty save the object in the centre lit by a suspended bulb. It's one of those trick boxes stage magicians make water escapes from. Designs carved into base and sides. A softball-shaped something sits inside. Starling leaves Donald and I to examine the box.

"What's in the box?"

"A demon," Donald tells me.

"Come on."

"You asked, chum."

"So it's a demon."

"Another guy, my associate, arranged it with your client. He wants to believe it is, okay, I say let him. It's whatever he wants it to be. It's his."

"I'm asking you. This other guy, associate of yours, was drunk when he said it."

"When I inherited it he wasn't in any real position to say."

"Inherited?"

"Something like that you don't have to steal."

"Doesn't look like a demon."

"What's a demon look like?" Donald Kerr's chin juts at an aggressive angle. "Could be something dredged up from the bottom of the sea nobody's ever laid eyes on. Not my place to know or not know."

"Why don't you want it?"

"Why's that matter? Not my cup of tea or whatever. It's mine now, but in a minute it can be his. He wants it. So let's make it his."

"What do I write on the invoice: Boxed Demon?"

"Not my problem, sport."

I step forward to examine it myself. Whether the box was built expressly for this purpose is beyond me. Inside: an oblong ball, faintly pulsating. Its scabrous outer layer looks like dead fingernails. I snap a few photos with my cellphone. When the cheque is cashed the amount transfers to Starlings' Centurion account. On the memo line I write: *Antique Box*. Blood spatters the paper. My nose has started to bleed.

I wait in the taxi while Starling speaks to a man across the road. He leaves the man standing beside the river and rejoins me. Our cab veers upriver to Chippewa. A harvest moon slit edgewise by an isolated cloud. The road bends past Marineland.

"Stop," Starling tells the driver.

The dreadlocked guy from the strip club is propped against a tree in the parking lot. His eyes are a pair of blown fuses. When Starling offers him a ride I resolve to find my own way home. We load the guy into the cab and I say goodbye. The cab's taillights flare as it accelerates on under an Oneida billboard.

Somebody's egged the Marineland ticket booths.

Sunbursts of exploded yolk. I worked here in high school. One time an animal rights activist with jaundiced eyes like halved hardboiled eggs shackled himself to the entry gates with a bicycle U-lock round his throat. The owner, a fierce Czech with pan-shovel hands, he'd gripped the protester by his ankles and shook him as you would a carpet. Roaring like one of the beasts he was accused of abusing. That was the autumn of my wife's pregnancy. Dad floated the idea of an abortion. My wife showed me a terminated baby in a Right To Life pamphlet. Nothing so much as a skinned guinea pig.

From the amphitheatre arises a yell— "Yeeeeearrrrgh!"—followed by a splash.

I walk down McLeod to Stanley. Mist gathers in funnels of light under the streetlamps. I trot along the breakdown lane. My father would wake me in the witching hours to run the gravel trail skirting Twelve Mile Creek. A gumshield socked in my mouth conditioning me to breathe past the obstruction. Taste of epoxy on my tongue: the same taste that fills your mouth driving past that glue factory in Beamsville. A sensation innately linked to boxing, same as the smell of the adrenaline chloride Dad swabbed in my cuts, through layers of split meat: it had the smell of silver polish.

A pickup blasts down the yellow line. The bed's full of young guys. Something of their circumstances—

so different than my own at that age—washes over me with the diesel exhaust.

My twenty-seventh fight, the one where the wheels began to fall off, was against Clive Suggs. Our weights the same but Suggs was a man.

We fought at the Lake street armory in a ring erected between decommissioned tanks. I knew Suggs was going to cream me. So black that when sunlight struck him there was a soft undertone of heavy blue about his skin. Clavicle bones spread like bat's wings from his pectorals. His wife had been there. His boy. I'd be fighting a father. I was a sixteen.

We boxers shared one change room. Suggs caught my eye and winked. Not an unfriendly gesture. He had his own problems with a wife giving him hell.

"Boxing at your age," she said. "You must have a death wish."

"Me, baby? Naw. I got a *life* wish."

My father made a gumshield for me by joining two mouthpieces together. Glued slightly off-kilter so my lower teeth jutted ahead of the uppers. A forced underbite kept my teeth from clicking, which prevented shockwaves coursing down my jawbone into the cerebrospinal fluid occupying the subarachnoid space around my brain, which would have cold-cocked me. He cut holes in the silicon so I could vacate air without opening my mouth.

It worked. I took shots that rolled my eyes so far back that the ligatures connecting to my eyeballs stretched to snapping. I was overtaken by this blackness where all I could hear was the scuffling of boots and thack of my heart. All I felt were bands of fire where the ring ropes touched my back. I'd sink back into my skin conscious yet likely concussed. Hoovering air into my nose. Expelling it in a mad hiss through holes in my gumshield. My father strapped oversize surgical Q-Tips to his wrist with a blue elastic band like they use to bind lobster claws. He'd soak them in adrenaline chloride 1/100 and between rounds stuff them so far up my bloody nose the pain of those Q-Tips poking what felt like the low hub of my brain made the nerves at the tips of my fingers spit white fire. And I never gave up. I should have. You can toughen every part of your anatomy save that glob of goo in your skull.

Strangest thing about a savage beating—one of those *within-an-inch-of-your-lifers*—is how everything's the *best* the following day. You wake up, sun streaming into your room: *The most beautiful sunlight ever.* Eat a bowl of oatmeal: *Goddamn if this isn't the best thing I ever ate.* Look out the window see a butterfly: *Mr. Butterfly, you're the prettiest creature.* If you're lucky to have a girlfriend and if she's kind enough to kiss those spots that hurt—"*Every* spot's hurting, honey"—the feel of her lips will drive you into a whole other dimension of pleasure. That terminal day-after sweetness is so addictive.

Suggs starched me with a honey of a left hook that no mouthpiece or the direct agency of God could have averted. After the ref raised his hand, Suggs reached over the ropes for his son. Perched him on his shoulder. Never had I seen any two people so concurrently, radiantly happy. For the son: the elemental joy of being in that ring, one arm slung round his pop's neck. For Suggs: that rare opportunity to share a personal triumph. You and me, boy! *You* and *me*. I suppose I became part of what may stand as Clive Suggs's finest hour—sad, considering: he pulped a kid with no future in the sport in a ring erected between WWII tanks at a bout watched by fifty. But his boy didn't know that. And it may not have mattered. To his son, Clive was mythic in those moments.

Suggs knocked over a Gales Gas and earned a jolt in the Kingston penitentiary. "So he did have a life wish," my father remarked. "A ten-years-to-life wish." He works at a retirement home now, I hear. That's just how the wheels roll in these southern Ontario towns, and I roll on it same as anyone.

But . . . that look Clive Suggs's boy gave his Dad. That myth-making look. I've never given my father that look. And my son has never given it to me.

The Falls tumble grey to match an overcast sky. A subdued crowd gathers along tarnished railings surveying the basin to watch Colin Hill go over the cataract.

"You'd've figured a bigger turnout," says Abby.

She's training again following a shoulder injury. She returned from vacation overweight and this, she says, had really set her father off. Dylan holds her hand as we come down Clifton Hill. On the patio of a dismal karaoke bar a rotund shill dressed as Elvis croons "Are You Lonesome Tonight?" His Tonawanda accent makes it sound he's singing, "Are you loathsome tonight?" We find a spot amongst the railbirds. Down in the basin Wesley Hill stands at the stern of his boat.

"I got to pee."

"You peed before we left, Dill."

"That hot chocolate," he reminds me.

I take Dylan's hand to lead him across the road. He says he can go himself.

"That arcade across the street should have one. Come right back. I'm watching."

Abby asks after my father. She knows all about the operation he'd botched some time ago. A wayward incision in somebody's prefrontal lobe. The patient's identity was protected by privacy statutes.

"I'm not saying he was drinking beforehand, but when you fall to pieces have the grace to admit it," I tell her. "Stop dicking around in people's heads."

Where's Dylan? Abby follows me across the road into the arcade. The attendant occupies a Plexiglas bubble with a police-car cherry rotating above it.

"See a kid?" I ask him. "Short, a little chubby."

"We get a lot of chubby kids in here, dude."

The arcade's rear door leads into an alley that empties onto Clifton Hill. Abby and I trudge uphill pressing our noses to the odd window. The air is quite suddenly full of fibreglass insulation; it sweeps down to the Falls in a pink drift. Abby's face is clung with pink flakes. Fibreglass stuck to windows and the street. Dylan comes down the sidewalk in the company of a man. They're holding hands. He's covered in pink. There's blood under his fingernails where the fibreglass cut in.

"Where the hell did you go?" I say, my seething anger barely contained.

"No place to pee."

The man points to a construction site. "I found him up there."

"Jeffrey?" Abby says to him. "Are you Jeffrey, from Sarah Court?"

Older, taller, but unmistakably so. Jeffrey, one of Mama Russell's special "boys."

"Abigail. Nicholas. This is your son." His inflection makes it less question than assertion.

"Only mine," I say. "We're here for—"

"Colin Hill." Jeffrey brushes pink out of his hair. "A block reunion."

He speaks as if he's joking but there's no smile. Jeffrey always was an odd duck. Same as the rest of Mama Russell's reclamation projects.

By the time we make it down, Colin Hill has already gone over. The crowd is buzzing. In the basin, Wesley Hill's jonboat has been joined by a tactical ambulance speedboat. Flashing red lights. Flashbulbs pop along the rail.

Mama Russell is there, and she greets us gladly. She's wheelchair-bound. Her silver hair is bobby-pinned up around her doughy face. She fusses over Dylan. Who is either scared of her or disgusted by her.

A flake of insulation has gotten trapped under Dill's eyelid. We say goodbye to Jeffrey and Mama Russell and drive to the walk-in clinic. Dylan sits on Abby's lap in the waiting room.

"She smelled like the old mall," Dylan stage-whispers into Abby's ear.

"Who did?"

"That woman in the wheelchair."

He winces, as if understanding it's not a terribly nice thing to say about someone so aged.

"She smelled how?" Abby wants to know. "How does a mall smell?"

"He means the Lincoln mall on the westside," I say. "With the boarded-up shops and the busted mechanical ponyride, right, Dill? Before it was bulldozed."

Dylan nods. With one eye closed due to the fibreglass, he's tipping this perpetual wink.

"Sort of musty?" When Dylan nods again, Abby says, "Old people can have peculiar smells. You may smell like that someday."

He's sincerely amazed. "People change smells as they get older?"

"Go smell a puppy," Abby tells him. "Then go smell an old dog. People are the same."

A nurse flushes his eyeball at an eyewash station. She fits him with a breathable eye patch. Abby tells him he looks like a pirate. I sort of wish she hadn't done that.

Lastly—and I mean, obviously—let's talk about Pops.

Once, after we'd returned from a run—Dad harrying me with: "Push it, milquetoast!" and me thinking: *What trainer worth his salt calls anyone a milquetoast?*—Frank Saberhagen, my dad, made me lie on the driveway with arms and legs spread. He traced my outline with sidewalk chalk.

"Look at yourself," he said, forcing me to look at my chalked outline. "Disproportionate as hell. Midget-legged but long-armed. A gorilla'd be jealous of that wingspan. So *use* it. Keep your opponent at bay. Otherwise I'll be chalking your outline inside the ring. After you've been knocked onto queer street."

This was Frank Saberhagen's idea of constructive encouragement. He missed his calling as a motivational author; his unwritten bestseller's title could have been: *Get Tough, Moron!—The SABERHAGEN Advantage*.

Another time we're at the boxing club. I'm sparring with Mateusz Krawiec. My father's in my corner. Mateusz's dad, Vaclav, is in the corner opposite. Vaclav was at that time the reigning "Sausage King" of southern Ontario: his Polonia kielbasa won the competition held every summer in Montebello Park. Dad felt Vaclav's win had given him a swollen head.

Me and Mateusz went through the usual paces— Mateusz now works at Nabisco as a safety inspector; cute Polish wife, two kids—both of us evenly matched except that he was a southpaw. He kept giving me the Fitzsimmon's shift to bounce stinging lefts off the bridge of my nose.

"Overhand right!" Dad hollered. "Shift with him, then go smashmouth on his ass. O.T.S.S.!"

O.T.S.S.: Only The Strong Survive. Shortly thereafter, Mateusz battered me with an accidental low blow.

"Call your kid the Foul Pole," my father cracked. Vaclav offered a deadpan: "Jah, Foul, ha-ha, jah."

Something was percolating, but with my father

you had to wait and see what permutation his unreasoning animus would take.

When a session ends it was customary for trainers to shake hands. My father stepped through the ropes with menace in mind. Butcher versus doctor. Their professions bore out physically. My dad was tentpole-limbed and spider-fingered. Kraweic looked like he split hog femurs with a friction-taped axe. You really couldn't beat my father for unadulterated perversity of character.

"Hey, Sausage King," he said. "You're brown-bagging it today. My compliments."

"Vhat?"

"You're brown-bagging it," Dad said amiably. "Here's a sackful of knuckle sandwiches."

In his defence it was the eighties, when the term "knuckle sandwich" was not hopelessly outdated. But what he did next was indefensible: took a wild, looping swing at the Sausage King. Should you find these circumstances improbable, all I can say is that if you knew Frank Saberhagen, you'd know he defies most sane probabilities every day of his life.

Dad's fist pelted Vaclav's ear. "*Vhat*?" said the Sausage King. I wondered if he was having a tough time hearing out of his punched ear or if, more likely, he was merely shocked at being hit by this mouthy fucking twerp. While Vaclav pursued my father in a blooded rage, Mateusz and I felt compelled to square off again. I shifted this time. Came over with my right. Gloves off, no headgear. I crushed the poor sap's nose. Blood mushroomed between Mateusz's fingers. Vaclav ceased his pursuit of my father to tend to his son.

"Overhand right, Nick!" Dad said triumphantly. "Told you."

That's how my father operates. He'll force you into positions where you must stand beside him. Now it's become a private joke. Whenever one of us gets on the other's nerves, it'll be: "Someone's fixing to feast on the brown bag special."

"Wouldn't it have been great," he said afterwards, "if I'd said the bag lunch line then nailed him proper?"

There are points in time you recognize your father as holding none of the special powers that as a child you believed he must. To see at heart he is careless and as often as not confused, that he smashes up things and people and it isn't that he doesn't care so much as he's done it enough to know he is more than capable of it and not entirely able to correct what he's set wrong. Plus he's a bastard. He's my dad, so I can say it. Cavernously narcissistic.

We lived on a block with a teenage halfway house and the terminally unemployable Fletcher Burger. He savoured the idea of living amongst his financial inferiors. But I've had more fun in his company than any other human being. If you conceptualize fun as a string of adrenaline dumps. But it's dangerous when the merrymaker becomes convinced that's all he need ever provide. As he'd inflicted himself upon me, made his pursuits mine, he'd hedged the odds of us sharing more "moments" than Mom and I. Though I'd never claim that as his clear-sighted aim.

Grown men weep at his feet for what he does in the operating theatre. A saviour complex has to fuck with a man's head. But he realizes he's an asshole. Regarding my mother: "Don't know why she bothers with me, Nick." In grade school I'd come home to a message on the answering machine from Mom, who Dad said had taken a "personal vacation": *You goddamn stinking shit. Don't call, don't come for me. You get away, you just stay away . . . Frank?* She sounded lost. Forsaken. *Frank . . . ?* You hear people claim they're "crazy in love." Plenty of us, yeah, we are. Chemicals exploding in our brains. Perpetually doing the wrong things with the wrong people for the wrong reasons. A chain of bad judgements and miscalculations: ten, fifteen years frittered away. I don't want to come off as a killjoy. But only the most deluded wouldn't be a little skeptical, right?

My father loves me. I know this much. But his love is brash and undisciplined and inwardly focused. He needs it to reflect back upon itself. Creatures of colossal egotism cannot simply give something away.

My mother said once: "I always hope you understand how much I love you." I do, partly as it exists in opposition to how my father expresses it. Mom's is a practical love with one obvious motive: to protect what she's put on this earth. A care-packages-of-boxer-shorts-and-mac-and-cheese sort of love. With Dad's I'm always fighting somebody. Him, mainly.

Dad knows I love Mom more. I've calibrated this using those means we use to reach such understandings and yes, I do. I think he's okay with it, too. In order for me to love him equally he'd be forced into concessions he has consistently proven himself unwilling to make.

I book the week of Dylan's suspension off. Each morning I wake him he hisses: "Zee light! Yar, zee light, she burns!" He's drawn a skull-and-crossbones on his eyepatch and sporadically fancies himself a pirate. A vampire pirate: synergy!

We go grocery shopping at Superstore. Dylan wanders into women's clothing and returns wearing a bra. The proverbial over-the-shoulder boulder holder, it hangs to his bellybutton. Any woman wearing such a contraption would occasion my father to note: "Whoa—it's a dead heat in a zeppelin race."

"Put it back."

"For Mom?"

"Not her size. But it pulls your whole look together."

This only encourages him to vamp it up. He struts down the shampoo aisle and performs a high-toed buttonhook round a Prell display, grabbing a bottle as a microphone to launch into "Viva Las Vegas," which he'd heard that Elvis impersonator sing. A woman my age with no ring laughs. I am cognizant of using my son as a lure. His Vampire phase is waning. These in-between spells, casting about for a new persona, I'm most vigilant. Next he'll be a rocket-powered tree sloth or a cannibal banana who eats nothing but his brother and sister bananas.

"These are the cheapest toothbrushes you can buy," he says, showing me one.

"You have a toothbrush. You want that one?"

He gawps at me as though I've perpetrated some arcane form of child abuse. I thought he was bargain-shopping.

I pick up a massive block of toilet paper, thirty-six rolls. On up the soft drink aisle for two cases of diet cream soda. The ringless woman comes down the aisle. Her eyes fall upon my cart and I'm horrified she's got the impression my life consists of drinking diet soda on my enormous toilet. For a full decade I never had one such thought. The band on my finger stood as proof to womankind: one of you accepts me. All prospects of remedy are exhausting in mere conception. Find a sitter for Dylan to spring me for a night at Fredo's under the Niagara Skyway, rucking in with the basset-eyed divorcees and sundry wastoids, clamouring for Ms. Right, Ms. Right Now, whatever's on the hoof. Cruising Toys R Us for single moms. Explaining it to my son: "This is Daddy's new friend, Trixy. We met at a speed-dating junket down the Lucky Bingo. She'll be sleeping on Mommy's side of the bed strictly on a trial basis . . ."

Dylan presses his lips to a pack of cheap blade steaks and whispers: "Fresh blood." In produce he gets on hands and knees reaching under a display of coloured potatoes. They're severely reduced and, judging by the smell, well on their way to becoming vodka. He comes up with a dented can of mushrooms cowled in spiderwebs.

"See?" As if I'd doubted his gathering instincts. "Can we get them?"

"The can's bulgy. You'll get botulism." Wrap both hands round my throat, pretend I'm throttling myself. "*Gak*! Plus you don't even like mushrooms."

He darts down the adjacent aisle, Confectionary, and returns while I'm comparing sodium contents on warring brands of cornflakes.

"Dad! Daddy-Daddy-DaddyDaddyDa—"

"What, Dylan? What the hell is it?"

He drops the tub of gummy worms on a low shelf.

Prods it between boxes of Mini-Wheats with his toe. Saws an arm across his nose.

"I love you."

Next he spies boxes of Animal Crackers.

"Can we go to the zoo?"

"You're not on vacation, sport-o. You're being punished, remember?"

"Like a field trip. To give me knowledge."

"How about the butterfly conservatory?"

He traces a finger round the lion's head on the cracker box. "Butterflies . . ."

"Fine. The zoo."

The next day is cool and edged with coming snows. Clouds cast indistinct shadows on Stoney Creek grape fields where field hands tend canebrake fires. Dylan's in full-on vampire mode.

"Listen to zee creatures of zee avternoon," he says as we drive south on the four-lane highway. "Vhat beeoootivul music zey make."

"I'm taking my son to the zoo. Not a vampire. Besides, a vampire's a scummy creature. They got to kill to live."

"What if you keep victims in your basement? Take their blood out with a needle?"

"Bleeding prisoners? Worse."

Offseason zoos are depressing. Polar bears with hotspotted fur snuffle at frozen blocks of fish bobbing in the oily water of their enclosure.

The monkey house viewing area is empty. Piped-in jungle noises: roar of lion, caw of toucan, the steady beat of bongos as you hear in films where pith-hatted explorers get cooked in cauldrons by needle-toothed headhunters. The poor monkeys look as if they've been plucked off banyan trees in their native lands, dropped into a sack and dumped here minutes prior to our arrival. One swings down to the floor of its enclosure and creeps forward on its belly. It's scrabbling through the bars at a wad of chewed gum balled up in its wrapper.

Dylan presses his forehead to my hip. "Can I give him it?"

"Monkeys shouldn't chew gum."

Instead we sprinkle puppy chow from a coin-op dispenser in the carp pond. Dylan's fascinated by the voracious surges of their liquid pewter bodies.

"That thing with Missus T," I say. "What made you do it, Dill?"

"It was a dare."

"Did you enjoy it? The rubbing? If you did . . . you're at an age of weird body feelings. Confusing stuff. You can talk to me, right?"

"I talk to Mom on the phone."

"Who dared you? Cassie Mulligan?"

"Sadie."

"Is she in your class, this Sadie?"

"She's my online friend."

"How old is she?"

"A little older than me. She's very . . . pretty?"

"Her photo on the computer screen, you mean. How did you meet?"

"She friended me. On MySpace."

"And she told you to do that to Missus Trupholme?"

"It'd be funny to play a joke on my teacher. Then Cassie could film it."

"Cassie's friends with Sadie, too?"

"Sadie's friends with everybody." He bites his lip. "Don't tell anyone."

How could it be possible that someone nobody has seen is the most popular person in my son's class?

"Dill, you've got to stop interacting with this person. Are you listening? Want me to chuck your computer in the creek?"

"Computers at school. Everywhere."

"This is not me trying to hurt you."

"You let Cassie punch me."

"God. Where'd that come from? Sadie could be some filthy old man in a basement."

"Can we go see Mommy?"

"Is that why you wanted to come to Toronto—to visit your mother?"

"We're close by. You could come."

"No, I couldn't. Listen, bud, Mom needs time alone."

"Alone from me?"

"Yes. No." Pat his knee. An ineffectual but easy gesture. "Not you."

"Doesn't she love you anymore?"

"You never stop loving someone. Entirely."

"So she could come back. We could live in the same house."

"You shouldn't pin much hope on that."

Early that morning I wake. Down the hall: the *tap-tap* of a keyboard.

I catch my son bathed in the glow of his monitor. No cape or eyepatch. A normal ten-year-old. The gutted remains of a clock radio are spread about his desk.

"Go away, Daddy."

He doesn't even look at me. Eyes on the computer screen.

"Who are you talking to?"

He spreads his hands over the screen. This angry tickling sets up inside my bones. I take his wrists. One of his fists comes free and strikes me. I pull him off the chair. Drag him into the hall.

"Is it her? Is it? I told you to stop talking to whoever the hell this is."

He swivels his wrists as though I've hurt them.

Perhaps I have.

"I hate you."

I sit at his computer. I'm struck by the orderly layout of his disassembled clock radio. The LCD display, circuit board, and plastic casing laid out in obscurely geometric patterns. Screws collected in a pill bottle scrounged from my medicine chest: Reminyl, which I take. It's usually prescribed to Alzheimer's sufferers to address short-term memory deficiencies.

Microsoft Messenger is running. Sadie's screenshot is of a cute girl in pigtails. Chatroom semaphore renders much of the conversation unintelligible: lolz, rotflmao, kpc. Sadie is discussing a new nightgown. How snugly it fits. I scroll up and am shocked, terrified, to find a conversation about my wife, myself. Our split.

Sadie: *dillie? dillie-sweetie? u there?*

Dylan: *THIS IS DYLAN'S FATHER*

After thirty seconds or so, words start to scrawl across the screen.

Sadie: *hey mr. dillie. i know all about u.*

Dylan: *ARE YOU A PERVY OLD FART? I COULD CALL THE POLICE*

Sadie: *. . . lol . . . i'm a cute giiiirl . . . i like to snuggle . . .*

Dylan: *MY SON SAYS YOU ARE FRIENDS WITH EVERYONE IN HIS CLASS*

Sadie: *dillie-baby told u that? such a sweetie-petey!*

Dylan: *DYLAN'S TOLD ME LOTS*

Sadie: *. . . lol . . . no he has not . . . dillie hates u, mr. dillie . . . like poison hates u . . .*

Dylan: *STAY AWAY FROM MY KID YOU STUPID FUCKER*

Sadie: *awwww, threatening a pretty wittle giiiirl . . .*

Dylan: *HAVE YOU ARRESTED CREEP STAY AWAY*

Sadie: *ur not the boss of me . . .*

[USER SADIE HAS LOGGED OFF]

There is part of me that struggles to believe this is even happening. Another part is wondering what, exactly, is happening. I print off the conversation.

Dylan's sitting cross-legged in the hall where the walls meet, faced away from me. He rocks forward until his skull touches the wall. I don't know if he's crying but if so it's silently. I want to hug him yet am furious for reasons I can't articulate. There is a cold fierce tickle inside my bones.

Niagara Regional Police HQ is a labyrinth of pastel green hallways, solid-core walls, and turret-mounted video cameras. I'm buzzed through a steel-plated door buttressed by bulletproof glass into a bullpen furnished in outdated Dragnet motif.

Danny Mulligan meets me at the coffee urn. He fills two cups. "You pay your taxes, right?" he asks before handing me one.

He leads me to his desk. His Laura Secord letterman jacket is hung over his chair.

"You still talk to Abby Saberhagen?" he asks.

"You and her dated back when, hey?"

He wiggles his ring finger. "Spoken for, now."

And Abby cries herself to sleep over that.

"Dan—"

"Lieutenant Mulligan."

"Right, Lieutenant. About Dylan."

"Not my jurisdiction. Try Juvie services. Or Scared Straight."

"No, it's . . . he's being harassed. Stalked. Something."

"Not my jurisdiction. Talk to the principal."

"Cassie, too."

"Cassie's involved?"

"I think so. They've got this friend. Dylan calls her a friend, anyway. An online friend. He's never met her. Nobody has."

"And *Cassie's* involved?"

"All that with the cellphone—this person, young girl or so she says, put them up to it. She's computer friends with everyone in class."

"This is your suspect?"

"Right. Sadie."

"Sadie who?"

"Sadie-the-perverted-old-man-posing-as-a-girl-stalking-my-son."

"I'll stop you right there. It may actually *be* a young girl. Infatuation isn't a crime."

"What if it's an adult? This person has . . . has infiltrated our kids' class."

"Nick, I'm backlogged. Got a case where a baby was almost drowned in the toilet at Wal-Mart. I've got a pursuable lead on that. Sort of."

"Mine's not?"

"Technically, anything's pursuable. If you have the manpower." He sips coffee. Skins his lips from teeth as if he'd slugged down a shot of gutrot mezcal. "Listen, I'll contact Missus Trupholme. We can sit down with the class and talk about the dangers of Internet predation."

When he can't find any scrap paper on his desk, Mulligan rummages his blazer pocket, finds a folded-over leaflet and absently writes his home number on its bare white back. He hands it over to me.

He says: "How's Dylan?"

"Your girl's a bombthrower."

"Takes after her old man."

"Nick, it's your father."

"What's the matter?"

"Just come over."

Rain fell earlier tonight. Shredded silver mist rolls up the streets to form halos around streetlights. I'd driven Dylan to Toronto for the weekend. He ran to his mother under the candy-striped overhang of her new condominium complex. I stayed in the car.

Sarah Court. Two lights burning: one in an upper window of Mama Russell's house, the other in my father's kitchen. His face is furred with a three-day beard. His skin hangs in doglike folds around his jawbone. He's drinking peach zinfandel from a box.

"I went into the hospital today," he says. "Surgery review board. To revoke my license. I scanned the incoming patient list. Abigail Burger. Emergency admission. You'd better drive."

On the way to the hospital my father's popping the passenger door ashtray open, closed, open again. The booze fumes coming off him are positively kinetic.

"Remember taking me to the LCBO on my thirteenth birthday?" I say, because he's in a self-pitying mood and that's when I prefer to needle him.

"I never. Your birthday? Never, Nick."

"Dragged me in on the way to mini-putt. They were out of your brand of gin. *Whersh the damn Tankeraaaay . . .*"

"Uh-huh, in that stupid lush voice. As if I've ever spoken that way. Ever."

"Were you drinking before that procedure?"

He avoids the question.

"You know, bail may be set at a million. I'd put the house up. Think your mother'd put hers up, too?"

"Why the hell would she?"

"For old times' sake."

"What about trial costs?"

"That's me off to Brazil. Non-extradition policy."

"Skip bail and Mom loses her house."

"I wasn't serious."

We cut across the parkway. Over the guardrail stands the brickwork of textile mills turned into low-rent apartments. A ladder of red pinpricks where tenants smoke on fire escapes.

"I took your mom to a cocktail party once. She didn't know anyone and held it against me. I went off to find a drink. She's chatting up some guy. Guy says, 'Your husband, what's he do?' and your mother says, 'Oh, he's a sonofabitch,' and the guy says, 'Whatever pays the bills.' Ha!"

We get to the hospital. The elevator rises to a white-walled ward sharing the floor with the neonatal clinic and the Norris wing. Fletcher Burger sits on a chair in the hall. At first I think he's drunk. But it must be shock. The man's groggy with it.

"At the gym," he tells us. "The weight bar fell on her . . . her throat."

Abigail's on a hospital bed in a paper hospital gown. Veins snake down her arms and trail under plaster casts. A throat incision barbed with catgut.

"Warmup lift." Fletcher rubs his thumbs over his fingertips. "I don't know how but her arm broke."

"Tracheal stent," Dad says. "How long before they opened her airway?"

"Brain scan showed black spots, is all I know. Her eyes. Frank, they turned *red*."

Outside the hospital wind shears across Lake Ontario around every angle this town was built upon. Wires of dread twist through me. My oldest friend. My prom date. Guess I thought we'd marry. Even when I was married—and loved my wife, truly—I felt I could have as easily been with Abby. But my son never would've been born in that scenario. A son, maybe, but not Dylan: the exact genetic prerequisites wouldn't have been present. Plus I'd end up with Fletcher Burger as a father-in-law. One self-obsessed man rampaging through my life was enough.

I leave my father with Fletcher and walk along to the Queenston Motel. A smorgasbord of ravaged faces and sclerotic livers. The lonesome thoughts of the patrons pinball round the dank air, glancing, rebounding, horrified at themselves. An old man eats a submarine sandwich the way you do a cob of corn: he looks like an iguana with a dragonfly clamped in its jaws. Another guy wears a leather vest with nothing on underneath. So insanely over-tanned his skin is purple. This leathery turnip of a head. The woman between them wears a hot pink tube top. Twin C-section scars grace her midriff, inverted 'T's overlapping like photographic negatives aligned off-kilter.

I order a greyhound. My wife's drink. The bartender gives me something that tastes like liquefied Band Aids. "Summer of '69" starts up on the Rockola jukebox. Pink Tube Top gets up on the sad postage-stamp of a dance floor. Breaks out that old Molly-Ringwald-circa-*Sixteen-Candles*, shoulders-forward-shoulders-back-slow-motion-running-in-place move. "Yeeow!" goes The Dragonfly. "Yip-yip-yee!" goes Leatherhead and he slither-slides up there with her. Now they're doing some spastic's version of the Macarena. Now I recall why I don't drink: it curdles my benevolent worldview.

The Hot Nuts machine is empty. There are no fucking hot nuts in the Hot Nuts machine. The red heat lamp is beating on a glass cube.

"Turn off the fucking Hot Nuts machine," I tell the bartender. "Some dumb bastard's liable to burn himself on the glass."

The barkeep lays a hand on the bartop. Large, scarred, knuckles crushed flat. A mean-ass scar descends from his ear to the dead centre of his chin: a chinstrap welded to his flesh. Am I going to scrap over a Hot Nuts machine? I've fought for less. Forty-odd times in gyms and clubs, a greyhound racetrack, the parking lot of a Chuck E. Cheese's. All to show for it a periodic openmouthed vacancy in my memory.

My father said I fought with absolutely no regard for my welfare. A man who had made peace with his forever-after. But you have to acquaint yourself with the notion, before even scuffing your ring boots in the rosin, that not only will you be hurt—there's no honest way you came out of any fight unhurt—but that you'll be hurt badly and repeatedly by an opponent who, in the hothouse of that ring, hates you. You cannot batter another human being into unconsciousness unless you harbour some hatred. The second hardest part of boxing is accepting your need to suffer. The hardest part is welcoming that necessary hatred into your heart. I'd stepped between the ropes never believing I could have a wife, a boy, people upon whom I was depended. I can't fight knowing how any punch—even one thrown by a spud-fisted bartender—could be the one to bust that all apart.

The cab drops me off a block from home. I'm so dehydrated that I steal up to the side of a house, twist the spigot on the garden hose and suck at stale plastic-y water like a poisoned dog. At home I'm nearly drunk enough to call my wife, *ex*, but it's late and Dylan is there. I don't want to be *that* father.

I'm absentmindedly rooting through my pockets when I turn up that leaflet with Danny Mulligan's number on the back. I turn it over. On the front is a naked woman, red-haired and busty. Pink stars over her nipples. A larger pink star over her crotch.

What the fuck? What the fuck.

"Sixty-Nine Cent Phone Fantasies," the operator greets me. "Our titillation experts are sweet and sexy, dom, sub, Black, Asian, naughty nurses, hirsute, leather lovelies, Daddy's little girls, fat-n-sassy, whips and chains, kinky, mincing, slutty secretaries, southern dandies—"

"Fine," I say. "That one."

. . . click . . . *buzz* . . .

"How y'all doing this faahn evenin'?"

"I'm . . . Jesus, are you a guy?"

"That's not what you asked for?"

"I didn't think I'd need to specify."

"I talk to whoever switchboard patches through, man."

"Well. Everyone's got to make a living."

"All with little mouths to feed."

"You got mouths to feed?"

"My own. And my dog, who I'm fixing to get back. So, you horny?"

"Not really. Anymore."

"We could give it a whirl. What're you wearing?"

"A parka and earmuffs. Hey, listen—you ever go through a stage where everything comes apart at once?"

"Pal, you're talking to a middle-aged male phonesex provider."

"I just got back from the hospital. A friend I've known forever, she's been hurt. Her father . . . my dad. Dads. Close with yours?"

"He's dead now."

"I'm sorry. My own boy says he hates me. What made him hate me? But I think, well, I hate my own dad sometimes. More than some. You got kids?"

"Me? No. Crimped urethral tube. Childhood soccer mishap. My wife left me over it."

"Over a crimped urethra?"

He says: "Other shenanigans, too."

"My ex-wife," I say. "This one morning we woke up. I told her how gorgeous she looked first thing."

"Right. No makeup, the tousled hair."

"Tousled, yeah. She gave me this arch look and asked me how long I'd taken to think up that line. But it just came to me. After that I felt compelled to . . . only so many times you can tell someone they're beautiful and not have it take on the ring of redundancy, right? After awhile you hope it's a given."

"My ex took up with a greasy surgeon. I'm gonna carve him out a new asshole one of these days and you can take that to the *bank*."

"What am I paying sixty-nine cents for?"

"Sixty-nine cents is the connection fee. This is running you five bucks a minute."

"Then listen to me."

"I hear you. Give it to me, baby. Lay it on me, stud."

"For Christ's sakes. I'm trying to say something important so—would you? Anticipate my needs. Act professional."

"Sorry."

"Hate, hate, hate. I've had more thrust upon me the past months than the rest of my life combined. I'm not a guy people should hate, am I?"

"You sound nice. Intense. A bit like your dad."

"What?"

"I said a bit like my dad."

"You know something? You're a piss-poor phonesex provider."

"I know."

"I'm hanging up."

"I sort of knew that, too."

When Dylan was three he caught poison ivy at Martindale pond.

The pond lies in a gully where an old roadway washes out. I took him fishing. We sat onshore amongst old catfishers perched on grease tubs with poles clasped in liquorice-root fingers. He'd get bored and go romping in the woods. I'd ascribed to an immersion theory of child rearing at the time. Let him lick a dog. Put bugs in his mouth. Build that immune system.

The poison ivy started as splotches on his thighs. Threads crept to his groin. He clawed it onto his stomach up to his armpits. The pediatrician prescribed calamine lotion. Dylan still had fits. Dad gave me lotion laced with topical anaesthetic.

I stood him in the bathtub, naked. My fingers went wherever ivy lurked: toes, thighs, belly. Felt odd doing that but he was so trusting. I worked lotion into his back. Cleft of his bum. I felt so close to him. A casual intimacy I thought could go on forever. To this day I'll feel it: a phantom *thack-thack* on my bare palms. My fingertips so close to his heart.

Only Danny and Cassie Mulligan show up to my Bullying Symposium.

Mulligan had sat down with Trupholme's class to talk about Internet predators. Sadie in particular. One of the more awkward experiences of his life, he told me. "Soon as I spoke her name, this eerie stillness. Like that movie, *Village of the Damned*. Kids with glowing blue eyes and test-pattern faces." Afterwards he'd handed out invitations to this Symposium, which had been my idea.

My son's school days have since turned hellish. He was the one who ratted out "Secret Sadie" to the grownups. Now he was being teased mercilessly in the insidious ways modern technology affords: IMs, text messages. Someone spat in his pencil case. When

I picked him up yesterday he had a wad of grape gum stuck in his hair. It took half a jar of peanut butter to untangle it.

During recess I'd idled in my car overlooking the playground. Dylan ate Nerds alone on the teeter-totter. Behind the fence stood a woman. Rainboots and an umbrella on a sunny day. A man dressed like that you'd think was a molester. Could be her womb was barren. I trailed her down the street before recognizing her as Patience Nanavatti, the fireworker's daughter.

On the day of the Symposium I lead the Mulligans into my family room. Finger sandwiches in a ruffled plastic tray. Dylan's on the sofa. No cape. The other day I asked after his new persona. He said, "I'm nobody. Just stupid old me." His mother's looking into having him finish the school year in Toronto.

"You should've called everyone's parents, Nick, to make sure they got the invites."

Mulligan's the sort of guy who, you're waiting for an elevator, he'll push the button again. Even though you've already pushed it. Even though it's lit.

The DVD I'd taken out from the library is called: *Bullies: Pain in the Brain*. The cast is comprised of little Aryans. An omniscient narrator asks questions:

"Jonathan, is your gang fun?"

Jonathan: "It's super. I used to be in a different

gang but they started bullying. I didn't feel right about that, so I left and started my own gang!" Calliope music kicks up.

Jonathan dances with the members of his new gang. They sit down to read books quietly.

"What do you know about bullying, Amy?"

Amy: "I was in a gang that started bullying. It was hard not to join in when they picked on others." This hardened ex-gang member is a seven-year-old in barrettes and a turtleneck sweater. What gang could she possibly belong to? The Thumb Suckers? The Bedwetters? After thirty minutes the ex-bullies and ex-victims form a conga line and dance off the edge of the screen to "Islands in the Stream."

Afterwards Mulligan shoos Cassie and Dylan outside. We head upstairs to Dylan's computer. He surfs to Youtube. Types 'Trupholme Joke' in the search box. One result. He clicks the video. It's Dylan rubbing against his teacher. A bundle of pixels available to anonymous eyes. Mulligan scrolls to the comments.

I hate u, dylan! looozer!

He should die . . . lolz!!

And, from SECRETSADIE:

Omg! what a total drip! if I wuz him, i'd kill myself and get it over with!

It wrenches my heart to see such hatred. So

bloodless. Cowardly. I want to seek out their fathers. Those who've fostered under their roofs such horrid monsters. Bash them to bone paste.

"I sent it onto the Internet crime division. How's Dylan's frame of mind?"

"He's ten, Dan. Overweight. Picked on in cyberspace. This one." Pointing at the cutesy moniker of SECRETSADIE. "Is encouraging him to . . ."

Out in the backyard Dylan pulls the padded seatcover off a lawn recliner. Earwigs scuttle into patio cracks. Cassie shrieks. I should have put the patio furniture in the shed by now. My wife usually reminds me.

Dan clicks on SECRETSADIE to open a fresh window: *Clips viewed by this poster.* He clicks the only other video: *Colin "Brink Of" Hill NF Stunt.*

The scene opens on the Falls. Grainy footage of Wesley Hill in his boat. The angle zooms out to spectators clustered along the railing. In the left corner, fleetingly, I catch sight of myself and Abby crossing the road. The viewfinder sweeps Goat Island and the Skylon Tower. Pink flakes congest the air. The lens climbs Clifton Hill to zoom on a construction site. I see Dylan in a mesh of raw girders on a concrete foundation slab. He's ripping with his bare hands at a giant plastic-wrapped insulation brick. He is joined by Jeffrey, Mama's boy. Together they tear at the bricks. The camera captures the steel filigree of a knife in Jeffrey's hand. My son is obscured by pink. The vantage returns to the river, where Colin Hill's barrel goes over the cataract. The camera pans the basin, shifts abruptly to the barrel floating past the spume. It's broken open. Colin's arm is a white branch crooked over the rim. Wesley Hill enters the frame. He lays his son's body in the belly of the boat. Whatever clothes Colin was wearing had been sucked off by the water. A thatch of dark pubic hair and the rest of his body is whitish-blue. His legs are all twisted together like a figure skater's in mid-Salchow.

"Criminal mischief," says Mulligan, I guess in reference to Dylan's fibreglass-ripping. "Not that your son's old enough to be charged. It just doesn't seem something a well-adjusted ten-year-old would do. You know the man he's with?"

"Jeffrey, yeah. He used to live down the street."

"From here?"

"No. As kids. On Sarah Court."

Back downstairs Mulligan tells our kids they have to stick together. Rough lately, he knows, but your Dads will fix things. Cassie asks if we'll come to school and beat up the bullies. Dan places a hand atop his daughter's head. His fingertips pulse like a heartbeat.

"What's this?"

Cassie grits her teeth. "What?"

235

"A brain sucker. What's it doing?"

"I dunno."

"Starving." He kisses her head where his hand had been. "Beat them up yourself."

That evening I take Dylan to his grandfather's house. I find him on the back porch with Fletcher Burger. The two of them could've crawled out of the same bottle. Despite their drunkenness there's evidence—a bodily gravity between them—of a serious conversation having taken place.

"The champ!" Fletcher rocks boozily to his feet. "And the little champ!"

I hug him. It comes as a surprise to both of us. That he's sitting here, drunk, while his daughter's in the hospital . . . this enrages me.

"What are you two talking about?" I say.

"Well," Dad says, "Fletcher here has just finished giving me an object lesson in cowardice."

Fletcher heads home shortly after this. Dylan goes inside to watch television.

"He's not wearing the cape."

"He's quits with that."

"Weird habit. That girl folded him up like a K-Way jacket in the ring."

I'm amazed at my father's ability to link unattached grievances into a single incoherent insult. No use getting my dander up. Arguing with him is like eating charcoal briquettes: stupid, pointless, and ultimately quite painful.

"Fletcher and I were talking about being fathers," he says to break the silence. "How hard can it be, you know? The butcher's a father. The plumber. Mailmen."

"And, what—you failed?"

Now it's Frank Saberhagen's turn to wallow in silence.

"My last fight I lost to a pipefitter from Coldwater," I say.

"Didn't have to be your last."

"We fought at the Lucky Bingo. The whatever it is, scoreboard, was still lit up from the last game that afternoon. B-17. I-52. He drove up on a Saturday. No cutman. No cornerman. By himself. Knocked me out Saturday night and drove home Sunday. He was back fitting pipes Monday morning. I was never going to be the middleweight champ. Not of the world. Not of anyplace."

"You'll never convince me of that."

Ride the horse until it dies. A phrase you'll hear around clubs. It's often spoken by trainers behind their boxers' backs. Ride the horse until it cannot prove its worth or meet its stable costs. If it's not dead, cut it loose. The bloody unvarnished truth of what happens everyday in many walks of life. You wish that horse no ill will but business is business.

Truth is, I could accept and even get behind that

reasoning. But it's nine shades of brutal when your own father's your jockey.

"I was a boxer like the guy who strums guitar Monday nights at Starbucks is a musician."

"You'll never get me to see it that way."

"Yeah, Dad. I know."

Work keeps me on the road. I fly to Hawaii to watch fifteen rust-acned fishing trawlers get dynamited off the coast to serve as fish habitats; it earned the cardholder several million points when written off as a charitable donation. To London for the sale of Damien Hirst's "The Physical Impossibility of Death in the Mind of Someone Living"—a thresher shark preserved in 4,666 gallons of formaldehyde—at Harrod's. To Florida to cut up Conrad Black's card. I take exquisite joy in this. When American Express dispatched me to hand-deliver his card years ago, Conrad held it against his chest. "Black"—tucking it into his shirt pocket—"on Black." I laughed, as I'd assumed was his expectation. He told me not to act like a "jumped-up little twerp and sycophant." I was later dispatched to oversee his purchase of Bonkers, a Glen of Imaal Terrier that cost 750,000 British pounds. Conrad bought it for his second wife, who fussed over it all of three weeks before offloading it on one of the Puerto Rican housekeepers at their Palm Beach estate.

Diverse legal imbroglios prevent Black being present to hand his card over. I cut it in half in front of his assistant, a wet-behind-the-ears Vassar grad—then into quarters and eighths and sixteenths until it looks as if it passed through a wood-chipper. An act which I find insanely gratifying.

Next I see my father we're faced across his kitchen table. I've come directly from the airport spurred by his strung-out voicemail message. Between us: a styrofoam cooler with ORGANIC MATERIAL on the lid.

Black rings like washers circumference Frank's eyes. I'd guess he's been crying but I've never actually seen Franklin Saberhagen cry.

"It showed up this morning. I decided I'd better drive Dylan up to his mom's for the weekend."

"You better not have been . . ."

"God damn, Nick." Running a hand through the wet ropes of his hair. "A little credit?"

"You're sweating—"

"I haven't touched a drop. That's why I'm sweating."

I lift the cooler lid. A cloud of dry ice vapour. I see what's inside. I close the lid.

"Sensitive biological material," Dad says. "They'll degrade shortly."

"For . . . ?"

"Yeah. They're from the Eye Bank . . . an anonymous donor. You drive."

Streetlights strobe the car windows to illuminate the contours of Dad's havocked face. The cooler sits in his lap. I cut through the orchards. At a pumpkin stand a woebegone Canada goose stands like a sentinel on a frozen squash.

"OR room four," he says as I drive. "Teaching lab. We'll put on scrubs, wheel her in ourselves—"

"Ourselves?"

"You're my assistant."

"If we get caught?"

"Seeing as I'm suspended? Jail. I was probably going, anyway. You're that worried?"

"Who are you all of a sudden, Montgomery Clift? Just shut up."

Service elevator to the fifth floor. When I try to pull scrubs over my street clothes my father tells me it's not a bloody snowsuit. We wheel a gurney into the elevator and on into Abby's room. She's sleeping. Dad injects her with ketamine so she won't wake up. I grasp her feet, Dad under her armpits. An awful smell, which Dad identifies as burst bedsores.

Up in the OR, Dad runs instruments through the autoclave, fills a syringe with local, selects suture thread so thin the plastic pouch containing it appears empty. The ticking tinnitus of strange machines. An acrid undernote my father says is burnt bone dust.

He dons glasses I've never seen him in: Buddy Holly style, magnified lenses screwed into the lower hubs.

He removes the eyes from the cooler. White balls threaded with burst capillaries, ocular stems attached, in a vacuum-sealed bag. They roll into a surgical tureen. With a dexterity I've rarely seen, he slices round their base and tweezes up the topmost layer. He holds one up on the scalpel's tip: invisible but for their rainbow refraction in the lights. Inserts the tip of a syringe below Abby's eyes. Bubbles where local collects beneath her skin. Further injections behind the cups of bone holding each eye. He has me hold her eyelids open while inserting ocular spreaders.

With a cookie-cutter instrument he traces the circumference of Abby's eyes. "Sweat," he says. "Damn it, Nick, *sweat.*" I dab his forehead with a swatch of surgical gauze. He tweezes out Abby's destroyed corneas. Deposits them on her cheeks. The blue of Abby's eyes *too* blue: this quivering naked vibrancy. He shapes the donor corneas until they are of acceptable size. Lays them over her eyeballs. Stitches fresh corneas to the edges of old. Gently clears away the blood occluding her eyes. The useless corneas are still stuck to her cheeks. He pinches them between his fingers. When they stick to his fingertips he blows as one does at an eyelash to make a wish. Twin scintillas land on the floor, lost on the tiles like contact lenses. Dad grins. Walleyed and a bit batty-looking behind those giant lenses.

Afterwards I idle on the sidewalk. Smoker's row: patients, orderlies, nurses filing a concrete abutment. In wheelchairs and hospital blues, dragging vital sign monitors and oxygen tanks. A snatch of a song comes to me: *The saddest thing that I ever saw / Was smokers outside the hospital doors.*

A guy stands in light shed by the ambulance bay. Shuffling along the halogen-lit brickwork. His fly is unzipped and his shirt's buttoned all wrong. His hair—long, the last time I'd seen him—was razed to the scalp. I walk over.

"Hey, how are you?"

Colin Hill offers me the most open, beatific smile.

"How do you do?"

He speaks as if a baffler down his belly prevents him from raising his voice. Slack features. Shaving cream crusted in his ear-holes. His smile goes on and on and on.

"We lived on Sarah Court," I tell him. "As kids."

He rubs a palm over his scalp as you do a foot that's gone to sleep. The muscles mooring his jaw tense. The frustrated noise he makes is, I'm guessing, laughter.

"I remember." He extends both hands in front of him, palms facing me, touching his thumbs then spreading his arms to their furthest ambit. The

242

sort of panoramic gesture a shady condominium developer makes to encompass vacant swampland where he plans a timeshare resort. "I remember . . . everything."

My euphoria sours. Colin faces the wall again. He hunts until he finds what he'd lost: a ladybug crawling in the grouting. He slips a pinkie finger into the gap. The bug perches on his nail. We're approached by an old man in a housecoat and winter boots.

"You got matches?" he asks us.

"Would you like a cigarette?" Colin says.

"Did I say cigarette? I said matches."

Colin's expression is wounded. The old man intuits things.

"I got a briar, son." He pulls a pipe from his housecoat. "Bastids at the home won't let me buy matches."

"But they let you roam around at night?"

"Roam?" he answers me. "What am I, a cow?"

He takes Colin's Zippo. We stand in fragrant cherry smoke, which must bother the ladybug as it lifts off from Colin's fingertip. "Oh, pooh," says Colin.

Our fathers have met in the hospital foyer. Wesley shakes my hand with a tired smile, then zips up Colin's fly. It's decided we'll go for a drink.

"I can drink a damn beer," declares the old man, as though one of us had challenged his ability to do so. Wesley asks his name.

"I'm Lonnigan," he says, and when he smiles his face is vaguely familiar—but in this city everyone's face seems vaguely so.

"Mr. Lonnigan—"

"Who said mister?"

"Okay, Lonnigan, come on."

Wes takes his son's hand to guide him down the sidewalk. Lonnigan lifts the odd car door to see if it's unlocked. At the Queenston Motel the Hot Nuts machine remains empty. Charred peanut specks stuck to hot greasy glass. Colin cadges a handful of loonies off his father and makes for the Manx TT Superbike video game. We take the window booth. When beers arrive, Lonnigan tells the bartender to put his on our tab and joins Colin at the video game.

"Your son . . ." Dad asks Wes.

"Barrel couldn't cope, Frank. They who built it said it'd been tested to so-and-so many psi but that water's a beast. Seals burst. Colin died a bit down in the dark. But I think he'd probably do it again. Just how he's made. When I baled him in he reached for my hand. Instinct? I don't know. He did reach. They did one of those—stuck him in a tube and went at his head with magnets . . ."

"MRI."

"Right. Black specks. All over his brain. None of the major neural centres."

I ask can it be fixed.

"No more than you can fix the rotten spots on an apple," Dad says.

"Jesus, Dad."

"I don't know it's the worst thing," Wes says. "Hope this doesn't come off bad, but I understand him again. For so long he was alien to me." He stares into his glass. "In some ways he's back to the kid I taught to shave before he had hairs on his face. Standing next to me in the bathroom, shoulders barely clearing the sink ledge. I lathered him up and he shaved with one of his mom's old pink leg razors. Thing is—and Frank, you'd know it—even as your kid gets older there's something of that child about their faces."

"A hell of a burden, Wes, your age."

"Yeah, Frank. Fine motor skills coming along. He'll find a job after therapy. But yeah."

A black man in orderly whites presses his face to the window. Shakes his head as he steps inside. Lonnigan spots him coming and chugs his beer before the orderly can take his glass away.

"You old cabbagehead. Who let you out?"

"Must've been *you*, Clive," Lonnigan cackles.

"You crazy goat. I'm'na handcuff you to a bedpost."

"You try and I'll sic the CNPEA on you faster than you can say Jack Robinson. Canadian Network for the Prevention of Elder Abuse—ho *ho*. I know people."

"Am I safe in believin' you ain't wrapped an automobile round a tree tonight?"

"Goddam fine driver, me. I don't wrap trees."

"Wrap your ancient dodo ass round a tree, is what I ought to do."

"CNPEA." Lonnigan clucks at the orderly. "Remember that."

"He says you brought him in," says the orderly, who I instantly recognize as Clive Suggs, the father who KO'd me years ago. "Why do such a thing? Old dude in his housecoat."

"He was insistent," says Dad.

"Well, he is that."

Clive sits for a beer. On duty, he admits, but what's one going to hurt?

"You want to know what?" he says, easing into his miseries with the air of a man slipping into a well-worn pair of slippers. "That old potato-head steals cars. Joyrides. A teenager do what he do, that boy's a hooligan. An old man do the same and he's full of beans. Discrediting the myth aged folk can't do nothing. Some kind a hero. He even stole a honeywagon."

"A what?"

"A kind of a septic truck," Clive tells me. "Suck the wastes out of pay toilets."

"He is peppy."

"Demented pain in my ass, what he is."

After another round, this pleasant fuzz edges everything: sort of like beholding the world from inside a cored peach. Colin and Lonnigan switch their attentions to the Claw Game.

"Go for the big white bear," Lonnigan instructs him. "Don't fiddle-fart around with them junky trinkets."

"Mister L," says Clive. "You played out your leash. Time to go."

On the way out Lonnigan checks up in front of Dad.

"I wasn't there for what happened to your dog," he says. "After I found out, I left for good. Can't say I could've done much. That woman had her ways. But you knew all about it, didn't you, doctor?"

Clive grasps Lonnigan's elbow. Dad drinks his beer with a distant smile. Soon thereafter Wes also says his goodbyes.

"I wish you boys well."

"Same to you, Wes," Frank and I say, nearly in unison. "Good speaking."

Two pairs of men move down the sidewalk. Lonnigan propped up by Clive, Colin by his father. Wes opens his truck door. Helps his son into the cab. Lashes the seatbelt across his hips.

"Hell of a thing," says Dad. He goes on to tell me

Abby got back to her room alright. The eye bandages would stay on for a few days. Patterns and shapes would come before too long.

"When they discover you did it?"

"Same as stealing a car and changing the shabby upholstery. You still stole it. My best friend's daughter. What can you do?"

"Best friend? Most days you hated Fletcher Burger."

"Christ, Nick. Never hate anyone. Fletch was a fuck-up, okay, but I mean, heaven's sakes—who isn't?"

After their divorce, people got the impression Mom stuck Dad with the corgi as a final screwjob. But Dad loved that dog. When Moxie developed persistent pyodermas, or hotspots, Dad rubbed the dog's skin with benzoyl peroxide ointment stolen from the hospital supply room. Here was a creature who made no specific attempt to be loved. Which was why Dad loved him. The night Moxie died, Dad found him walking circles in the yard. When he picked him up, Moxie vomited blood with such force he blew out both pupils. The last minutes of his life that dog was blind. Dad tried to force-feed him Ipecac but Moxie died gracelessly, blood all down Dad's shirt, the corgi's stiffening legs stuck out of the cradle Dad had made of his arms.

The car wends through stands of jackpine—telephone pole firs—on a strip of one-lane blacktop. Dylan's in the passenger seat. He's been expelled from school. If there is such thing as a mercy expulsion, my son was the beneficiary.

He'd vomited down the playground's corkscrew slide. Climbed the ladder, stuck a finger down his throat. Then he slid down through his upchuck. Iris Trupholme found him sitting at the bottom. Trousers soaked with puke.

The teasing had been nonstop. Someone put a dead frog in his lunchbox. Curly hairs in his PB&J.

"Years ago I had a Pakistani boy, Fahim," Trupholme told me. "Another boy had one of those laser pointers and shined it on Fahim's forehead, mimicking the red dot worn by Hindus. The boy's father had put him up to it. That sort of informed hatred has to be inherited. This with the pubic hairs is similar. Until you're older, a hair is a hair is a hair. Most of the kids shouldn't even be growing them yet."

Last night I'd received a call from the American Express head office asking for further photos of the Antique Box that had been bought by client 622, a Mr. Starling Bates. The cellphone images I'd sent were apparently too indistinct. I was told that Starling maintains a residence in Coboconk.

I'd called my ex-wife to see if she'd take Dylan

for the night. No answer. I packed him up in hopes of dropping him off through Toronto. Gridlocked on the Don Valley she told me sorry, she had evening plans. A date? Jesus. I'm not at all prepared for that.

We stop at a zinc-roofed restaurant, The Dutch Oven. All Dylan wants is Easter Seals Peppermint Patties from the coin-op machine.

"Dill, eat something proper. A Denver omelette."

Dark, fatigued bags under his eyes. I order the omelette and buy four Peppermint Patties. He plays with them like poker chips: stacks them, lines them in a row, a square, a diamond. He isn't wearing his cape anymore. I ask who he is now.

"Black."

"What do you mean—a black person?"

"Black the colour. A cloud of black gas coming out of the ass of a sick car."

This helpless sense of frustration and fear. My kid vomited down a corkscrew slide, then slid down and sat in his own upchuck. What does that even *mean*?

The sky is blackening by the time we reach Coboconk. I grab a room at the Motor Motel: five units in a field outside town. Our room is clean, with a queen-sized bed. I tell Dylan we could ask for a cot, but he says it's okay we sleep in the same bed. I'm not going to leave him here alone.

It's dark by the time we reach Starling's cottage.

All the other units strung around the lake are winterized and empty.

"Listen to the radio, Dill, okay? And stay put."

My knock is answered by the dreadlocked guy we picked up outside Marineland. I follow him into a vaulted chamber. Starling is in a wheelchair. His head is bandaged, one eye covered. His hands similarly wrapped and his legs swaddled in woollen blankets. His arms shrunken, somehow shrivelled: alarmingly, they look like penguin flippers. His left ear is fused to the side of his head as if his skull is devouring itself.

"Are you alright?"

"It's painless." Starling smiles. His body is just so *warped*: like he's been stabbed in the guts and he is gradually curling into the open wound. "How is your boy?"

Had we ever spoken about Dylan?

"Fine. I took him to the zoo."

"Zoo. Oh my," says Starling, and smiles. I immediately wish he hadn't. "I toiled at a zoo. With bears. All males. Bear society is a lot like ours, only the hierarchy's more bald. One bear, an albino named Cinnamon, got it worst. He rode a tricycle in a midwest circus; when the big top folded he came to the zoo. Undersized, genetically inferior. The others made sport of him. Every day each bear inflicted some casual hurt. They pissed on Cinnamon; his coat went yellow from white. Skinnier and skinnier. That's when they took to raping him. A big black bear, Chief, mounted poor Cinnamon first. The zookeepers felt this was the natural order. As one said: Better fuck-er than fuck-ee."

Starling laughs and laughs. A vein fat as a night crawler splits his forehead below the bandages. His fucking eyeballs are sunk so deep into their sockets it's impossible for them not be to touching his brain.

"Kids can be that way, too, Nicholas. Singling someone out for torment."

I'll find the goddamn box myself. Doubling down the hallway, I pass a partially open door. A wide, dark, metal-walled loft. The box is in the centre lit by a spotlamp. My camera whirrs as celluloid spools through the flashbox. Whatever's in the box seems to have sprouted fresh appendages.

I take a new angle. Twin facts register simultaneously.

One: Dylan is standing on the opposite side of the box.

Two: whatever's in the box has tubes growing out of it. Wriggling . . . *tubes.*

I lay my hands upon Dylan. Shake him far too hard. My adrenaline is redlined. My son's face is as vacant and bare as the surface of the moon. Blood drips from my nose into his hair. My heart batters the cage of my ribs primed to burst right through.

"Did you get all you need?" Starling shrieks after me. "Did you *SEE*?"

Back at the motel Dylan won't move. The heat's drained right out of him. I reef the motel covers back and lay him down fully clothed. He's not shivering or moving much at all. I head outside for our bags. A pickup pulls into the neighbouring unit. A woman's laughter plays out its open windows. Three people get out of it.

"You make loving you hell," the taller and ganglier of the two men says.

"Husha, dumb dog," says the woman, before stepping inside with the other man.

I go back inside and get into bed with my son. His face is grimed with sweat. I flatten his hair with my palm. Touch my lips to his head. His knapsack's open on the tabby-orange carpet. Inside are bits and pieces of things he's stripped apart. Everything in Ziploc bags. Orderly and arranged.

"What do you hope to accomplish doing this?" I ask him hopelessly.

"I'm going to put them back together," he says. "In different ways. I have all the pieces. I'll put them back together and make them even better than they were before."

"It doesn't work that way, Dylan. You don't have the skill or know-how. None of this stuff was made to go together any differently than how it came out of package. When you take it apart with no idea how to put it back together, you end up with junk."

He sits up. Unlaces the hiker boots his mother bought. Clodhoppers. He starts tugging the thick laces through the eyeholes. I want him to disagree with me, shout at me, but he's concentrating on his boots. Stripping them apart, too.

"We'll find a new school. It'll be okay. I promise, Dill. Swear to God."

After awhile the silence turns mammoth, oppressive, so I take a shower. The yellow water reeks of sulphur the way all water does this far north. Lewd goings-on come through the pressboard walls. The rhythmic knock of a headboard. A man shrieking: "Sweet darlin' Sunshine!"

I return to an empty room. The door's wide open. I step outside with a towel wrapped round my waist. The tall gangly guy sits outside the adjacent door.

"Did you see a kid come out?"

"Ain't seen nothing," he tells me wretchedly.

I step back inside. Dylan's hikers sit at the foot of the bed. Laces tugged out, tongues lolling over the toes. The utility closet door is ajar. I open it.

Next to my argyle sweater hangs my son on a noose of knotted bootlaces. Dylan's face is as blue as a sun-bleached parking ticket . . .

My son has a birthmark on his shoulder. It looks like a pinto bean. During his Steam-Powered Android phase this birthmark became his "on" button:

"Power up Android Dylan," I'd say, and press it. Dylan's head would rise, arms cocked stiffly by his sides. "Android . . . Dill . . ." he'd go, in robot-voice, ". . . needs . . . pudding . . . for . . . power . . . cells."

At recess another boy told him if you had a birthmark it meant your parents hadn't wanted you born. Dill agonized over it all day.

"Dylan, that boy's a creep," I told him. "How could your mother and I not want you born? You're the best and most precious thing in our lives. Believe me?"

"Okay. I believe."

. . . Rip the hangar rod off the wall, plaster dust and the jingle-jangle of hangars. Dylan's knees crumple as he falls face-first tangled up in my sweater. I try to pry the noose off but the laces are dug so fucking deep into his throat. A sobbing tension in my chest, agonizing compression pulsing ever-outwards. My vocal cords splinter as I let it loose. Blood's blurring into the whites of his eyes. I claw my fingers under the laces and my shoulders pop loosening them. My son's not moving but oh so warm. Prop one hand under his neck and open his airway as I'd been taught at Red Cross training. Settle my lips over his and blow. My breath disappears into the dense loaves of his lungs, circles around and back into my mouth with the taste of stale mucous and something else, slick and vile like gun oil. This cold throttling terror is sharp and blistering as blowtorched masonry nails clawing the surface of my brain.

Specks. *Specks*. Thousands upon thousands. I cannot see for their accretion.

BLACK SPOT

PIPES

Pipes. Is how I see you. All human beings. Pipes. As you have running through your home. Transporting fuel, water, wastes. All you often see of a pipe is their mouth, in the form of a drain or toilet bowl. People are pipes through which different substances emit. As a boy I understood out of Mama emitted food, a bed, blankets, smacks, a home, limits, broken glass. Out of Cappy Lonnigan: tobacco, cuss words, larcenous advice. Out of Teddy: moans, burn holes, crying jags, blackened ants.

I saw the colour, texture of their emissions. Out of Mama's pipe flowed burnt orange fluid. Out of Cappy's: bright blue liquid that when he laughed transformed into moths. Out of Teddy's: muddy goo stubbled with dead crickets or rusty nails.

Twist a water tap, water pours out. Not so people. Some days I could do such a thing as comment on Mama's new haircut—which often made her orange fluid flow brighter—but instead her liquid turned black-*black*, full of twitchy, screamy things. Next she committed acts meant to hurt me in ways that I am incapable of being hurt.

Cappy was a journeyman pipefitter. "I've been a journeyman everything," he would say, "including husband." He said pipes connect odd ways. People connect odd ways, too. Their colours change when they merge, the way mixing different coloured paints do. I study emissions. Colin Hill's fluid flowed sun-hot yellow. Abigail Burger's flowed pale violet until her father yelled at her, at which it blazed hemoglobin-red. When she came to our house after her squirrel was shot, Patience Nanavatti flowed with burping lava. But Mama ran so dark that day, all the lava bled right out of Patience.

Out of my own pipe emits grey substances the consistency of gruel.

My pet's name: Gadzooks! An Eastern grey squirrel suckled on scalded milk. When the neighbourhood kids gathered all our squirrels to play, he was hounded by his siblings. But Gadzooks! was terribly fierce. He once tore the head off a greensnake in an eavestrough. Devoured a family of silky pocket mice nesting in Mama's walls.

Last night Gadzooks! dashed out my apartment

window, down the drainpipe onto the road. A car ran over him—over him, you understand, not ran him over. The tires did not flatten him. Still, he was dead. By the time I rushed to the street, his legs were stiffening. Trapped under that car, the roaring engine, pinned in that wash of exhaust. Any man overtaken by such unreasoning forces so, too, would die of FRIGHT.

Now: Gadzooks! is in a shoebox. On a bluff overlooking Ball's Falls. On top of the box is a silenced Glock 10mm handgun. I am in my vendor's blues. I am digging a hole.

Wipe my brow. Pulse check. Fifty-eight bpm. Heft the gun. Adjust for windage. Empty the magazine into an elm. Collect the shell casings. Gadzooks!: into the hole.

Voices arise. I kneel at the bluff's edge. Three men with a blue barrel. Colin Hill, the stuntman. Wesley Hill, his father. A third young man I do not recognize.

Colin Hill strips at water's edge. Afterwards, he crawls onshore after plummeting. He ignores his father's outstretched hand.

My name is Jeffrey. My mother smoked crack cocaine.

An addict of loose moral virtue, says Mama, who

died giving birth. "A defiance of nature," Mama said. "A ripe apple pushed out of a rotted one." My mother died with chalky lips, Mama says.

Three pounds, nine ounces. They called it a miracle when I failed to die. Six months with casts on my elbows so I would not pull my joints apart with my frantic infant exertions. Mama keeps the casts—so small you cannot even fit a finger into them—to remind me I was once so pitiful.

There is a stain on my brain the size of a cocker spaniel's paw print. Occipital with spread to parietal, temporal lobes. Only dead black meat.

"Your mother was a crackhead," Mama says, "and your poppa was a sunbeam."

The black spot is no physical bother. My fine motor, balance, speech skills: all tip-top. My pulse rate, excellent. Yet I fail to experience pain as others do. As a six-year-old I stuck my finger into a stationary bicycle ridden by Mama's sometime boyfriend William "Cappy" Lonnigan. "What a nutty thing to do, kid!" My finger hung by a shred. The paramedics said I was "the stoniest little trouper" they ever saw.

Sundays Mama took us to church for ablution. The congregation swayed.

"Feel it, darling?" We were all Mama's darlings. "The LOVE?"

I do not feel LOVE. RAGE. SYMPATHY. They live

in the black spot. I have woken howling odd places in twisted bodily positions, never knowing why. I see guests on daytime talk shows. Emotion-torn faces crumbling apart under studio lights. Comprehension eludes me.

Mama took me to a movie. In it, a boy with massive facial deformities taught a blind girl to "see." He put a hot potato in her hands: RED. Cotton batten: CLOUDS.

Mama showed me a photo of baby chickadees: LOVE. A soldier in a ditch beside a bombed farmhouse: LONELY.

Cappy Lonnigan arrived, drunk, while we were at it.

"It's the blind leading the blind."

Good, evil: I can differentiate. But I am not impelled to pursue one path to the exclusion of the other. I camouflage myself through conditioned responses. Were a lady to set her head on my shoulder at a car wreck, I could identify her emotion as GRIEF.

"What a waste," I could say. I could mean the cars.

I often find myself trapped in difficult emotional waters. But I can tread water. I employ conversational strategies. One is to repeat what someone says, slightly altered. If I was at a funeral for those killed in that hypothetical car wreck, that same lady might say: "What a pity. They were far too young. So much promise."

"Too young," I might try. "Such promise."

Or at a supermarket. A boy making a scene his mother is helpless to arrest. A fellow shopper could whisper: "Someone should tame that little brat."

"Whip him," I might say, that being how a lion tamer tames his lions. "Whip that brat."

I also have trouble fitting warring notions in my head. Like: the first time I saw a banana I realized you had to peel its skin to eat its insides. That banana had been given to me by a human. The two knotted in my head. Snapping the top off a banana sounds a lot like snapping the neck of a small, armless, legless, yellow person. I do not eat bananas. Ever. Or welcome yellow objects into my proximity.

"You got a case of the brainfarts," Cappy said when I tried to explain.

"That's vulgar," said Mama. "Call them cramps."

"Whaddaya mean—like, menstrual cramps?"

Farts within my brain make me mistake prone. Example: Cappy would bring Mama breakfast in bed. "Great way to spice things up in the ole sack-a-reeno, kid." Beyond that, he never elaborated.

One afternoon Gadzooks! quarrelled with a robin. I shinnied up the tree—I had beaten Nicholas Saberhagen in a climbing contest, even though his father made him climb trees daily—to spy eggs in the nest. I brought them home, cracked them into a skillet. Eggs so small fried rapidly. So tiny on that big white plate. I arranged pretty blue egg shells around. When I presented them Mama was HAPPY. Until she studied closely.

"Jeffrey, where did these come from?"

"From the tree in Mister Burger's yard."

Mama shrieked. I mustn't go stealing eggs out of nests. But I worked especially hard to get those eggs. Farmers stole eggs from under chickens' bums. An egg was an egg . . . ? I only wanted to spice things up in the ole sack-a-reeno. For Mama.

I stock for Vend-O-Mat Incorporated. Class-A Vending Machine Technician. Member of Vending Machine Union Local 104. At my other job I am, at best, a hobbyist.

I restock claw machines at bars. The key: place a plush teddy bear in the centre of the cube surrounded by cheap trinkets. The claw is too weak to pick it up, but fixated drunks waste many coins trying. I service Hot Nuts machines, too, but the only place that has one stopped paying their maintenance fee.

Machines are logical. When I twist my multi-use flat barrel skeleton key on a Beaver 970 gumball dispensing unit—same insides as every Beaver 970 dispensing unit—I instantly spot the problem. Usually a torn-apart gumball in the ratchet mechanism. Or if I open an Aaxon frontload dual-cycle washing machine, I will usually find a 3/4-inch washer stuck in the coin slide. You can look into any machine to know exactly what is wrong. How to fix it.

Weeks ago I was at a school, stocking a Slim Line Mark X—voted Most Reliable Dispensing Unit by the Independent Vendors Association—when a boy interrupted me.

"Vhat are joo do-ink, blah?"

"I'm a stocker."

"Zee Night Stalker?"

Gym shorts. A cape. Fat. A short, fat vampire boy.

"I stock vending machines."

"Do joo stock Nerds?"

"I do not stalk anybody."

"Nerds zee candy."

"Products in boxed form do not vend well. Also tube form. Certs vend poorly."

"But, blah!" Fists clenched. "*Neeeeerds!*"

He says this the same way Marlon Brando shouted "*Steeellla!*" in *A Streetcar Named Desire*. The fat vampire boy chin-pointed at the Slim Line Mark X.

"It ate my dollar last week. So I kicked it."

"Never kick them. This one weighs a thousand pounds. That is how much a female grizzly bear weighs. Five people a year die from vending machines tipping on them. Squished."

"Whoa."

There may be some Nerds in my truck, I said. He tagged along.

"Should you be in gym class?"

"Jeem eez strictly for zee blood bags."

"Us alone in a truck full of treats. I could get in trouble."

"Vy?"

"I could be a molester."

The fat vampire boy squinted at the sun. Pulled the cape over his head. Wind goose-pimpled his bare legs. There was a case of Strawberry-Lime Nerds stashed under a box of Mallomars.

"Seriously? Wow, thanks."

"Do not eat them all at once. You are fat already, as I imagine you must know. You risk hyperphagia. Childhood onset diabetes."

I checked my pulse. The boy asked what was I doing.

"Your pulse is the most reliable indicator of overall health."

I showed him my wrist. The radial vein popping through tightened skin.

"Check here."

Instead, the boy clutched his crotch.

"I don't feel anyzing. I yam zee valking undead!"

I helped him locate it properly. On his wrist. He looked DISAPPOINTED.

The day I arrived at Mama's she baked angel's food cake. Aside from Cappy, I cannot recollect who was there. Cases—when angry, Mama called us by our Social Services case number—came, went. I ate plentiful welcome cake. She took in cases other systems would not abide. Social Services paid a premium. We dressed alike: tan trousers, hush puppies. Flowbee haircuts.

"Built like a brick shithouse": Cappy's term for Mama. Legs thick as Japanese radishes. One night a big case, Gothia, experienced an episode. Mama weathered his ravings then slapped him. A skull-rattler. She pounced on Gothia's back. Her callused hands on Gothia's head sounded like sledgehammers breaking open a cement sack. Her pet expression was "Gadzooks!" The night she beat on Gothia, every time she rained down a blow she yelped, "Gadzooks! Gadzooks!"

Mama was also prone to what she called "spells." During one she came out of the bathroom with dental floss wound round her fingers so tight her fingertips were bloodless.

"Who left this? I'll have a DNA test done, so help me God! This is not the *brand we use in this house!*"

How did she identify used dental floss by brand? She was convinced somebody, a stranger, had broke into her home to floss their teeth—also, they would have had to bring their own floss. One of Cappy's *whores*, in all probability.

"Three wolves and three sheep deciding what to eat for supper," said Cappy Lonnigan, regarding life in Mama's house. "Who says democracy works?"

He was her on-again off-again boyfriend. When he found work at the Port Weller dry docks—"I'm hell-on-wheels with a riveting gun, kid"—they were on. When contracts were scarce, so was he. My understanding of human behaviour is that people fall into one another's orbits out of an inability to exist alone.

"Type of woman you'd call *brassy*," he said of her. "Way a cabaret torch singer is brassy. Big teeth, big hair, big . . . overall. Throwing herself out there not giving a sweet tweet. Except she isn't really pretty enough to pull it off."

Cappy would be around two months, gone six. Mama sniffed his itchy feet. A Sarah Court ritual: Cappy Lonnigan on the lawn in his boxers while Mama flung his possessions down.

"Rotten-ass bastard, heave-ho! Come round here, I'll bust your nuts off!"

"Crazy bitch—you threw my record player out the window!"

The Divestment was followed by The Reconciliation: Cappy would show up hat in hand.

Eventually he stopped coming round. Last I saw of him for years, he stood in long johns while Mama hurled his belongings out-of-doors.

"Limp-dicked goat! See you again I'm chopping it off!"

Cappy shoved his property into a sack he'd stashed under the porch for this eventuality. He sat beside me on the stoop.

"Shrink your world. Pin everyone under your thumb. Every minute of every day, assert control." He brought his thumb, forefinger together. "If your kingdom's small enough and everybody owes, anyone can be Queen."

The girl with the *Blade Runner* haircut dances like a robot.

I drink a Shirley Temple. My employer sits with Nicholas Saberhagen. I am not sitting with them. I see them across the strip club. Another woman, her name is Diznee, asks may she dance. On my lap. Asks: am I a conventioneer? For fifty she will take me to the motor lodge to "suck on it." No, thanks.

My employer is joined by Wesley, Colin Hill, a dreadlocked fellow. I order a five-dollar steak. It arrives with tiny green potatoes.

I head out the back exit. Ignite the cube van. My employer exits the front door. Into a cab with Nicholas Saberhagen. I tail them down Bunting onto the QEW. Their taxi curls along the Niagara river past the hydroelectric plant. Into a warehouse lot lit by security lamps.

I park beside the gates. Cross the road to a bench overlooking the river. Check my pulse. Log it. My employer reconnoitres. Transparent molasses flows from his pipe.

"You?"

"Yes," I say. "You?"

This is all we say. I know what I am supposed to do. Inside the warehouse is a box. The leaden cover draped overtop is of the same material as X-ray vests. I roll it into the cube van, drive to Coboconk. Halfway there I veer into the breakdown lane. I crack the hood to find the source of the persistent hiss. Before long I reach the understanding that it is emanating from inside my skull.

Cappy Lonnigan taught me to hotwire a car.

"I spent six months in a Tallahassee lockup for car-nicking," he told me. "Roaches big as matchbooks chewing my toenails. A southerner, Muddy Phelps, taught me. *I'm'na shew yew tuh hut*whirr *a vayheckle, son.* Muddy's what you'd call a recidivist criminal. One time I'm bending elbows with Muds—some bum tells ole Muds his mother wears army boots. Well! Muds tells that bum he's gonna come to where he slept, creep in a window, and slash his weasel throat.

Slaysh yer way-zaal thrut. A man was able to get his point across, those days. Anyway, you find yourself an unlocked car. With a flathead screwdriver bust open the wheel collar. Pop the steering lock and touch the red wires. Easy as a beagle bitch in heat."

The car I stole was a Cadillac Coupe de Ville belonging to Frank Saberhagen. The night I leapt off the train trestle with Colin Hill. I broke the Cadillac's steering collar, popped the locks, touched the wires. I could barely see over the dashboard. I ran over a hedge on the corner of Sycamore.

The train trestle bowed over Twelve Mile Creek where it met Shriner's Creek washing into Lake Ontario. We climbed rotted rungs nailed to the pilings. Colin Hill's pipe flowed rabbity orange flecked with dark blue.

"Still want to?" Colin said.

I failed to view it as a matter of want.

"I will."

The water so cold my heart nearly burst. I surfaced. Colin Hill bobbed alongside. Smiling. Or had the river wrenched his face into the expression?

Days later Wesley Hill stopped by to apologize for Colin's actions. Mama led him to the sofa. I watched through the upstairs railing.

"I'm deeply sorry, Clara," Wesley Hill said.

"I don't have eyes in the back of my head." She gripped Wesley's skull. Ruffled his hair. "You, neither. Boys will be boys."

"They could have been killed. But God works in mysterious ways."

"I wouldn't say mysterious. I wouldn't say so at all."

Mama hugged Wesley Hill. "Been worse on top of bad for you, hasn't it?" Next she touched his knee. "Your poor wife. Frail as a leaf."

Her hand cupping Wesley Hill's kneecap. He restated his apologies. Left.

"That ridiculous man thinks I took liberties," Mama told me later on. "The very idea . . . fetch me a tissue." Her face was hard when I returned. "Do me a favour, Jeffrey. An itsy-bitsy one. After all I've done for you. A silly prank. You LOVE Mama, don't you?"

LOVE I do not comprehend. Loyalty, yes. Loyalty means do as you are told.

That night I broke the head off the sand-cast dog on Wesley Hill's front porch with a five-pound mallet.

Frank Saberhagen's corgi, Moxie, once forced itself upon Mama's sheepdog.

Excelsior lay on the sidewalk when Moxie "bum rushed"—Cappy's term—her haunches as if he aimed to "drill for Texas tea." The dog must have "one hell of a Napoleon complex," as he was "giving that ole girl what-for."

Excelsior shook Moxie off. Moxie persisted with clumsy jump-thrusts. Excelsior mule-kicked the corgi. Moxie did a backwards somersault into Mama's marigolds. Which he urinated upon. Cappy laughed. I struggled to understand what was funny about a small neutered dog doing sex with a big spayed one. But Cappy laughed, so I did. How my laughter sounded in my ears: a man in a crowded room shouting in a foreign language.

Excelsior developed pyrotraumatic dermatitis. Bacteria on the epidermis caused coin-sized lesions or "hot spots" to occur. Mama blamed Moxie, who had a similar condition.

Mama sat the dog in her lap. By then only Mama could touch her without being bitten. She trimmed hair round the spots with surgical scissors. Dabbed them with cortisone cream. When Excelsior died, Mama's spell lasted a week.

Mama has known Colin Hill since he was "knee-high to a duck's behind." She wants to watch him go over the Falls in his barrel. I wrangle her thick body into my minivan. Guide her wheelchair to a spot along the rail.

"I wen' da turlet." Mama's words have been slurred since the operation. "Loog a muh bug."

I went to the toilet, she's said. *Look in my bag.*

I lift the blanket covering her dead legs. The

pouch is three-quarters full. I unclip the stint, walk up Clifton Hill with a bag of warm urine. I kneel at a sewer grate, squeeze Mama's urine out. Uphill is a construction site encircled by a cyclone fence. The fat vampire boy stands on a concrete slab. His cape licks in the wind.

"Hello," he says to me. "Blah!"

"What are you doing?"

He points to bricks of insulation. There are holes in the plastic where his fingers punched through.

"Ripping zem."

"Why?"

"A pink blizzard vood brighten zee day."

"You are a strange boy."

He touches his upper lip to his nose. Snorts as horses do on cold days.

"I yams what I yam and it's all that I yam."

I pull a pocketknife from my trenchcoat. Stab a brick. Wrenching movements slash the plastic. The boy grabs one flapping sail. Flakes blow downhill. The boy is laughing very hard. It is interesting to see. Clifton Hill has gone pink. Next Nicholas Saberhagen, Abigail Burger are coming.

"Don't tell," he says. "*Please.*"

He tenders his hand. He wishes me to hold it. I do. Tendons tense along Nicholas Saberhagen's jaw. His pipe flows red. I let go his son's hand. They come down the hill to say hello to Mama.

"Dylan, is it?" *Dywaan, iw ii*? "Handsome darling."

Mama points to her cheek. Dylan kisses it. With Mama's gaze averted, the boy wipes his lips.

Mama took old Seamus Finnegan to the lake.

Seamus was the father of the richest oilman in the world, according to Mama. Seamus Finnegan boasted excellent health before a series of strokes rendered him paralyzed. Balanced sidelong on his wheelchair, he peered along his nose at the quivering knots of his fingers. His sole joy: watching Canada geese congregate on the lakeshore in Port Dalhousie. One afternoon Mama turned Seamus Finnegan away from the geese.

"Someone's getting overexcited," she said.

Seamus Finnegan's chair was aimed at a runoff. Snags of rebar clung with lily pads. Seamus Finnegan moaned.

"Husha, darling. Make yourself sick."

MANIPULATIVE? This is asking a colourblind man to appreciate a rainbow. Yet if I was Mama's favourite Monday, Teddy was her favourite by Tuesday. She said I ought to be more like Teddy, who drew lovely pictures. So I drew one: black blobs. Horrid! Why not fireworks, as Teddy did?

Mama acted out "dramas." Mama the star, everybody else the supporting players. The kitchen was her stage.

"Teddy: be Beatrice Klugman, that nelly from Children's Aid. Stand there like a stunned cow." Teddy: empty-eyed behind Coke-bottle glasses with melted frames. "Yes! Jeffrey, you be the Social Services Ombudsman. Scratch yourself—he's got psoriasis something awful—and mumble."

"Er, em, homina homina . . ." I would go, imitating Ralph Kramden.

"Perfect, darling!"

"You got any matches in this house, woman?" Cappy would say. "I got to watch your twisted little productions, least let me smoke my pipe."

"How can I have matches with eight-oh-four, a known P-Y-R-O, under my roof?"

Teddy, me, were allowed to draw on the driveway with sidewalk chalks. Once I had been allowed to set up a lemonade stand. Lemon-lime Kool-Aid mixed with hose water. My only customer, Fletcher Burger, said: "This tastes scummy as hell." Next Teddy drank a whole jugful. On a sugar high he doused an old recliner in Mama's garage with nail polish remover. Set it on fire.

From then on: no lemonade stands. Only sidewalk chalks.

Teddy's drawings were all the same. Splooges of orange, red, yellow but at their hearts, shapes as creatures may look with their bodies wrecked by flame. One afternoon Frank Saberhagen returned from a vigorous run with his Nicholas. He swung round the court on his bicycle before stopping at our driveway. His pipe flowed static green. He considered my picture: a man with broomstick legs. Belly following a strip of patching tar.

"You're missing his eyes."

I pointed out two holes in the driveway where air bubbles in the foundation had popped. I modelled the man around those pits.

"Beefy fellow," said Frank Saberhagen. "What's his favourite food?"

I said my own favourite food. "Fish, chips."

"Fish and chips?"

"Fish, chips."

He nodded, then picked up—*stole*—one of my chalks to trace his son's outline on their driveway. Afterwards he yelled at Nicholas, especially his "gorilla arms."

That night Mama came into my room with a pizza box. Also the mallet I used to break the head off Wesley Hill's sand-cast dog. She took Gadzooks! off the bookshelf. Shut him inside the pizza box.

"I saw you talking to that awful man today."

On the box was HEAVY DUTY in orange script. Cheapest pizzeria in town. Pepperoni with the texture of bologna. I did not know what putting Gadzooks! in a box or malleting him to death had to do with me talking to Frank Saberhagen. Had

Gadzooks! done something to make Mama wish to squish him? If she killed the squirrel I would bury him. As you did with dead things. Put them in holes.

"Don't ever—*ever*—talk to that horrid man again."

"Alright."

Inside the box, Gadzooks! made the same noises as when he had been only a baby.

Last autumn Mama collapsed. An emergency procedure addressed a saccular aneurysm in her brain. Surgical complications. Mama's legs no longer function. A machine now regulates her nocturnal oxygen supply.

Mama was homebound. Smashing her belongings. Urinating in her pants on purpose. I bought her a computer. Presented it with a red bow tied round.

From Your Darling.

According to her, Mama became "a regular computer nerd." I signed her up for *Cyber Seniors* at the library. Mama is online "24/7." She has many cyber-friends.

"Same as real friends," she says, "only less polite."

New friends keep Mama young at heart. You can reach out, she says, and touch anybody.

Cappy showed up after Mama's miseries. But she did not want him dragging his "ragged ass" back into her life. Allegedly he called her "fat as the queen of sea cows."

"Flat busted" though he looked, Mama did say Cappy drove a fancy automobile.

The night Gadzooks! got run over I visited Tufford Manor.

"Lonnigan?" said the black orderly. "You're his relation?"

"No."

"Shoot. Then you must be psychoneurotically disturbed."

"Pop by to offer my sympathies and she calls me ragged assed," Cappy Lonnigan told me, once the orderly located him. "Who put the potato up her tailpipe?" He went on in this vein. "She suffered a man before me. Don't know his name—do you think he could have surrendered even *that*? She grinded that bum down to a *nub*. She sure bled all the charm and romance out of self-pity. Days lying in the dark unwashed. Nowadays there's pills for that. She take pills?"

"Vitamins."

"What Clara can't admit is, she's sick-minded. Comes over her like a thundercloud. Turns her into somebody else—no: just a worser reflection. Pills are for weaklings. That's how she sees it. She hasn't a hateful heart. Just not an ounce of flex to her."

Sick-minded? Sick is vomit. What was Mama's mind vomiting? I went to the toilet. When I returned Cappy was gone. Also the keys in my jacket pocket.

I found him jamming my apartment key in the ignition.

"Let's blow this popstand."

"This is my minivan."

"What's that got to do with the price of tea in China?" He pointed out the hockey tape I'd affixed to the steering wheel. "What's this?"

"So I remember where to put my hands."

"Well, that's creepy. We should go tomcatting."

"You are wearing a housecoat."

"So? A man never feels so good as when he's got a full tank of gas, fifty bucks in his pocket, the night ahead of him. Yesterday's history and tomorrow's the mystery."

"The gas in the tank belongs to me. Do you have fifty dollars?"

"Did I say I felt good *personally*? A *man* feels good. A hypothetical. Jeez. I got to buy matches. Clive's canvassed every store in a five-block radius. *No matches for this man*—toting a Polaroid of me, as if I aim to light myself afire."

We drove to a Big Bee convenience store near the bus shelter. Inside, the overhead fans flapped like heron's wings. I brushed past a woman with a baby. Her back was turned to me. Cappy Lonnigan entered.

"No matches for the old man. He'll burn his hair off. Yeah, yeah. Where's the pisser?"

When we go outside, my minivan is gone. Cappy

removed one foot from its slipper. Wiggled his toes.

"You left it running."

"Hadda whizz. Who thought anyone would nick it?"

Emotion I do not grasp. Irony, yes.

"Thievery, Jeffrey. It's the lowest form of human behaviour."

The car is a rental. Ford Taurus. Car equivalent of Teflon: eyes slide off. On a static scale it would weigh twenty-two ounces over stock: mass of the Phoenix Arms 9mm affixed to the undercarriage. Exposed hammer. Satin nickel finish. It is the firearm equivalent of a Ford Taurus. Everyone owns one.

I rigged the car at a do-it-yourself garage. The gun's polished blue barrel friction-taped to the steering linkage. Stock U-clamped to the left rear wheel well. Trigger, recoil spring in the washer fluid reservoir. Hammerhead rounds in the passenger seat coils. Firing pin under my tongue.

Days ago I received my employer's call.

"Come. Now." *Click.*

I drove to the Niagara district airport. Boarded a Cessna Twin. Landed on a dirt strip near Coboconk. Drove the waiting car to my employer's. He lay on the floor of his lake house. He'd been dog-mauled, apparently. A plate of inflated flesh over his left eye. Webs of skin thin as bat's wings connecting his fingers.

"Slipper-footed space bugs," he kept saying.

When he was able to walk I helped him to the car. We drove until daybreak. A lab complex. Fletcher Burger. Men in scrubs. Whine of a surgical saw. Burnt bone dust. I leave with a cooler marked ORGANIC MATERIAL.

At the Coboconk dock I found Fletcher Burger's houseboat. I drove downriver to Happy Houseboat Rentals. I discovered Fletcher Burger had stolen the houseboat.

"That doggone prick," the owner of Happy Houseboat Rentals said when I told him where he could find it. "I should wring that guy's doggone neck."

My minivan was in the lot. Covered in maple keys. Fletcher Burger must have stolen it, too. There was a bucket of chicken bones between the seats. The upholstery stunk of fried chicken.

Flash-forward to right now:

I clear the U.S. border. Niagara Falls, New York. I drive up Pine Street. Men outside bodegas with bottles between their feet. Stop at Piggly Wiggly for a bottle of Faygo Red Pop. Ask for the bathroom key. Take the toilet paper roll.

In a parking garage near the Niagara Falls airport

authority I reassemble the gun. Blow off road grit with bursts of WD-40. Trigger hitch lubed with saliva. I empty the pop bottle. Stuff it with toilet paper. Fix the top over the barrel with duct tape.

There are rows of cheap units off 44th street. My employer's Cadillac is curbed with two flattened tires. In the apartment hallway I remove my shoes. Bread bags go over my feet, taped to my ankles. Skin lotion on exposed skin. Shower cap. Surgical gloves.

13A is unlocked. Tiny B&W TV. Mr. Turtle pool full of soil. Books: *Raising Earthworms for Profit. Harnessing the Mighty Nightcrawler.* An old video game unit. I play *Stuntman* with the volume off until James Paris arrives. His pitbull wears a plastic head-cone. Catgut racing its flank. He sees my gun pointed at his chest.

"Place the dog in the closet."

"Easy," he says. "What's with the bread bags? . . . my wallet on the boat, right? You can take the car back."

"You were told not to take it at all. My employer has a strong code of ethics."

He accepts this without rancour.

"I don't even have the cash to offer you double whatever you're being paid. You know, like in the movies."

He laughs. But his lips hardly move. He roots his pockets for a slip of paper. Name, phone number.

"Call her. She'll take my dog. Tell her she has to feed Matilda Iam's Scientific Diet, okay? None of that Purina bullshit. Liver pills everyday. Liver ailments are common with the breed. Mix baby food into her kibble for the complex proteins. Silly, I know."

"Silly."

"I was trying to raise worms." He nods to the Mister Turtle pool. "Garden centres, bait shops. Like drugs: there's gradients. You must establish a rep as a premium worm producer. Well, I guess they'll die."

"They will die."

I raise the gun. James Paris's forehead butts the bottle's plastic nubbins. He rocks forward on his toes. The weight of him on my shoulder. His heels do not touch the floor.

When a bullet enters a human body a number of things happen simultaneously. For small calibre arms such as mine, the unjacketed round—free of casing, propellants dispersed—weighs 110 grams; 132-grains ballistic calibration. Entering James Paris's forehead it will cause two types of damage: permanent cavity damage where the projectile tears directly into flesh; radial displacement of neighbouring tissue stretched in the projectile's wake. The pop bottle is a single-use silencer. All his neighbours will hear is a momentary high-pitched *tssst!*, like steam blowing the lid off a saucepan.

I pull the trigger.

Compressed gasses expand the bottle. Its base explodes into James Paris's face. Suddenly, his face resembles a red starfish.

. . . this could have happened—if not for the kiddie pool. You see, you bury bodies in dirt *outside*. Here dirt was *inside*. You must never bury a body inside. Unsanitary.

I lower the gun. A little moan comes from somewhere. I open the closet. Matilda sits on her haunches. A doggy cough: *houch-houch!* I am aware that James Paris should be dead. I am aware that he is not dead. But I *think* he is. I have had a brainfart. This is a very lucky thing, I think, for James Paris.

I drive to the Niagara Falls aquarium. Under the security halogens I break the gun down. I heave the parts into the basin. The border guards give me no hassle over the *canis domesticus*.

Mama's hysterectomy became a public showcase.

Her uterus was riddled with pre-cancerous fibroids. Adenomyosis: uterine lining thickening into the organ walls. Mama instructed her doctor to "rip out the plumbing."

Following the laparotomy Mama became obsessed with her pulse. Resting, active rates. She instructed us to check ours hourly. Log it in a notebook. It made Cappy Lonnigan CRAZY.

"Who gives a good goddamn about your *pulse*. It's beating. You're alive."

Mama's phantom hot flashes were unbearable. She wanted to "take in the days." Teddy, myself would push Mama around Sarah Court in a wheelchair. Mama had a bowl of M&Ms on her lap "for well-wishers." Neighbours made enquiries with eyes in the sky.

"Missus Russell," said Philip Nanavatti. "What's the matter?"

"Nothing but a little hysterectomy, dear."

Mama took this opportunity to approach Frank Saberhagen. The surgeon was drinking with Fletcher Burger. Pitting their children in some sort of contest in his garage.

"Your kid stole my Caddy what, six months ago? Thanks for pencilling me in."

"Mister Saberhagen—"

"*Doctor.*"

". . . I've undergone a hysterectomy."

Frank Saberhagen examined the sole of his deck shoe.

"Yeah? Those can be a bitch."

"I wished to discuss, civilly, Jeffrey's actions and my dog's treatment of yours some time ago. You can't blame Excelsior. Your corgi was eating squirrel babies."

Frank Saberhagen turned to me. "Jeffrey, right?"

I looked at Mama. She nodded so I nodded.

"Do certain colours scare you, Jeff?"

I peered at my shoes. The yellow band running over the toes I had coloured over with black marker. I was not SCARED of yellow. It did make me feel as I did riding the Tilt-A-Whirl at the Lion's Club carnival.

"Are there specific words you prefer not to say? Do you know about autism, Jeffrey, or Asperger's syndrome? Has your ward of the state told you about those?"

"Nonsense," Mama said through tight-gritted teeth. "Darlings, wheel me home this instant."

At home Mama smashed dishes. RAGING against the "rat-shit jack-bastard." The "hateful brute and lush." Were Cappy present he would have exclaimed: "She's on the warpath!"

"A rotten trickster," Mama told me. "As doctors are. Warp your body, warp your mind. You have a black spot on your brain because your amoral mother smoked drugs. That's why . . . that's why . . . *everything!*"

In the kitchen that night Mama crushed shards of bone china with a rolling pin.

"Pull that ground chuck out of the icebox, Jeffrey. Sloppy joes another night."

Mama crunched the china to sparkling powder.

Knuckled sweaty hair out of her eyes. She rolled the raw chuck through glass.

"All I ever want is to help. But people so seldom take the cure." Pinpricks of blood on her hands. "They spit the bit. You believe me, darling, don't you?"

I cannot tell what other choice I ever had. Under a gibbous moon I threw the raw meatball into Doctor Saberhagen's backyard.

Before dying, Gadzooks! chewed through my telephone cord. I have to go to Mama's house to call.

"Is this Patience?"

". . . it is."

"I call on behalf of James Paris. Who is dead."

"James Paris? . . . oh! Dead. Christ. How?"

"Police are stumped. His pitbull, Matilda, is with me. Old Family Red Nose. White coat. Brindle pattern over left eye. High stiffles. Clipped ears. A proud bitch."

"I knew him only one night. We met at the Legion in Fenlon Falls."

"Otherwise she must go to the Humane Society. For gassing."

"Gassing?"

"He wanted you to have the dog. Otherwise—"

"Gassing, gassing. My life may not tolerate a dog."

But she agrees to meet. I hang up. Mama is off at the Lucky Bingo. My elbow brushes the computer mouse. The monitor brightens.

A MySpace page. A girl in pigtails.

We meet at Montebello Park. Patience is Patience Nanavatti. She is wearing a floppy sunhat. Big sunglasses accord her face the aspect of a dragonfly. She is also pushing a pram.

"Jeffrey?" Chin tucked to her neck. SUSPICION. "From Sarah Court?"

I mimic her chin-tuck. "Patience Nanavatti?"

Matilda licks the baby's foot. The baby's name: Celeste. She grabs the air in front of her face. Patience Nanavatti takes Celeste's hand. She pins it gently to her belly.

"She is very scrawny," I say. "Have you seen a pediatrician?"

"She . . . no, she eats. Why won't you take Matilda?"

"This dog was not offered to me."

"She's yours."

Celeste emits hitching, painful sobs. Her eyes swivel so far back in their sockets it is as though she wishes to examine the inside of her own skull.

"Celeste is the toilet baby. I read of you both in the newspaper."

"Please." Is she soliciting help or begging me not to tell? "Jeffrey, please."

Patience Nanavatti tells me how she stole her. Then she fled up north but, finding nothing at all, she returned to the city. The police may be monitoring her home. I ask how long Celeste was in the toilet.

"Four minutes, maybe?"

Onset of advanced cellular decay: two minutes.

"Something is the matter with her brain."

"You don't know that."

I do not know what else to say. I say this:

"I will take the dog."

"Can't stand to see her gassed?"

"I will take the dog."

My employer is entombed in a wheelchair. Bandages clad his head, eyes, to the midpoint of his nose. Hands encased in gauze. He appears to have shrunk several sizes. His body is like an alpaca sweater sent through the wash. There is a large depression in the side of his head. A wet, red, glistening hole like a medical photograph of someone's wrecked vocal cords. Tonight he will be visited by Nicholas Saberhagen. My presence a precautionary measure. The dreadlocked kid, Parkhurst, who my employer says is a biographer of some sort, is curled up in a corner. I saw this person, Parkhurst, not too long ago. In the company of Colin and Wesley Hill.

When Nicholas Saberhagen arrives, I observe unnoticed from the top of the stairs. Nicholas asks permission to photograph the box. There is some commotion in the viewing chamber. Nicholas brought his son with him, you see. Somehow the fat vampire boy got into the viewing area with the box. Next Nicholas is bundling his son into the car. I follow them in my minivan. They pull into the Motor Motel. I park in a washout. The dark fluttering of wings in the trees. Time goes by. Nicholas exits his room in a towel. He retreats inside.

Next: bracing animalistic screams.

I get out of the car, walk across the road. The boy is lying on the motel carpet. Rope burns ring his neck. Nicholas Saberhagen pushes at his chest. He spies me. As if to spy a demon. I kneel beside them. There is a visible dent in the boy's throat.

"Your boy's trachea is crushed."

In my pockets: a notebook, a pen, a penknife. I chew off the pen's cap. I pry out its ink wand.

"The fleshy tube running down the boy's neck. You must cut below the obstruction."

"Do you have any idea what you're doing?" says Nicholas.

"The veins run here"—I trail a finger down the boy's neck—"and here. I know to avoid them. I know the trachea's consistency is that of a garden hose. I know about how hard to push."

I kneel patiently. The towel has fallen away from Nicholas's body. There is a dark stain on the tip of his penis. The boy's skin is presently the blue of a picture-book sea.

"Okay, Jeffrey. Go. Go."

I straddle the boy's waist. Set the knifetip horizontally across his windpipe below the Adam's apple. Drive the knifepoint in, then squeeze either side of the wound. Still too small. Insert my pinkie finger. The boy's tendons constrict around my fingertip. His slit trachea feels like a calamari ring. I thread the pen barrel in. Nicholas wraps the towel round his boy's throat. I find the carotid snaking past the boy's collarbone. Pressure stems the blood flow.

A man enters. He has the look of a SAD cowboy. His consort: a half-naked woman with a harelip.

"We called the medics."

A medical evacuation helicopter touches down in the gravel lot. I stand in the rotor wash as it lifts off. The helicopter ascends until it is nothing but a blinking red dot.

I return to the motel room. The closet door smashed. Contents of the boy's knapsack spilled over the carpet. Electronic equipment in Ziploc baggies. On the cover of his math booklet is a girl's name. Encircled by a lopsided heart. I know that name.

General hospital. Lea side of Valleyview Road past the ambulance bays. Midnight. Patience Nanavatti sits in the passenger seat of my Vend-O-Mat Dodge Sprinter. On my lap is a box of cellulose packing peanuts.

"It is sensible."

"You keep saying that. How will she breathe?"

"I will punch holes in the boxtop."

"She's not a turtle."

I stack cases of soda onto a dolly. Patience sets Celeste gently into the bed of packing material. She moans when I close the flaps.

"I'm a bad mother, I guess."

"But she is not your child. She never was."

I have made Patience Nanavatti SAD. I cannot understand why she should react so. I merely outlined the truth of the matter.

The elevator takes me to the fifth floor. As I am pushing the dolly round a blind corner, I nearly collide with a nurse. The nurse's patient is Abigail Burger.

Abigail is narcotically swollen inside a hospital gown. Her feet are covered in thick strings of blue veins, which I can see through her green paper shoes. The flesh of her face hangs in bags, as if fishing weights have been sewn under her skin.

"Gruh!" goes Abigail Burger. "Gruh!"

The most purely FRUSTRATED sound I have ever heard. Her breath is as sweet as baby food. She reaches for me. So strong. The nurse struggles to keep her in check.

"No soda machine up here," the nurse says. "You want the caf."

I double down the corridor into the neonatal ward. I carefully set Celeste in a plastic tub. Pluck stray peanuts off her blanket. To the tub I affix a note:

FORGIVE ME.

I pull into the horseshoe driveway of my employer's cottage. The moon stands upon its exact reflection on the lake. Hours ago he called:

"Je . . . uuuuuurt suh–*suh* . . ."

Then the phone line went dead.

I open the cabin door. All is very quiet. Except a cupboard rattles under the kitchen sink. I open it. The dreadlocked one, Parkhurst, has squirmed underneath. His body is bent round the gooseneck projection of plumbing pipe. His face appears oven-charred, but no: only blood dried to a glaze.

I shut the cupboard.

In the viewing chamber, the casement windows open upon a starless sky. A squirming mass the size of a medicine ball occupies my employers' wheelchair. On the floor beside it are empty bandage casings that still hold the strange shapes of whatever they once encased.

Inside the box is something holding the exact shape of my employer. Its skin is grey yet gleaming, silvery, shifting in the insubstantial light the way campfire embers will brighten in the wind. But as I watch, its flesh is paling to match the colour of my own. Its eyes are blobs of mercury in creased sockets.

With one fingertip the thing traces the box where each pane meets.

"Whoever built this did a very adequate job."

It opens its mouth against the glass. Puffs its cheeks like a blowfish. Deep down in its craw, little half-seen things are thrashing. It has no nostrils. But the quivering ball in the wheelchair has two slit-like dilations, side by each, fluttering in the manner of fish gills. They are the only feature it has, anymore.

"Are you scared of me?" the thing in the box asks.

I say: "I do not know what I am."

"If it makes you feel any better, neither do I."

It yawns. Blood emits from my nose.

"Eat the hearts of the innocent," it says. "Is that what you think I'll do?"

I say: "What will you do?"

"Go to Disneyland?"

"What are you?"

"Some call me demon, some say alien. Demon as it fits a ready-made definition, I guess. Alien as I don't match any categorized flora or fauna on earth. I wish I knew what I was. You are lucky to be part of a species."

It stretches, catlike. Snaps its jaws.

"Want to hear something funny? Although I don't know if it is. That whole concept is lost on me."

"Me, too."

"Your species finds it impossible to envision an alien entity lacking the body structure, appendages in some arrangement, of organisms found on your planet. Your most common alien representation? The "Grey Man." Big globe-like eyes. Legs, arms, fingers, toes. Or if not human-shaped, then spider-legged. Or tentacle armed. Still legs, still arms. Or exactly the same bodily specifics as you, except furry. All with eyes and mouths: only more or fewer than you, or smaller or larger. Your imaginations can only conceive of organisms here, on this planet, reconfigured. Do you understand the mammothness of the universe? That there must be life hieing to no forms found here on Earth? Creatures without heads, or eyes, or organs. Only human beings are self-absorbed enough to believe all life in the universe must resemble them."

Tiny openings appear in the nasal shelf above

its top lip. The ball in the wheelchair is now utterly featureless. It bulges convulsively. Then it stops quivering. The thing points to the still ball.

"I promise you I am no better or worse than he was. It's a one-to-one exchange." The gesture it makes invites my acceptance. "If that is a fact, then tell me: how can your world be any worse with me in it?"

I wipe my nose. Then I ask:

"How would I do it?"

"Just say the words. Hey!"

"There's something under the kitchen sink."

"Oh, you can leave that to me." The thing performs a jack-legged dance round its box. "Hey! Hey!"

I back out of the chamber. Blood is squeezing out of my pores. I close the front door. *Almost.* I press my mouth to that slit of darkness and whisper:

"I set you free."

One year Teddy and I missed Halloween. Chickenpox. Mama made us costumes. Teddy, a teddy bear. "My cuddly Teddsy-weddsy," said Mama, nuzzling him. I went as "Boxcar Jeffy," a hobo. Mama painted my beard with an eyeliner pencil. My bindle was filled with tube socks. By the time we got over the contagion it was November 2nd. Mama dressed us up to take us out anyway.

"Why should it matter?" she told Cappy. "Surely our neighbours have leftover candy."

On a cold night we went trick-or-treating. No jack-o-lanterns, except those that had been smashed by vandals or were decaying in trash cans. Mama knocked on doors around Sarah Court. Philip Nanavatti wasn't confident he had any candy. The holiday having passed, you see. Mama had not ordered the Nanavatti's squirrel shot yet.

"Come now, Phil," said Mama. "Surely your daughter could part with a few candy bars from her stash. For my boys' sake."

Philip dutifully rummaged up a few granola bars. Not all neighbours were so obliging.

"Tell the belligerent bitch to take a hike," came Frank Saberhagen's voice from the family room when his wife answered Mama's knock.

But Mama was persistent; we returned home with our plastic pumpkins full. I felt something indefinable for Mama. For what she had done. Was it LOVE? I could not say.

Cappy, speaking of Mama: "Like the moon, she's got her phases. When she's waxing, her LOVE's the purest, truest thing. But when she's on the wane . . ."

Squirrels gave every child on our block parasitic seatworms. Mama had "a bird" watching Teddy or me claw at our anuses. She ordered: "Don't flush!", then checked our leavings. At Shoppers Drugmart Mama bought a kit: Colonix Cleanse. Insisted upon administering it herself. Teddy, myself: naked on plastic sheets in the bathroom. Clutching our privates. We pried our buttocks open. Mama lubricated the plastic wand with flaxseed oil.

"Hold it, darlings. Hold it up there."

Cappy quarrelled with her over this.

"You force them to hold two pictures of you in their heads. One's this woman who feeds and houses them. The other's an ass-invading bitch-wolf."

"They can't give themselves bloody enemas, William."

"You're half devil, Clara. I swear. Three quarters, some days."

She envisioned a world where she was everyone's Mama. She sought to hurt her darlings as only a child can be hurt by its mother.

From my employer's I drive to hers.

Mama is in bed. Her sleep apnea machine hums. Mama removes the mask. Gulping inhales. Her eyes too round. Words mushed up. She cannot see the latex gloves on my hands.

She tells me a police officer named Mulligan barged in today.

"Investigating computer malfeasance. A ring of kids teased some poor youngster into a suicide attempt." *Suside ta-tempt.* "But I don't know my ass from my elbow with computers—do I, darling?" She nibbled her bottom lip. "He took your lovely gift away. As evidence. As if I'd even hurt a fly. He said my parole officer hasn't even been born yet. That's how long I'd be in jail."

Every act of kindness I ever experienced came at her hands. She never hurt me because she never found a soft spot. But she took me in. I called her mother.

I pull the pillow from beneath her head. I settle it over her face. Apply pressure. Her startled slurs are muffled by the stuffing. Her hand rises, trembling, to touch my elbow. Then it is all thrashing. Grunting. Growling. One dead leg slips off the mattress. I slide myself on top to straddle her. Her big breasts bunch under my groin. Her nails tear grooves in my forearms. Her chest deflates between my thighs. I withdraw the pillow. The muscles of her face have come unglued. I see the silver fillings in her molars. She has wet herself. That almond-y smell. Thin rasps exit her throat. I snap the oxygen mask back over her face.

I find some Q-Tips in a bathroom drawer. Sit back with Mama. I take each finger very gently. I remove my skin cells where they have collected under each fingernail bed.

SARAH COURT

Patience Nanavatti has been sleeping at my apartment. She is packed when I arrive. Grocery bags filled with Sally Anne clothing. Enough, she believes, to make a clean start.

"You're sweating," she says. "There's blood on you."

A blistering ache sets up in my arms, my shoulders. Lactic acid burn. Chloride torching the muscle fibres. Matilda noses between my legs.

"Lie down, Jeff."

"I am alright."

"Lie *down*."

"I will."

I lie on the bed she has occupied previous nights. I have slept on the couch. The scent of her is in the sheets. It is not a bad smell at all. Patience Nanavatti pulls off her sweater. Blue static sparks pop along her torso.

I do it out of LOVE. Mama used to say this. "If I am brusque or insensitive it is because we are familiar and I LOVE you." How much behaviour can you hide under the cover of LOVE? Allowances made to trample others because—because what? Because LOVE? Because you LOVE someone?

Patience Nanavatti lies beside me. We do not touch.

"I could take the dog," she says. "You, too."

To leave this town permanently—I do not know

it is FEAR I feel, simply because I do not know the colour that emotion bleeds. There is a brittle cracking sensation, localized to my chest, through which burst wires that wriggle as earthworms do. To vacate these streets, these sights of long acquaintance . . .

As Cappy Lonnigan says: *Yesterday's history, tomorrow's the mystery.*

"You must understand, Patience Nanavatti. I do not need you."

"That's fine, Jeff. I don't need you, either."

EPILOGUE

Summertime and squirrels abound on Sarah Court. The descendants of Alvin and Gadzooks! nest in trees whose outlines stand in calligraphic relief against the sky.

Nicholas Saberhagen's car rounds the bend where Clara Russell's house still stands. He pulls up in front of Fletcher Burger's house. Burger himself is long gone—*disseminated* is more apt—but the house is currently occupied by his ex-wife and daughter.

Nicholas's knock is answered by Abigail. Who is lovely in a violet sun dress. The scar on her throat is white, while the rest is tanned. She extends her hand to Nick, who receives it in a brotherly manner. They do not speak. Abby seldom does anymore.

They cross to the house where Nick grew up. His mother lives there now that her ex-husband is gone. Released on bail after his malpractice hearing, Frank Saberhagen booked clandestine passage to Brazil on a ship borne down the Saint Lawrence seaway.

He was bitten by a stowaway spider. Its neurotoxin induced seizures and severe priapism. Frank Saberhagen thrashed to death in an airless metal cabin on a banana freighter in the dead calm of the Atlantic ocean. His limbs flexed hard as bowstrings. Teeth clenched so tight his molars impacted. He also happened to perish sporting a trouser-ripping erection.

Though I give the impression of omniscience, it is not so. Whether Frank is dead or alive in fortuitous or inhospitable circumstances is really up to you. Stiff as a rod in a Brazilian banana boat? Fine. Should you wish to picture him in more charitable circumstances, well, everything is within the realm of speculation.

Dylan Saberhagen runs out to greet his father and Abby. Had it been me guiding this narrative, I suppose I would have let him die at the Motor Motel. Please try not to hold this inclination towards the most horrid variable against me. How svelte the boy is! Brain damage altered the appetite suppression centre in Dylan's brain. As has been said: the brain is a funny organ and it breaks in funny ways.

Nick's car wends up Martindale past the pond where Dylan caught poison ivy years ago. Nick unrolls his window to let air flow through his spread fingers. Wind skates up Abigail's legs to stir the hem of her dress. Nick's gaze momentarily wanders to that bare strip of thigh—a sight that once would have locked a thrilling tension across his chest—but now he only lays a hand on the armrest as the fabric touches his fingertips to resettle.

The Lion's Club carnival is on in Port Dalhousie. The heavenly smell of fried dough, or at least I've heard it described as such. The beach is studded with Tilt-A-Whirl, Zipper, bumper cars. All manned by a leathery roustabout. A pavilion christened "Our Poisoned Seas" is erected beside the marina. An oil-coated shark floats in a glass box of formaldehyde. Its black eyes stare over Lake Ontario.

An Educational Initiative Made Possible by Mister Conway Finnegan and Wal-Mart, reads the plaque beneath the shark.

The lake shore is teeming with residents awaiting the fireworks. A ferry crosses the lake, its windows bright as Kuggerand gold as if ferrying the sun itself.

Nicholas spots Wesley Hill and his son. They greet each other with great warmth. Colin has caught something he wants to show everyone. A lunar moth batters the cage of his spread fingers.

"You mustn't do that," Wesley tells his son, as he'd told him years ago. "Moths have a protective powder on their wings. If it comes off, it's like . . . well, you without your skin."

Colin opens his hands. The moth floats up into the night.

"Did I kill it?"

"He'll be okay," Dylan tells him. But everyone knows the moth will die.

You are all in this together. That huge thrashing teardrop of life. Consider the story threads. Where they start and end. A young pyromaniac enthralled by fireworks ends with fresh eyes in a woman's sockets. A car thief telling an odd boy how to hut*whirr* a *vay*heckle ends with an equally odd boy hanging himself in a motel closet—only to be saved by that first odd boy, now a man, who once stole a Cadillac belonging to the other boy's grandfather.

Some say the only way to break such chains is to leave the place they've been forged. Yet every town is essentially a box with an open top, isn't it? If you do not make the choice to step out of the box, well, can you really call it a trap?

Further downshore stands my benefactor, Jeffrey, with Patience Nanavatti. They should not be here, as they could be spotted—indeed, Danny Mulligan stands not far away with his daughter Cassie upon his shoulders—but Patience's father will be honoured with a fireworks fusillade tonight. Between them sits a bitch with a livid scar on her flank.

At the merry-go-round congregate the residents of Tufford Manor. Clive hands out blankets to his thin-blooded charges. William Lonnigan wipes away a runner of gossamer-thin drool descending from Clara Russell's bottom lip. She's by far the most docile tenant at Tufford Manor. Clara Russell causes absolutely no fuss at all. After all, she is alive in the sense a ficus plant can be considered alive.

I myself hover peripherally. The moonlight reflecting off my silver eyes tends to look alarming. When I alarm your species, you fuckers have a nasty habit of locking me up. Do you not enjoy my being here? I unnerve you. Yes, I do that. But it is quite possible I am not here at all. Could be it was only a box. You know, the sort magicians escape from. An empty, boring box. If that is what you would rather believe, well, I urge you to do so. It may even be true.

Dylan presses his forehead to Nicholas's hip. As he gets taller he will adapt this same gesture to elevated portions of his father's anatomy. He will press his forehead to the spot under Nicholas's rib cage, the crook of his elbow, the round of one shoulder. When fully grown Dylan's habit will be to wrap one hand gently round the back of his father's skull and press their foreheads together.

Nicholas's hand slips down to Dylan's neck until it brushes the tracheal scar on his throat. They both flinch. Years from now a girlfriend, Dylan's first, will kiss that scar. She will ask how he got it. Dylan will say he tried to hang himself as a boy. A hole was cut in his throat to let in air. He will direct her fingers to the thin but prominent scars near his ears, from the bootlaces, and the others, even smaller, made by his father's frenzied fingernails.

"What was it like?" she will ask. "The coma."

"I don't remember," is what he will tell her. "I don't know you're really supposed to."

"How long were you in it?"

"Eleven days. I woke in the hospital. Mom and Dad were there. I thought maybe they were back together. Patched things up or whatever. But they weren't. They weren't."

"Why did you do it?"

"Sad, I guess. Why do people do it all the time? Every day?"

He'll smile. She will think he is about to touch her but he will not.

As he grows older, Dylan will realize how so much of anyone's life is slip-slide-dancing along the edge of some karmic razor blade. Some of you get cut deep. Others get off unscathed. This town has a saying for instances of just such dipshit luck: *Even the blind squirrel will find a nut.*

All the people you've met within these pages will find happiness. You believe that, don't you? On a reduced scale, yes, but that scale reduces itself starting the moment you suck first breath. You organisms have so many flaws. Worst is how you seek to be happy at all times. Happiness is best when it arrives in modest measurements and in small moments. To ask for anything more is lunatic.

More often than not I think you carbon-based scraps of interstellar waste are not sustainable as a species.

But my, it is entertaining to watch you go about your business of extinction.

Now the fireworks begin to explode into the summer dark. *Oooohs* and *aaahs*. Last is Philip Nanavatti's finest creation. Globes of fire detonate, flaming umbrellas opening in the sky, tinting the lake every colour of their creation.

Spectators close their eyes. There it is. The Mushrooming Imprint.

And so the residents of Sarah Court make a wish. Each of them their own. Even though a fireworks display is not a regular outlet for wish-making.

What is it you would have them wish for? Well?

Make it that, then. Why not? Make it that.

ACKNOWLEDGEMENTS

Thanks to Brett and Sandra for taking this book on, and to Erik for providing such a brilliant cover. Thanks to my hometown. And thanks to Roald Dahl, whose story "The Man From the South" provided the basis for a scene in the third section. I mean, it's a pretty blatant rip, but I figure Quentin Tarantino already ripped it off even more blatantly in *Four Rooms*, so mine is, at best, a facsimile of a rip-off.

ABOUT THE AUTHOR

Craig Davidson has written three other books: *The Preserve* (as Patrick Lestewka), *Rust and Bone*, and *The Fighter*. His nonfiction has appeared in *Esquire*, *The Washington Post*, *Nerve*, *Salon*, *Real Fighter*, *The London Observer*, and elsewhere. Currently, he's hanging his hat in Fredericton, New Brunswick, where he is the deputy editor of an alt-urban weekly.